Sharing Their Wives

A 10-Story Hotwife Exploration Collection

Making Me a Slutty Wife
The Slutty Wife's Vacation
Slutty Wife Unleashed
Slutty Wife on Edge
The Slutty Wife's Desires
Making Me a Naughty Hotwife
The Naughty Hotwife's Staycation
The Naughty Hotwife in the Wild
Naughty Hotwife Unleashed
The Naughty Hotwife's Desires

Lacey Cross

Contents

Naughty Hotwife Unleashed

The Naughty Hotwife's Desires

Making Me a Slutty Wife

Book 1

Lacey Cross

Chapter 1

As I stroll into the vet clinic on Friday afternoon to pick up my cat, I think about my husband Ian's offer to open our marriage and allow me to fuck other men. For the last couple of months, we've been discussing the idea of me being a hotwife, and I've been hesitant. I don't need other men. Sure, the idea sounds appealing, but it's not worth risking my marriage over—at least, I didn't think so, but after a deep conversation last night, Ian made it clear that this is something he wants to try if I'm willing.

I find it hard to believe he wants me to fuck other people and then tell him about it, and that he doesn't want to go out and find himself a side piece as well. But he asked me to look up a bunch of stuff on the internet about hotwives, and I guess it's a legit thing.

Last night, after admitting that the idea turns me on, I finally agreed to it. Fucking other men with his permission sounds great, but I don't know how I'm going to find someone I actually want to do this with. Ian left it up to me to decide when and with whom for the first time. He wants it to feel right for me. But what if it never feels right? That's the problem.

The veterinarian clinic is deserted. It's a new clinic and I've never been here before. Buddy, my old-man cat, had a chipped tooth, and they needed to put him under to pull it. They wanted to keep him overnight to monitor him, so my husband dropped Buddy off yesterday and prepaid. All I have to do is grab my kitty and head out.

I sit down on a chair and wait for someone to notice I'm here. The pressure of the bench against my pussy reminds me I've been turned on all morning. I might have to go home and do something about it. After the talk with Ian last night, I had a sex dream where I was getting railed by a bunch of men in an alley. Not really what I'm into, but I guess my brain liked the idea in a dreamland.

Finally, the front desk worker pops out from the back room. She's a young, pretty woman with black hair and she greets me. "Oh hey, sorry. I didn't hear you come in."

Her friendly smile sets me at ease. "Oh, it's fine," I respond, as I return her smile.

She gestures toward the clinic area. "Come on back. We're closing early today and you're our last appointment. The vet wants to go over some things with you," she offers sweetly.

I follow her into an exam room. Since the office is new, everything sparkles and is spotless. The examination table is a long, brushed metal surface at waist height. The room is fairly bare other than a counter, and a bench against the wall, but that probably makes it easier to clean.

The front desk woman checks my cat's file. "Okay, wait here and I'll let Jace know you're ready."

I thank her and settle in on the bench. Pulling out my phone, I text my best friend, Sasha, to continue the conversation I had this morning with her about Ian's desire for me to fuck other men. We had to stop mid conversation so I could come and get Buddy. It looks like she messaged me while I was driving here.

Sasha:

Wait, did you take your cat to the new vet place on the corner of 64th?

What's this? This place has a reputation? I hope she's still on her phone, and I quickly reply.

When I see chat bubbles pop up showing she's typing, I relax. Okay, she'll give me the dirt.

Um...what the fuck is she talking about?

She replies with a big laughing emoji.

I actually laugh out loud at that. It's so messed up. But there's no way I'm paying some dude to fuck me. It doesn't matter how hot he is. Huh, who knew we had a gigolo vet in town? Go us.

She sends me another laughing emoji.

what he offers. Your husband said you could fuck someone else, so why not?

Oh God, she's crazy. I'm about to tell her so, but the exam room door opens, and I quickly set my phone down. My mouth drops open as the vet walks in.

Holy shit.

He's probably in his late thirties, and he's smoking hot. His dark brown hair is swept back, accentuating the deep blue of his eyes. His lab coat is unbuttoned over a pair of blue scrubs, which doesn't hide his powerful, fit frame.

I immediately can tell he's a dominant guy. He commands the room with his sheer presence, and I imagine being on my knees for him. Yep, I'm totally a thirsty slut.

"Hi, I'm Jace." He holds out his hand and I stand up to shake it. As my palm touches his, a tingle of desire ripples down my spine. Mmm, yeah, I'd take extra services from this guy, but no way would I ask for them.

"Hey, I'm Erin." My voice sounds breathy, but I can't help myself.

He shoots me a sexy grin. "Nice to meet you."

I try to hide how immediately attracted I am to him, and give him a soft smile. "Nice to meet you too."

Jace is taller than I am, and I imagine him bending me over the exam table. This is what I get for having a sex dream and not getting myself off this morning. I should have been playing with my toys instead of watching reality TV shows and chatting with Sasha until I had to come pick up Buddy.

Jace spends a few minutes going over how Buddy is doing and has a list of instructions for after-surgery care. He said it's all on the form, so once I know Buddy will be okay, I barely pay attention. I'm too busy looking at his thick fingers holding the paper and daydreaming about him dominating me.

I don't even know where the thought is coming from, but something about him exudes confidence and control. A desire to surrender overtakes me as my pussy pulses and I feel my panties grow wet. Yeah, I'm totally going to play with my toys when I get home and imagine this guy fucking me.

He's staring into my eyes deeply as he talks, and I can feel my pulse race as my body responds. The corners of his mouth lift and his eyes twinkle, as if he can tell what I'm thinking.

I'm suddenly unsure of what to do with my hands, and I rub them against my jeans self-consciously. I want to lick every inch of his gorgeous body, and then ride his cock like I'm on the Tilt-A-Whirl at the fair.

When a tap on the door interrupts us, it opens and reveals the front desk worker as she pops her head in. "Hey, is it okay if I head home? Everything is locked up."

"Sure, have a good weekend." Jace gives her that sexy smile of his and she blushes–yeah, I don't blame her.

She closes the door behind her and it's just me and Jace in the exam room again. Alone. My heart hammers as his eyes land on mine and electricity sizzles between us. Um, wow...I can tell he finds me attractive, but he's probably got all the neighborhood women drooling and hoping to fuck him. Hell, who knows how many people were in here already today asking for extra services. He might be exhausted.

There's no way in heck I'm going to fuck the vet—that just doesn't happen outside of books and movies—but I could flirt with him a little just to see what he says. I keep my voice silky smooth. "Does your office offer any extra services?"

The hot vet grins and he rakes his eyes over my body, making my nipples harden. Oh yeah, he didn't misinterpret my meaning. I wish he would rip my clothes off right here. His eyes burn with intensity. "Not if you're married. It's bad for business if an angry husband comes storming in."

He looks down pointedly at the wedding ring on my hand, and I almost laugh. Holy shit, Sasha was right. He DOES fuck women who come in. God, why is this idea so hot? Do I just want to be a number? It's a good thing I'm not seriously considering doing this... I don't think.

There's a noticeable bulge in his scrubs. Oooh, he's turned on. Shame and desire burns in my throat, and my brain blips out. All I can think about is fucking him, and I feel like such a slut.

I didn't expect to get so turned on by the temptation of fucking someone other than my husband. Talking about it was just theoretical, but being here with the possibility of it actually happening makes my pulse quicken with forbidden longing.

I fight the urge to sway towards him as a lusty feeling of warmth settles over me. Hell, why don't I fuck him? My husband wants me to. I can text Ian afterwards and tell him to come home prepared to hear about my slutty adventure.

Wet heat flares between my legs, and my body lights up as I make my decision. I'm going for it. It's time to make it clear what I want.

I keep my eyes glued to his as I run my fingers up his forearms and give him a coy smile. "I am married, but I have permission to play."

The corners of his mouth quirk as he moves closer and reaches out to finger a lock of my dark hair. I let out my breath and lower my eyes at his touch. "So your husband is fine with you fucking other men?"

He caresses my cheek, tracing along my jawline until he reaches my chin and tips it up so I'm gazing into his eyes again.

I hold my breath. The thought of fucking Jace makes me hotter than I can stand. I'm dying for him to press his lips to mine.

His words are like velvet. "Because I have to warn you, I'm not gentle and I like to share."

Um...share? The question must be in my eyes because he answers me. "You've got a beautiful mouth. I'd love to see your lips wrapped around my technician's cock while I fuck you."

Oooohhh…My pussy flutters, and a wild impulse rises within me. This is something I haven't done before. The idea of strangers sharing me makes my inner muscles clench. My husband didn't say I could fuck two guys, but he didn't say I couldn't either. Does one more cock matter that much? I take a breath and gather my courage.

I answer him honestly. "I'd like that." My heart races and I continue without thinking. "I want to feel your cock inside me."

His hand slips around my neck, and I lean towards him. I'm about to throw all caution to the wind and let this sexy stranger do whatever he wants to me.

The door to the room opens, interrupting us. I jump back from Jace when a guy in his twenties enters. He's got scrubs on and has a name tag, so he must be the technician whom Jace wants to see in my mouth.

The new guy smiles. "Hey, I'm Matt."

Hot damn. He's freaking gorgeous. Matt has short, blonde hair and deep-set, gray eyes. But the part that makes me warm and tingly is that his arms are covered with tattoos.

I never thought a tattooed man would do it for me, but Matt is hot. He's an Adonis of masculinity that makes my entire body ache. I love how he exudes a raw, sexy, male energy. He's definitely my type of guy, and he's definitely too young for me in any other circumstance but this.

Mmm, both of them together at once? Yep, I want this. I let out a breath and I try to compose myself. I'm acting like a wanton slut, but I can't help it.

Jace nods towards me and speaks to Matt. "Erin would like some additional services. Are you interested in joining us?"

Matt looks up and down my body, and his eyes take on a gleam. "Oh, yeah."

Shit, they do this together often? I mean, looking at them, I'm not surprised. This makes it even dirtier.

"Matt, why don't you go make sure Buddy is comfortable, and then come back so we can help Erin."

Matt grins at me and leaves. When the door closes, Jace turns to me and raises a questioning eyebrow. "I need to hear you say it. Say you want to fuck us both."

I didn't expect the need for explicit consent, and my mind whirls. My college years weren't crazy, so this is the sluttiest thing I've ever done in my entire life. I don't know if Ian is ever going to want me to do this again, so I better make this good. Go big or go home, right?

My brain buzzes as I imagine being their shared fucktoy. There's no question that I want this, but it's more than just fucking someone. There's something that my sweet husband can't give me and I think Jace can: I crave roughness. I want to be boneless with pleasure and sore when they're done with me, and go home feeling used. I want to be the ultimate slut who lets strangers fuck her and leave her dripping with their cum.

Oh, he's waiting for my answer. I lower my eyes again and my voice is soft. "Yes, please fuck me. Use me however you want to use me." Oh god, I feel a hint of shame for being such a slut, but I push it aside and add firmly, "You can do whatever you want to my mouth and my pussy. I want you both to take turns fucking me and filling my holes."

I peek up at him and his lips curl as if he's pleased and his gaze glitters with undisguised lust. "Good girl."

His 'good girl' sizzles my brain and the air becomes charged with sexual energy. Ohhhh, I think he's going to give me what I want.

He hooks his fingers into the waistband of my jeans and pulls me towards him. "It's time for you to undress so I can examine all your holes."

The next thing I know, he releases the button of my jeans and he's bending me over the side of the examination table. Since the table is too high for my feet to reach the floor, he has to boost me up. The surface is slippery and I grab the edge to hold on. I kick my sandals off while he pulls my jeans down, exposing my blue cotton panties. I would have worn something sexier if I had known this was going to happen, but he doesn't seem to care.

"What a good little slut." He rubs my pussy through my panties and my head spins. I love the harsh, dirty talk. He can call me whatever he wants.

As he peels my jeans all the way off, I study a chart on the wall that shows how to tell if your cat is obese. Yep, Buddy is a chonky boy. This entire moment feels surreal. Today was just a normal day. How did I get here?

He slips a finger under the band of my panties, seeking my clit. A pulse of joy in my core makes me gasp. Yeah, who cares how I got here? This is fabulous. If they spit-roast me, it's going to fulfill a fantasy I've dreamed about but never thought would happen.

I listen to the sound of his zipper going down while he continues to rub circles around my clit. Soft pings of delight radiate through me. Ohhh...th is is definitely happening. He moves my panties aside and pulls my hips up, spreading my legs apart with his. When I feel the head of his cock probing my slit, I don't dare to breathe, afraid I might accidentally wake up if this is a dream.

The pressure against my entrance increases, and then with one fierce thrust he buries himself to the hilt. My mouth falls open as I give a long moan from the intense bliss. My fingers grasp the side of the table tighter as he fills me. Fuck...this feels so good. I want more.

I peep out tiny cries, and try to push backwards against him. He digs his hands into my hips roughly and forces me to hold still. He lets out a harsh growl. "Let's get one thing clear, little slut. I'm in control." His hand moves to my lower back, and he shoves me flat against the cool surface.

I whimper and pant as I obey his command to lie still. I want more, so much more. His hands move from my hips to cup my ass and squeeze it tight before he plunges back inside me with one deep thrust. "Fuuuuck," I cry out as my hands clutch at the sides of the exam table. His thrusts become powerful and rapid. Each slam into me jars me forward. I struggle to remain in the same position, so he won't stop again.

"I think I found a pussy that needs testing," he mutters darkly as he plunges in and out of my slick folds. His words send shivers of delight through me. He can test that hole all he wants.

Suddenly, he withdraws, and I yelp at the unexpected loss. I'm addicted to his length already. An unfamiliar madness seizes me and I writhe and mewl out in protest. I need more—more of him, and I need to suck on Matt.

His voice brings me back from my fantasies. "Did I say you could move?" he scolds. I freeze, my body shaking as I fight an impulse to look at him over my shoulder. I need to remember this is his show. Biting my lip, I shake my head in response and whisper, "No."

His hands slowly trace the curve of my ass before moving between my legs again. I lift my hips without thinking, offering my dripping sex to him, and he rewards my efforts with two fingers delving into my tight channel. My juices drip over his fingers, and my breath hitches as he finger fucks me while spanking my ass.

Shit...fuck...I wasn't expecting him to spank me. He's not doing it hard, but a fuzziness steals over me and I can feel myself sinking further into the mindset of being just a fucktoy. This is what I wanted, and it's glorious.

I struggle to obey his command to not move. Each thrust of his fingers creates an inferno of need inside me. I'm moaning, and start mindlessly grinding against his hand and lifting my ass with every spank.

When he pulls his fingers out of my pussy and I feel him rubbing my asshole with them, I cry out. Oh god, what is he doing?

He wraps my hair around his fist and pulls my head back. "Stay still, you filthy slut. I said I had to examine you."

I squirm on the table as he continues to massage my forbidden hole. Fuck, this is so hot, and I'm loving the new level of depravity I'm willing to allow. I want to feel him inside my ass so much, and I've never had anal sex. If he goes for it, I won't stop him.

A whimper escapes me as he releases my head and grasps my hips. I inhale sharply, trembling as I await his next move. He forces my legs farther apart and I hold my breath. Is he going to do it? His hands spread my ass cheeks, and the tip of his cock nudges my asshole.

Oh god. It feels good. Tension coils low in my belly as the pressure increases and I expect him to slip inside at any moment, but he backs off.

His voice is low and strained. "We'll leave that hole for your next visit."

His words sizzle my brain, and I whimper when he plunges his cock back into my pussy. Ohhhhh, fuck. This is more intense than before. He feels so big. He stills and caresses my ass. I start to pant and let out a long exhale. God, it feels amazing. My pussy pulses in excitement and the rapture builds in layers.

I'm so far gone, I almost don't hear the door open until Jace laughs. "Took you long enough. Erin's been begging to suck someone's cock."

"Oh, yeah?" Matt's voice sounds amused, and I want to protest that I really wasn't begging to suck on anything, but I stay quiet. Whether or not I voiced it, I do want to suck on him. I want everything. If Jace had shoved his cock in my ass, I would have thanked him and asked for more.

Jace holds my hips firmly, and my body vibrates with intense pleasure as he pounds into me relentlessly. His rhythm drives me closer and closer to the brink of ecstasy. I can feel my orgasm about to peak, and I rock my hips back against him, encouraging him to increase the pace.

Instead of going faster, he pulls out and slaps my ass. "Get on all fours. It's time to see those pretty lips wrapped around his cock."

Mmmm, yes. I scramble down on the floor and close my eyes as Jace kneels behind me. The cold tiles bite into my knees, but I don't care.

"Be a good slut and let Matt use your mouth," Jace commands as his fingers brush against my clit.

"Yes, I'm a good girl," I murmur as Matt kneels in front of me and pushes the spongy head of his cock against my lips. I open my mouth eagerly, and he guides his shaft in. He tastes different from my husband, but it's not unpleasant. His cock is thick, and I swirl my tongue along the veins, enjoying his groan of pleasure.

Nothing matters at this moment other than both of them filling me. I'm a slut who wants to get used by whoever wants me. If there were more men in the room, I'd beg them all to fuck me. This is the dirtiest thing I've ever done in my life. I can't believe I'm being so shameless. I really am a slut.

I moan around Matt's thick shaft as Jace plunges into me again, and my body shakes with desire as my pussy spasms. This is beyond messed up, and I love it. My moans grow louder as both men ravage my mouth and my pussy. The tension builds quickly this time, and soon I'm close to tipping over the edge again. My thighs tense and my toes curl as I inch closer to my orgasm.

Matt and Jace fuck me harder as I moan and try to match their pace. I lose myself in the bliss of their cocks driving into me, sucking harder as Matt pumps in and out of my mouth.

"Mmm, mmmm..." I groan loudly around him, struggling to take every inch of his cock. Matt responds with a loud grunt, "Oh, fuck. That's it, baby."

It feels so good and I bob up and down, swallowing him all the way until he hits the back of my throat. I choke, but don't stop. I need to satisfy them both, and I force my throat to relax so Matt can slide in and out easier. Whenever Jace whacks against my ass, it forces Matt further into my mouth. They're fucking both my holes at an unrelenting pace. This is so wonderfully dirty.

It's not long before I lose all semblance of control. My legs tremble as Matt and Jace work in tandem, alternately plunging into my mouth and my pussy. The ecstasy builds until I can't take it anymore. I explode, and a loud moan escapes my mouth as waves of rapture crash into me. My pussy quivers around Jace's cock as the bliss continues to spike.

Neither man stops pounding into me, even as I melt underneath them. When Matt shoots his cum down my throat, I drink every drop. "Mmm, yes, good girl. Swallow every bit," he says huskily.

I savor the flavor of his essence on my tongue and revel in the feeling of being used. Who knew I would like this so much?

Jace picks up speed behind me, and his harsh breathing tells me he's close. He's grunting in pleasure as his thrusts become faster, and soon his groans of ecstasy echo through the room as he empties his hot seed inside me.

"Ah, fuck," he sighs before pulling out. A rush of his cum mixed with my juices splashes on my leg and it shocks me back to my senses. I'm on my knees in the middle of the exam room with two guys I just met, and all I want is more.

I lean forward and rest my head on my arms, whispering hoarsely, "Wow."

Both men laugh in appreciation.

The men talk briefly while I float in a daze of joy. Matt leaves the room to check on my kitty, and Jace cleans me up with some wipes and helps me dress. When I'm ready, I stand there staring at him awkwardly. How does he end these encounters with other women? Does he wish them a happy life? I can't think of what to say, and I'm relieved when Jace speaks first.

"Erin, that was wonderful. Are you all right?"

He brushes away a strand of hair that is sticking to the side of my face and tucks it behind my ear. I can only nod yes. My head is spinning and my legs tremble, but I feel incredible. My body feels deliciously used, and my mind is mush. I've had plenty of great sex, but this experience is easily in the top five. It's not even that I took two men at once, though that was incredible. It was the depravity of letting my vet fuck me in his office and use me like a toy while sucking on another worker that made it a mind-blowing experience.

Shit, I hope Ian still lets me fuck other people. I don't want this to be a one-time thing. I want to be a hotwife now.

He puts his hands on my shoulders and gazes down into my eyes. "Are you okay with driving home?"

This time I can find my voice and do more than just nod. "Yeah, I'll be fine. Just a little overwhelmed."

He gives me a gentle kiss on my lips. "It's not always like this. You're a very special person."

I can't help the rush of joy I get from his words. Even if he says that to all the women, it's still nice to hear.

He pulls out his cell phone. "Can I have your number so we can talk later?"

It doesn't cross my mind to say no. "Yeah, sure." I rattle off my cell phone number and he punches it into his contact list.

"Thanks." He winks at me. "It's always fun to get to know someone outside of a one-night stand."

I don't know why since I just fucked him, but I feel shy. This entire experience has been intense, but in a good way. He runs a hand through my hair tenderly, and it surprises me when it feels so natural.

I want this to continue, whatever this is.

He touches his forehead to mine, and we stay that way for several moments before he steps back and walks me out to the lobby. Matt is waiting with my cat in the carrier, and I wave goodbye to the guys on my way out.

On the drive home, I hum to the music on the radio, thinking about how crazy this day has been. I can't wait to tell my husband all about it, and hopefully he wants me to continue being a hotwife. Hell, I just gave my number to the vet, so maybe someday I'll fuck him again.

This hotwife thing could work out nicely after all.

CHAPTER 2

I almost call Ian while I'm in the car, but I figure it's better to wait until I can focus on the conversation. I hope he doesn't get mad that I took on two men. It's not like they were both in my pussy, so it'll be fine, right?

He gave me permission to fuck other guys if it felt right. And this definitely felt right. Two hot, well-hung men devoured me. I love how they fucked me until I was almost mindless with lust. I need more of that in my life.

After I get home and make sure Buddy is fine, I sit down in the living room with a bottle of water and a snack so I can text my husband. When I woke up this morning the day seemed so ordinary, and now I feel as if my life has completely changed.

My hands shake with excitement as I type.

Erin:

> Something crazy happened today. Do you want the details now, or later?

Ian:

> I'm stuck on a stupid Zoom meeting and it's boring. Tell me now.

Erin:

> Okay! Remember your request from last night? About fucking another guy? Well, one just kind of fell into my lap today. It was the vet, and he invited a co-worker to join in. So I got to play with them BOTH! I guess I'm a hotwife now. I really hope that's what you want to hear, because I loved it.

My fingers hover over the screen, not sure how much more I should write. It takes forever for him to respond, and when he does, I giggle.

Ian:

> Fuck, I have a tent in my pants. Did they come inside you?

Mmm, oh yeah, they filled me so much it was running out of me.

Erin:

> They sure did.

Ian:

> Was it just your pussy or did they fill other holes?

Um...holy shit, Ian is totally into this.

Erin:

> My pussy and my mouth.

Ian:

> Which did you enjoy more?

A delicious naughty feeling shoots through my body as I think about the two men. It's hard to compare because they didn't both fuck me, but Jace is closer to my age and I loved his dirty talk. I don't want my husband to feel threatened, so I try to be cheeky.

Erin:

> I prefer your cock.

Hah, tell the truth.

I can't lie, but I can change the subject.

This is silly. You have a hotwife now, who you can play with as often as you want. Come home so I can fuck you.

I feel bad for him if he has a raging erection. Poor baby is going to just have to wait until he gets home. I look and it's barely 3pm. Shit, he won't be home for a couple of hours. This is going to be torture for me as well.

You're changing the subject, but fine, I'll wait for the details. I want you naked in bed when I get home.

It's a date.

I rub my nipples through my shirt and pull at the stiff peaks. I need Ian's mouth on my breasts tonight. The girls didn't get much attention today, and I'm feeling needy. I'm tempted to touch myself and use a toy, but I want to wait for Ian. Tonight is going to be fun.

Oh shit, I better tell Sasha what happened. That will entertain me for a bit. She'll be amazed at my sluttiness. I type away on my phone with glee and get lost in conversation with her.

I'm naked in bed with my eyes closed when Ian gets home. I'm playing with my tits and have a vibrator pushed into my wetness while I daydream about my slutty vet appointment.

My eyes snap open when he walks through the door. I shoot him a lusty smile and remove the vibrator so he can see the moisture coating my fingers. "Welcome home, honey. Would you like a taste?"

He takes a step towards me, but instead of diving for me as I hoped, he strips off his clothing slowly. I lick my lips when I see his cock. It's standing straight out, hard, and glistening with his pre-cum. When he sits on the bed, he growls, "No, you're going to come up here and straddle my lap so you can ride my cock while you tell me about what you did with the vet and his employee."

A delicious shiver races through me. When did he get so bossy? I like this version of him. I climb into his lap and guide his hardness to my pussy, moaning from delight as he fills me. My body tenses for a second and then relaxes as I adjust to him. He likes it when I'm on top.

"Okay, I'm not sure where to start."

His mouth lands on mine, and I lean forward and wrap my arms around his neck as I rock against him. He tastes spicy and warm—like I'm home. My pussy contracts around him and his hands wander to my tits. He pulls a breast to his mouth and sucks. His touch is so familiar, and I moan, "God, this feels so good. You know just what I like."

When he flicks his tongue around my nipple and sucks harder, I moan louder and grind on the base of his cock. This is why sex with my husband is always going to be better than with anyone else. He knows exactly how to give me the most pleasure. After so many years together, we're like a well-oiled machine, and the experience today highlights that. Fucking other men was fun, and was an amazing experience, but coming home to Ian is what makes it awesome.

As I bounce up and down on my husband's thick shaft, I share the details of my crazy day. I tell him about what Sasha told me, and how I propositioned the vet. I explained what they both looked like, and paint a vivid picture of how they fucked me. Telling Ian about my slutty exploits is erotic, and I slam down harder on him with each new admission.

Once I think I'm done with the story, I'm about to fuck him furiously and try to get him to blow his load, but I realize I left something out.

"Oh, honey…"

He rolls us over on the bed so he's on top and feasts on a breast before answering. "Yes?"

A spiral of desire makes me arch against him, and I'm breathless when I speak. "I forgot to mention something."

"Mmm hmm?" He switches breasts and sucks on my other nipple harder than usual.

I squeal from the pleasurable pain and buck against him, forcing his cock in as deep as he can go. Fuuuck, he's driving me insane.

He tugs on my nipple with his lips and murmurs, "Tell me."

Fuck! Okay. "Jace didn't fuck my ass, but he fingered it."

Ian stops all movement and looks up at me. "You let him stick his finger in your ass?"

Oh, shit…is he pissed? I open my mouth to tell him he didn't actually stick his finger in, but I don't have time to think because Ian sits back on his heels, lifts my ankles onto his shoulders and hammers into me. His eyes bore into mine with ferocity. "You are MINE," he grunts. "That means all your holes are mine."

"Yes…yours," I moan and close my eyes as the bliss builds. His possessiveness thrills me. I am his. My husband's cock fills my pussy to perfection; no other cock is better.

"Good," he growls and redoubles his efforts, slamming into me with such vigor I can tell I'm going to be sore tomorrow. I welcome the pain.

When he reaches down and slides his thumb past my asshole's tight ring of muscles, I groan from the unexpected pleasure. His voice is harsh. "I own this too."

The idea that I belong to him makes me go half out of my mind and my muscles tighten as I spiral towards my climax. "Ian…Ian…Yes…Ohhh god..." I'm practically screaming as he fingers my ass while his thick shaft pumps in and out of my pussy with hard, fast strokes.

"Fuck, Erin." Ian grunts and swivels his hips, drilling into me with a primal need as his thumb penetrates deeper.

Pleasure slams into me, and I feel as if I'm flying as a wave of ecstasy radiates throughout my entire body. It's a soul-shaking orgasm that sends me shooting sky high.

My husband goes wild when I climax, fucking me with abandon. He removes his thumb and grunts as he gives one last thrust and empties ropes of his sticky cum deep inside me.

"Mmmm...." I mumble as he collapses on top of me, nuzzling into the side of my neck.

He whispers, "You're the best," and a warmth steals over me.

I hold him tight, running my fingers gently down his back as our bodies cool down. My pussy is deliciously tender and tiny spasms of delight continue to ripple through me, but my brain is humming. I never expected him to fuck me so hard. Was it because I let Jace play with my ass? Maybe we both have secrets that turn us on.

We move onto our sides and I snuggle up against his chest. He pulls my hand to his mouth and kisses the pads of my fingers one by one. "I love you," he whispers. "So, you'll do it again—fuck other men? You want to be a hotwife?"

I nod. "Yeah, I'll totally do it again."

"Thank you."

I glance at his face. "For what?"

He kisses me tenderly. "Trusting me, indulging in my fantasy."

"I wanted to do it," I protest. He needs to know I didn't do this just for him. I wanted to fuck Jace and Matt.

He grins. "Yeah, my slutty wife loved getting it in two holes."

"Mmm, I did."

I bury my head in his chest and inhale his familiar scent. Shit, what a wild day it's been.

We're both quiet for a few moments until Ian shocks me when he pipes up. "I enjoy seeing this slutty side of you. If I invite my friend from the office over to fuck you, can I watch?"

Holy fuck, who is this man I married?

I thought fucking a stranger would satisfy my curiosity, but now I want more. Ian asking to watch is the icing on the cake.

I purr, "Yes, my love. I'll fuck whoever you want while you watch."

And it's true. I'm officially the ultimate slut and I'm going to get as much cock as my husband allows. It's time for a new chapter in our marriage, and I'm excited to see where this is going.

The Slutty Wife's Vacation

Book 2

Lacey Cross

CHAPTER 1

As Sasha and I approach the entrance to the casino and hotel, I glance down at my outfit and smile. This weekend is going to be fabulous. My tight black miniskirt and low-necked, slinky blue tank top make me feel sexy.

I feel a little guilty for going on vacation without Ian, my husband. He's stuck at home while I'll be having fun and making questionable decisions. He insisted I go and enjoy myself. Plus, Sasha had a discount voucher for the hotel that was about to expire if she didn't use it right away. So, I need to stop feeling guilty that he isn't here with me; he loves me and wants me to have a good time.

As Sasha and I wheel our suitcases to check-in, she interrupts my thoughts. "What's on the agenda for this evening, hot stuff? We have time for a bit of gambling before dinner. Do you want to give the slots a go?"

"Sounds like a plan," I say.

Sasha and I have been friends for years, and she's like the sister I never had. We get along famously, and I share everything with her. Her sparkling personality brings lightness and joy into any situation—and she's the one who helped me become a hotwife.

A month ago, my husband and I agreed that if I found someone I wanted to sleep with, I should pursue it. The next day, I flirted with my cat's attractive veterinarian and became his plaything. Being double penetrated by him and his technician has been the highlight of my year.

Afterwards, my husband enjoyed the thought of watching me fuck another guy so much that he asked if I'd fuck his friend while he watched. Mmm...yeah, that was a wonderful night as well.

But that brings us to this weekend. Ian said if I wanted to, I could find someone to sleep with, but he had one request: he wants to watch over video chat. It's not likely I'll find someone to have sex with in the next couple of days, but Sasha knows the agreement. She told me if she needs to make herself scarce for a couple of hours while I get busy, just toss her twenty dollars and she'll entertain herself and play some slots.

She's so funny and supportive, and it almost makes me feel guilty that her husband isn't willing to share her. She sighs wistfully about how she wishes she could fuck other guys as well and tells me she'll just live vicariously through me.

The line for check-in is unusually long. Maybe they're all here on discounted vouchers. I survey the lobby while I wait for the cue to advance and notice an attractive man looking me over. Hmm, interesting. He's not being too obvious, and I receive a much-needed ego boost because he obviously likes what he sees. A pleasant tingle runs down my back, and when we reach the check-in counter, I'm sure my cheeks are rosier than usual. Sasha notices the guy too and wiggles her eyebrows at me as we give our names and a credit card to put on file.

As I'm handed my keycard, Sasha gives me a knowing grin and teases, "He was checking you out."

"Oh, please...no, he wasn't."

I play it off, even though I noticed his glances. I'm surprised he wasn't eyeing Sasha. With her beautiful blonde hair, striking blue eyes, and petite frame and big boobs, she usually gets most of the attention from men. Not that I don't clean up well. I'm attractive and feeling sexy tonight...and I'm the one who can actually fuck someone if I want to.

As we head towards the elevators, I'm still confused about why the hotel and casino are crowded. You'd think a discounted weekend would be empty, and that's why they were tempting people to visit. Hell, maybe we're all just cheap bastards who only visit when we can get the rooms at a reduced rate.

As we pass a conference room, a sign catches my eye and I stop abruptly. The sign is welcoming veterinarians to a conference. My eyes widen with shock, and Sasha turns around when she notices I'm not moving.

I point at the sign. "Seriously?!"

She laughs at my reaction. "What? Rumor has it you enjoy being fucked by hot vets. Maybe you'll find another one."

My pussy hums in delight at the thought, making me giggle in response to her suggestion as we continue towards the elevator. My slutty side is all set to take another ride on a cock that isn't my husband's.

When we get in the car, I push the button for our floor and mutter, "If there's a conference here this weekend, why did they give out discounts?"

Sasha shrugs. "Maybe you should stop questioning the universe and instead be excited about the possibility of fucking a sexy vet."

I give her a sidelong glance. "There're hundreds of rooms in this casino, not all with veterinarians. Plus, there are women here for the conference, too. I won't be able to tell which guys are vets—I'm no vet whisperer. There aren't any signs on doors telling us 'hot vet in here', right?"

"All I hear is you whining about being allowed to fuck whoever you want this weekend while I have to behave. Just pick the nearest smoking hot guy and tell him you've got a pussy that needs an exam and see how he reacts."

Oh God, she's nuts. We laugh as the elevator dings and opens on our floor. My spirits lift as we walk down the hallway. It would be fun to fuck a hot vet again. I'm just not sure how to go about finding one who wants me and will fuck me on video chat. Jace, my cat's veterinarian, wouldn't object to showing off on camera to Ian, but he's half a state away. We've texted a few times since I fucked him, and he's definitely looking to set up a playdate again while Ian watches, but the timing hasn't worked out yet.

Our hotel room is nice, but not lavish enough that we'd want to spend all weekend holed up inside. I'm sure that's calculated to keep us down on the main casino floor and spending money. We drop our luggage off, and while I'm in the bathroom freshening up, I daydream about fucking a train of sexy, muscular men. My husband didn't say I could fuck multiple guys this weekend, but he didn't say I couldn't either. I should probably find just one first before my pussy makes these elaborate plans and then gets disappointed. Once I find one, then I can ask Ian if I can have more.

I'm giggling to myself when I join Sasha back in the room. She glances at her phone. "About damn time. We need to hurry."

Jeez, we've got plenty of time to gamble. It's not like we're on someone else's schedule. I don't want to tell her I was busy daydreaming about being a mega slut this weekend, so I hurry and follow her out the door.

The first thing I notice as we enter the casino area is how many sexy guys there are. Yup, definitely an excellent selection to choose from.

Wait, why are there so many attractive men here? It's like the Twilight Zone and I'm in an alternate universe where all the men are hot and willing to fuck me. I wouldn't mind a portal to that universe.

Sasha nudges me, and I shake my head to clear my daydream. She tips her head towards a guy. "Hey, look at that ass. It's fucking yummy. Prime real estate. Do you think he's packing more than just that tight ass?"

Yeah, I wouldn't mind taking a bite out of those buns. I check out the guy's delicious looking ass while rolling my eyes. "You have the filthiest mind—he's hot, though."

The guy turns his head to look in our direction as if he knows we're discussing him. My body tenses with surprise and disbelief as I stare at Jace. What are the chances? The odds of us landing in the same place as Jace are slim to none, but here he is. Sasha squeezes my arm, and I have to pry my eyes off Jace to look at her.

She winks at me. "Have a good time tonight, Erin. Your husband said to tell you to not forget the video chat."

My mouth falls open, and she giggles as she strolls away through the slot machines. I'm rooted to the spot in shock, but my entire body lights up when Jace's velvety voice brushes against my ear.

"Hello, Erin. Are you going to be a good girl for me tonight while I fuck that sweet pussy of yours?"

Oh my god, yes. He doesn't need to ask me twice.

I spin to face him. "I can be very good."

He chuckles as he wraps an arm around my waist, tugging me closer. My mind races. Should I try to find out how he and Ian set this up now, or do I just take him up to my room so he can use me all night long? It only takes two seconds for my body to hum at his touch and for me to know what I want: fuck first...talk later.

Jace is just as sexy as I remember. He's in his late 30s with dark brown hair. He's taller than me, with a powerful, fit frame. I know exactly how well he's able to hold me down and fuck me hard, and my pussy flutters in response to the memory.

His deep blue eyes gleam as he smiles at me, and his hand skims lower, squeezing my ass. He leans forward and presses a kiss on my neck, teasing my skin with his lips before pulling back to whisper in my ear, "Let's take this party to my room. You've been a very naughty girl since our last visit. I'm going to need more than just your pussy tonight."

Excitement surges through me, and I suck in a sharp breath. Shit, Ian and I didn't discuss what holes could be used this weekend. Last time I was with Jace, he indicated he wanted to use my ass the next time he saw me. When I told Ian about it, Ian got so worked up by the thought that I didn't know if he'd be okay with it. I didn't bother asking about having anal this weekend because I wouldn't want to experiment with someone I don't know, but with Jace...mmm, I'd let Jace fuck whatever hole he wants.

Jace's lips capture mine, and we share a heated kiss that leaves me panting and wanting more. How the hell does he do this to me? I just have to look at him and I'm immediately in the mindset of being his fucktoy, wanting only to please him. If he asked me to do something, I would, without thinking. It's insane.

He grasps my hand and pulls me along with him towards the elevators. I'm assuming this was all planned and that's why Sasha was in such a rush, but I'll get the story out of her tomorrow. Jace mentioned going to his room and not mine, so I don't have to worry about Sasha. She's a big girl and can take care of herself tonight.

As we wait for an elevator, his fingers caress mine, sending ripples of joy down my spine. When the doors open, we're alone and he presses me against the elevator wall and ravishes my mouth as the doors close. Holy fuck. I melt into his kiss and lose track of time, forgetting where we are. He runs a hand up my inner thigh and under my black skirt. Since my skirt is tight, I can't give him as much access as I'd like, but I'm able to spread my legs enough for him to rub my pussy through my panties. I groan with pleasure. I want to feel him inside me—right now.

The elevator dings and comes to a stop. The doors open, snapping me back to reality. Three people are waiting outside, and my cheeks flush as Jace removes his hand from between my legs. There's no doubt about what we were doing. A woman titters and the two men smile at me as we pass them by. I silently wish them all good luck for the weekend and hope they get laid.

Jace pulls me along the deserted hallway, stopping at a doorway at the end. Instead of pulling out his keycard, he presses me against the wall and kisses me deeply while kneading my breasts with his massive hands. I can feel his hard cock through his jeans, and I don't understand why we're not in his room with his cock in me yet.

I push at him and give him my best sensual purr. "Take me inside. I need you."

He nibbles on my neck, and for a moment, I think he's going to ignore me. My head spins as a delicious shudder shoots through my body. God, he's intoxicating.

"First," he murmurs as he licks and sucks on my neck. "You have a choice to make."

"A choice?"

Like...which hole? A spark of concern zips through me because I don't know if I can make any decisions while my head is swimming. I want him to fuck me and not give me a choice.

He grips my waist and grinds his erection against me. I can hear the smile in his voice. "Yes. Do you want one or two...?"

His hands wander back to my breasts, and I'm confused. When he pulls on my nipples, I moan, "One or two what?"

"Cocks."

He swoops down to give me a bone-tingling kiss before I can reply. Am I hearing things? His hands slip under my tank top, and he lifts it above my head, exposing my black lace bra. My arms are in the air and he drops my shirt on the ground as he pulls the cup of my bra down to expose one breast before moving his lips to my nipple.

Holy fuck, we're in the hallway! I frantically glance both ways, but we're still alone. His teeth graze my nipple, making me forget that he asked me a question. Mmm, that feels amazing. His tongue flicks my nipple while he works the other breast out of its bra cup with his fingers.

Wait. Did he ask me about two cocks? My brain is mush from the plea-sure of his mouth on my breast, and I try to form a sentence. "Two...two guys?"

He grins around my nipple in his mouth and gives it a hard pull of suction before letting go to answer. "Matt came with me this weekend. He's in the room. Are we telling him to leave or stay?"

My mouth forms an 'O' as all thoughts drain from my head except for being spit-roasted by Jace and Matt again.

Jace laughs at my expression. "Your husband said it was your choice. He'd love to watch you with us both, but you decide."

Holy fuck. If Ian wants to watch, the decision is already made. I'm desperate for both of them again, and Ian's been my only concern. My pussy gets wetter as I think about explode. My husband wants it after all. What else is a girl gonna do?

"So, Erin, what will it be? One or two?"

I wrap my arms around Jace's neck and press my lips to his. "Mmmm, two please!"

CHAPTER 2

I don't bother adjusting my bra, and Jace grabs my tank top from the floor. Excitement surges through me, and I feel like an absolute slut as we step into the hotel room. Had I known what was in store for me before the trip, I wouldn't have been able to sleep for days. When I get home, my sweet husband can ask for all the blowjobs he wants. He deserves many, many blowjobs.

I pause with my tits hanging out of my bra when I see Matt on the king-sized bed, naked and ready for us. His cock is hard, and he's stroking himself. His face lights up when he notices my bra pulled down, and he strokes faster.

What if I had said no to their proposition? That would have been a bit awkward, but let's be honest…I doubt anyone thought I'd say no. Hell, my husband probably assured them I'd pretend they were my favorite rollercoaster and ride them both all night long. And once Jace said my husband wanted to see me with two men, how could I say no to that? I snicker to myself. A girl's got to take one for the team occasionally to make her husband happy.

Matt is still impossibly sexy. He's in his mid-twenties, with short blonde hair and those yummy arm sleeve tattoos that still just do it for me. I'm more attracted to Jace just based on his being an older dominant man, but Matt is smoking hot. My mouth waters when I think of sucking his glorious cock again.

Jace presses up behind me and massages my breasts, pulling on my nipples and making my toes curl from the pleasure. Fuck, this is good. When he turns me in his arms and claims my mouth with a savage kiss, I moan against his lips as a wild, sharp need ripples through me.

His voice is rough with lust. "I want you on your knees, sucking my cock, but first you need to call your husband. He's waiting for you."

My legs nearly give out when I picture my husband sitting in the living room, staring at his laptop, his cock hard and aching as he waits for me to video chat. I bet he's stroking himself right now. Ian is an amazing lover and is generous in bed, but lately I've been the aggressor with sex. Now, he's taken charge, and this is a wonderful surprise.

Jace rubs his thumb along my bottom lip. "Go on, be a good girl and call him. I'm sure he's getting impatient."

Mmm, yes, I'll be a good girl. There's a dresser with a TV on it a good distance from the bed that will give a full view of the action. Setting my purse there, I dig my phone out and call my husband on video chat. I'm not surprised that he picks up immediately. When his face fills the screen, he's wearing a wide smile. A wave of love for him washes over me.

"Hi babe," I say and blow a kiss at the screen.

His eyes shine as he gives me a sly grin. "So, do you like your surprise?"

I pan the phone around the room to show him Jace, sitting at the foot of the bed, and a very naked Matt. "If you're talking about these two hot guys you arranged to fuck me tonight, then yeah, very good surprise."

"Good. Now it's time for you to show me how well you suck another guy's cock. Get your clothes off. I want to watch."

His words sizzle my brain, and it takes me a moment before I can think. Jesus, what has gotten into Ian? He's never this demanding. Yeah, I fucking love my husband.

I prop the phone up against the TV so it's facing the bed. I stand in front of it and cup my breasts. "Is this a good view?"

"Oh yeah, baby. Wonderful view." Ian rustles around, and I can tell he's doing something with his pants—probably opening them so he can stroke while he watches.

I giggle and blow him another kiss. "Enjoy the show."

He blows me a kiss back as I quickly kick off my shoes and unzip my skirt, letting it fall to the ground. I'm wearing black panties to match my bra, and I slow down to give the guys time to appreciate what they're about to have. I face the bed to tease them, rolling my hips and slowly peeling my panties down my legs. Ian moans his approval from the phone behind me.

It's a little weird that he's not in the room, but just knowing he's turned on makes this even hotter. I unhook my bra and throw it aside, cupping my full breasts and giving them a squeeze, watching as the men in the room react. Jace growls, his hand sliding down to squeeze his cock through his jeans while Matt moans and strokes his shaft more quickly.

Jace smiles, and his voice is low and commanding. "Now get on your knees and crawl over here. You're going to show us how good you can suck cock."

I feel a thrill of submission course through me as I sink to my knees and crawl towards the bed, my breasts swaying with each move. I stop in front of Jace and look up at him. "Should I start with your cock or Matt's?"

Jace chuckles, his gaze raking over my body. "Mine."

I lick my lips, my mouth watering as I kneel between his muscular thighs and reach out to unzip his jeans. I pull his cock out and grip his shaft firmly in my hand. With a slow, deliberate pace, I take him into my mouth, my lips sliding up and down his length. The taste of him is salty and sweet, a delicious combination of masculine muskiness and undeniable desire. As I lap up each drop of pre-cum, the sensation of him against my tongue sends pleasure zigzagging through me. It's too bad Ian can't see much from this angle.

Jace lets out a strangled groan, his hands fisting in my hair as he starts moving my head up and down his length. I take him deeper into my mouth, my tongue swirling around his cock. For a few moments, the only sound in the room is the wet sounds of me slurping on him.

Jace keeps guiding my head up and down his cock as he says, "Can you hear this?"

The sounds of me sucking on him fill my ears, and I assume that's what he's talking about. "Uh huh," I murmur around his cock.

"This is the sound of you learning to be a good girl."

My stomach flutters from joy, and a warm fuzziness floats over me as I bob up and down rhythmically. I want to be his good girl, and I'll do whatever it takes to get him to say it.

I can feel every throb of his cock, and I'm curious to taste him since I didn't last time. When his cock spasms, he pulls my mouth off him before he comes.

Looking up at Jace, I ask, "You don't want to come in my mouth?"

Jace shakes his head. "Oh no, I'm going to come deep inside that pussy of yours. Now go show Matt what he's been missing."

I crawl up on the bed and over to Matt, my heart racing with anticipation. He's leaning against the headboard, and I approach him from an angle that gives my husband a side view of my body. I want to make sure Ian gets to see the action since my back was to the camera while I was sucking on Jace.

I take Matt's cock into my hand, feeling the heat and weight of it as I slowly stroke him. Looking up at him, I ask, "What would you like me to do?"

Matt's eyes darken with lust. "God, I've been daydreaming about your mouth for weeks."

Shit, that's hot. I get a jolt of pleasure from him admitting he's been thinking about me.

As I sink my mouth down on Matt's cock, my lips stretch around the thick girth of it. I work my tongue, licking his shaft as I take him deeper into my throat. I get a moment of déjà vu as I think about how his cock tastes different from Ian's. It was the same thing I thought the first time I was spit-roasted by these two. But now that I have more experience sucking cocks other than my husband's, it's not as weird to have a unique taste in my mouth.

Matt's moans of pleasure fill the room, and when I feel his balls tightening against my chin, I almost giggle. He was stroking so much before that he might come quickly. I won't mind, especially not since he's been thinking about me all this time. He was probably stroking and imagining me sucking on him, and now he gets to enjoy the real thing.

When Jace moves behind me on the bed and rubs his cock up and down my wet slit, I moan my approval. Matt swears as he tries to hold back his orgasm. As I pull my lips off him, I stroke his slick cock, watching it swell and twitch under my touch.

With a swift movement, Jace plunges into my pussy. I cry out in pleasure as his cock stretches me out and fills me completely. Jace groans, his fingers digging into my hips as he pounds into me, his cock hitting just the right spot to drive me wild.

Oh...my...god. I give a long moan from the intense bliss before I suck on Matt's cock again. I bob my head up and down, trying to keep my movements synchronized so that every time Jace slams into my pussy, it forces Matt deeper into my throat. Matt's leg twitches, and I can tell he approves of what I'm doing. Saliva drips down his cock as I work him over, my fingers wrapped around his thickness as my mouth glides up and down.

I turn my head as best I can to make sure the phone is still upright. It is. I can only imagine how this looks to Ian. He's got a side view of me while I'm sucking on Matt and getting plowed by Jace. Too bad the phone is too far away for me to see Ian clearly. I'd love to see him stroking himself while another guy fucks me.

Jace draws my attention to what he's doing when he growls, "Do you like being a little slut for us?"

"Yes," I moan around Matt's shaft.

Jace continues to talk dirty. "Is that because you're just a filthy slut who wants a cock in all her holes?"

His words send a shiver of delight through me because it's true. I've been daydreaming about Jace fucking my ass for weeks now.

"Admit it," he demands darkly. "Admit you're just a filthy whore who wants to be used all night and have all her holes filled."

Fuck...I can't think when he talks to me like that, and my brain blips out as Jace hammers into me.

A sharp slap to my ass makes me cry out around Matt's cock. I lift my head off of him and grind back against Jace. "Yes. God, yes, just a dirty whore who wants to be used."

Jace says, "Good slut," as he fucks me steadily.

I focus back on Matt's cock, putting my lips around him and sinking down to the base. When his cock pulses against my tongue, I suck harder, and he explodes with a groan. I swallow his cum as best I can as it spurts down my throat. Now that I know I've made one guy come, I'm desperate to make Jace blow his load as well.

As Matt slips free of my mouth, I glance back at Jace. "Fill me. Please?"

"Not yet," he says.

Dammit, I want his cum inside me. My orgasm is building, and I know if I get his cum, it will tip me over the edge. My pussy is trembling and clenching around his cock.

"Please," I beg. "Come inside me. I want to feel it."

"That's a good girl," he chuckles. "Now get on your back. I want to get you off before I shoot my load into that sweet pussy."

Jace pulls out, and I want to scream with frustration. I need him to come so badly. I've never been this crazed for a man's cum before.

I practically dive onto the mattress and roll over. Once I'm on my back, Jace hovers above me and captures my mouth, his tongue tangling with my own. My entire body tingles from the pleasure as his hands roam over my breasts, massaging the soft globes as he deepens the kiss. I sigh, and he releases my lips as his mouth travels lower.

Trailing soft kisses along the sensitive skin of my neck, he lingers on my favorite spot, sucking and licking until I'm sure I'll have a hickey before the night is over. Fuck, that's hot. I want him to brand me.

I squirm beneath him, pushing my breasts against him, urging him lower. He's torturing me with his kisses, and I desperately need more. I want everything he can give me.

His lips finally land on my nipple, and he swirls his tongue around the taut bud, gently biting the swollen flesh. My pussy floods with wetness as I buck beneath him. I'm going to go insane if I don't come soon.

He glances at my face. "Patience, my little slut."

Oh, fuck this. I moan out my displeasure, and his mouth moves lower. He plants a row of kisses along my ribcage and navel before burying his face in my soaked pussy. I nearly lift off the bed as he sucks on my swollen clit, sending a rush of sensation throughout my body.

"Ohhhh, god," I cry out as he slides two fingers into my hot channel, finding just the right spot as he pumps them in and out.

I whimper, arching my back as the intense pleasure builds in layers. When his fingers speed up, it sends me over the edge. I cry out as I explode. Waves of ecstasy ripple through me, and he continues to suck on my clit, prolonging the pleasure.

After the last spasm subsides, I collapse onto the mattress. I lay limp while Jace kisses my inner thigh. He traces his lips along the soft skin until he reaches my knee before kissing his way back up my other leg. I'm quivering beneath him, my body thrumming with excitement, and I can't believe how turned on I still am.

His eyes burn with passion as he gets to his knees and positions his cock at the entrance of my pussy. He grins wickedly as he enters me in one hard thrust. I cry out at the exquisite pressure of my pussy adjusting to his thick shaft again. He stills for a second, and my breathing returns to normal while I relish the feeling of having him buried inside me.

I turn to look at the phone on the dresser and blow kisses towards my husband as Jace slides in and out of me. The erotic sounds of his cock thrusting in my wet pussy, combined with his labored breathing as he nears his climax, drive me wild. I look back at Jace as he hammers into me harder and harder, his thick cock pounding into my soft, wet pussy.

I wrap my legs around Jace and hold on to his shoulders as my climax builds. When Jace leans down to claim my lips, my toes curl and my whole body stiffens from pleasure. He groans, thrusting one last time as his warm cum splashes the walls of my pussy, triggering my release. A sharp pleasure runs from my fingers to my toes, and I moan and writhe as he fills me with his cum. My pussy spasms around him, milking him dry, desperate for every last drop.

Once my climax recedes, I can't help the delirious giggling that follows. Jace pulls out, rolls onto his side, and I relax. Fuck, that was good.

Matt chuckles. "Don't get too comfortable. You're not done yet."

What? I turn my head to look at him. He's erect again, his cock pointing towards the ceiling, begging for attention. Yeah, guess I'm not done yet.

Jace strokes my hair and tilts my face towards his. His mouth meets mine, and he kisses me with such intensity that it takes my breath away. My heart is pounding with anticipation, and I want nothing more than to have his cock buried in me again, but he has other ideas.

"Roll over like a good slut, and get on your hands and knees," he demands.

I do what he wants without hesitation. I'm just their fucktoy for them to play with. My pussy is throbbing and desperate for more. Oooh, wait. Now do I get it in the ass? Wait...I need to talk to Ian first. I can't have that.

Matt gets off the bed and moves to the other side so he can climb on behind me. I relax a little when I realize Jace didn't put me in this position to fuck my ass. Mmm, does this mean I get Matt's cock in my pussy tonight, too? I'm not sure why I assumed I'd just be sucking him off like I did before. This is like a double treat.

"Time for your second round. Do you think you can handle both of us, or are you too tired?" Jace asks, teasing me with the possibility that they might stop.

"Bring it on."

Hell, I feel like the biggest slut at the moment, and I could probably take on an entire battalion of hot veterinarians. I'm insatiable, and I love how dirty I feel. I revel in my new hotwife role.

I wiggle my ass and look over my shoulder at Matt. "Fuck me, please. I want you inside me."

He presses in behind me, wrapping one hand around my waist and using the other to guide the tip of his cock to the entrance of my pussy.

My core melts at his touch. I need him. "Please...hurry."

As he eases his cock into my pussy, I'm flooded with pleasure. I moan loudly as I push back against him, needing all of him inside me. Ohhh, god. They can use me all night long if they want. I'll be the best fucktoy there is.

"Fuck me hard, please. Don't be gentle," I beg.

"Like this? Is this what you want?" Matt pants out as he hammers into my pussy.

I grip the comforter as he rides me. I can feel my breasts bouncing with every thrust. I'm not sure I can answer him, so I moan, "So good."

My husband loves it when the pleasure short circuits my brain and I can't talk. I really hope Ian is stroking as he watches. I want him to be enjoying this because I'm not sure I want to stop being a hotwife. This is wonderful.

Jace kneels next to the bed so he's directly in front of me, and his thumb brushes my lip. I know what he wants. I part my lips, and when his thumb enters my mouth, I suck on it. He watches me intently as I reach for his cock. I grasp it in my hand, and his eyes flash with lust.

His voice is low and strained. "I'm going to fuck that pretty mouth of yours."

Mmm, yes. When he moves his cock towards my mouth, I flick the head with my tongue and he growls in appreciation.

He strokes my hair and whispers, "Keep being a good girl."

He holds my head in place as he pushes his cock past my lips and into my mouth. I can taste myself on him, and it's like licking an Erin lollipop. The thought makes me giggle, but I quickly become distracted by how deeply he's fucking my throat.

Jace's eyes are focused on his cock driving in and out of my mouth, and when I look up at him, the corner of his lips lift. It's obvious that he likes this, and my pussy spasms when I realize I'm going to get another load of cum from both of them.

Holy shit, I love my life, and I adore Ian for arranging this. I can't believe he planned it all out for me.

Matt's thrusts intensify, and I know he's going to come. He gives several last thrusts before he empties his seed into me. I let out a muffled moan, and a burst of pleasure shoots through me as my orgasm takes hold. My entire body trembles as my muscles contract, waves of rapture rolling over me.

When my tremors stop, I continue sucking Jace's cock as Matt climbs off the bed and sits in a chair. My arms are shaking, but I want Jace to finish down my throat. The way he's making short and quick thrusts as I suck harder tells me I won't be disappointed.

Jace grabs the sides of my head, pumping furiously into my mouth as my lips slide over the thick length of his cock. My mouth is stretched wide open, and it feels so dirty to have my lips wrapped around him, especially knowing my husband is watching. I love being the center of attention.

Jace lets out a low growl as his cock erupts. He spurts into my mouth, and I do my best to swallow the hot, salty liquid, but there's so much some drips out. It runs down my chin when he withdraws from me. He drops his forehead on mine as we pant for air.

"You've been such a good girl," he whispers, and I flush at the compliment.

When Jace gets off the bed, I collapse onto my stomach. Oh god, I feel so used. It's glorious.

Jace puts on his jeans before picking up the phone to talk to my husband. "Ian, I want you to see how pretty this little slut is when she's used and well fucked. Do you like my cum all over her face?"

The only noise coming from the phone is a strangled groan. Jace angles the camera at my face as he wipes his thumb across my chin, clearing up some of the mess. I smile at the camera, knowing I probably have a goofy grin. I'm cum drunk from all the fucking and enjoying my slutty facial. I've never had so much cum in one night before, and I can't say I mind one bit.

Jace puts the phone in my hand, and I'm looking at Ian. My voice is a soft purr. "Hi, baby."

"Hello, my sexy wife. I love you. I fucking love you." Ian's voice is shaky, and I'm pretty sure he just blew a massive load while watching.

I giggle. "You look happy. Did you like that?"

Ian smiles at the screen. "Yeah, it was awesome."

I blow a kiss at the camera, my chest flooding with warmth. This man is perfect. I have no clue how I got so lucky, but I'm thrilled he enjoys watching me with other men.

"You better be ready to get fucked the moment you walk in the door," Ian teases me.

I give a soft laugh. "Okay, I can't wait to see you and give you all the attention you deserve."

My pussy spasms at the thought of my husband driving his cock deep inside me. I'm going to show my appreciation for everything he's done by riding him for days when I get home.

"I can't wait. Have fun, baby. We'll chat tomorrow." Ian ends the call.

I stretch out my legs, enjoying how relaxed my body feels.

Matt and Jace have been quietly cleaning up. Now they sit in the chairs, dressed and looking at me with smiles.

Matt is the first to speak. "Thank you again, Erin, for a wonderful time."

Jace nods in agreement. "You were amazing and a good girl."

My body hums from his praise. "Yeah, maybe we can do this again at home while my husband is in the room watching?"

Matt's eyes spark with interest, but he turns to look at Jace for direction.

Jace's lips twitch with a smile. "Sounds good to me. I'll contact Ian and set something up."

They stand, and I can't resist sitting up and pulling them into my arms for a hug. We're laughing, and I give them both a quick kiss before getting cleaned up and dressing.

Jace escorts me to my hotel room, making sure I can get in with my key. Before the door opens, he pulls me into his arms for one last deep kiss. I melt against him as his tongue sweeps through, caressing and exploring my mouth as he trails his hands up and down my back. He's turning me on again, and I want to fuck him in the hallway right now.

When he releases me, we share another long gaze. I don't think he wants to go, but he forces himself to say, "Goodnight, Erin."

I step through the doorway, turning around to give him a little wave. "Goodnight, Jace."

As I close the door, I realize Jace didn't even try to fuck my ass. What's up with that? He makes me admit I want it in all my holes and then doesn't even give it to me? A warmth of wetness from my pussy makes me giggle. Yeah, fucking dom guys. He's going to make me desperate for it before he gives it to me. I mean, it's not like he was going to get it tonight without me talking to Ian, but he should have at least tried!

Sasha isn't in the room yet, and I assume she's still playing slots. I'm giddy and laughing at myself as I fall onto the bed, my entire body drained from all the orgasms.

Yep, Ian deserves blowjobs for days. I'm the luckiest slut alive.

Slutty Wife Unleashed

Book 3

Lacey Cross

Chapter 1

My hands are over my closed eyes and my heart races with excitement as my husband, Ian, leads me to the spare room. He claims he has a surprise for me, and I can't wait to see what it is.

"No peeking," he reminds me.

I giggle. "I'm not looking, but don't let me trip."

"We're almost there," Ian says and stops walking.

My curiosity gets the better of me and I finally ask, "Can I open my eyes now?"

He's been keeping me out of the spare room for an entire week. All he said was that he was creating something for me.

"Sure. You can look," Ian says with a smile in his voice.

I drop my hands and blink twice to clear the spots from the sudden change before gasping in shock as my jaw drops. The bed is gone, and in its place are two long couches against the walls, new side tables, and in the middle of the room, a shiny silver pole sticking up from the floor.

Holy shit, Ian got me a stripper pole! I squeal with happiness and throw my arms around him. I've been talking to him for a year about wanting to take pole dancing lessons, but I never imagined he would actually want one installed in our house.

He kisses me soundly and laughs at my delight, and when I let go of him, I examine the rest of the room. There's new lighting in the ceiling and a stereo and speakers. He went all out. The floors were already hardwood, so he didn't need to do anything different with them, but he installed a wall of mirrors across from the couches.

"This is amazing. Thank you so much!"

He grins broadly, amusement twinkling in his eyes as he hugs me. "I hoped you'd like it."

Yeah, this room isn't going to be open to family when they visit anymore. I'll just tell them it's now a storage room, and keep the door padlocked if I have to.

Ian's never done anything like this for me before, and my hands shake with excited energy. I approach the pole and study where it's attached to the ceiling.

My voice is bubbly and I start talking fast. "Is it secure? Have you tested it out already?"

When I imagine Ian dancing around the pole to test it, I smile. My sweet husband probably wouldn't dance for me, but I know he'll enjoy watching me.

I pull on it and I can tell it's going to hold my weight. I can't help teasing him with a sly grin. "So, what made you decide to do this?"

As if I didn't know. He just wants to watch his slutty wife pretend to be a stripper.

Ian leans against the wall, crossing his arms against his broad chest. His eyes darken with desire. "You became a hotwife because I asked you to, so I wanted to do something you've been asking for."

I open my mouth to protest that I'm not fucking other men just for him, but he continues. "Plus, you'll look sexy sliding all around that pole. I'd be crazy not to encourage that."

Well, that seals it. There will definitely be a lot of shows for him.

Ian sits on the couch, reaching for a bag I didn't notice before from underneath a side table. "There's more to your gift, too."

More? He motions me over to him as he fishes something that looks suspiciously like lingerie out of the bag and hides it in his lap. As I get closer, he lifts his hands up to reveal a see-through black teddy. Yeah, that seems more like a gift for him. Hell, everything so far is a gift for him, but it's something I've wanted, so it's sweet of him.

I purr at him. "Ohhh, you're going to wear that for me? I initially thought you said you got me a gift, but you're the one who's getting a gift here. The teddy would look sexy on you."

He chuckles, shaking his head and pulls me into his lap. "Not me. You'll be wearing it when Jace and Matt come over next weekend to watch you spin around that pole for us."

My brain freezes for a moment as a delicious tingle spreads over my body. Jace is my cat's veterinarian that I fucked one wild day at his office while his technician, Matt, used my mouth. Later, Ian arranged a surprise for me to fuck them both on a casino trip while he watched over video chat. I envision swinging around the pole in the black teddy with the three men staring at me, waiting for me to get naked and fuck them. Holy shit, he already arranged it?

Oh god, what if I suck? My heart races with unease. I haven't had any training. What if I make a complete fool of myself?

I can feel my face flush as I bite my lip and hesitate. "Shouldn't I learn how to first?"

He rubs my arm in soothing circles. "Baby, you're gorgeous, and whatever you do is going to be fucking sexy. All you need to do is swing around it a bit and you're going to have us drooling."

Hmm...I climb off his lap and test out the pole again, twirling around it to see how it feels. He settles back onto the couch and smiles at me. He's not worried about a damn thing.

Hooking my leg around the pole, I arch my back and wink at him. "Like this?"

The bulge under his jeans is noticeable, and his voice is husky. "Yeah, that works."

He's probably thinking of me in the teddy. I get a jolt of courage and try a few more poses, working out the best ways to balance with my leg hooked around the pole. Pretty soon, I'll be able to do some decent choreography. I wonder how much dancing the men expect me to do?

Unhooking my leg, I turn to Ian and strike a pose that I think might be seductive. I run my fingers through my hair, thrust my tits forward, and put an extra roll to my hips. I slowly approach the couch and pull off my shirt, glad that I'm wearing one of my favorite bras, a wisp of purple lace.

"And what else should I do that night with you guys?"

His eyes wander down to my breasts, and knowing he's turned on by what I'm doing gives me a zing of pleasure straight to my clit.

"I'd like to watch you have sex with them," Ian replies, his voice growing rough. "But only if you want to."

Oh God, he's nuts. As if I'm not going to want to fuck their brains out once I get worked up playing stripper for them. I hold in my giggle as I unbutton my jeans and peel them down my legs.

I tease, "Watching me suck another guy's cock gets you hard, huh?"

A flush creeps up his neck, betraying the heat stirring within him as he watches me step out of my jeans. I turn my back to him, then bend over to pick them up. When I stand and glance over my shoulder, I catch him adjusting his crotch.

I lean down, sticking my tits in his face as I take off my panties. He hums in approval as I toss the underwear to the side and straddle him. His erection nudges my soaked slit through his jeans, and I grind on him briefly before sitting in his lap. I hope he didn't plan on wearing these pants all day. He's going to be a mess when I'm done with him.

My hands roam over his muscular arms, loving how strong he is. And he's all mine. I lean in close to kiss him, flicking my tongue against his.

Pulling back a fraction, I murmur, "I love the stripper pole. Thank you."

He grins, and I can tell he's satisfied that I appreciate his gift.

I nibble at his earlobe. "So why isn't your cock inside me yet?"

In an instant, he flips me over and I squeal in surprise as he presses my back against the cushions. Oh shit, I guess he's taking me at my word. As he fumbles with his pants, I wrap my arms around his neck and I giggle at his enthusiasm.

He guides his cock into my pussy, and I moan as I lift my hips off the cushion to meet him. Mmm, this is perfect. When he's fully sheathed in my pussy, he grazes my neck with his teeth as he fucks me. With each plunge into me, a sharp jolt of bliss travels from my pussy to the rest of my body. I tangle my fingers into his thick brown hair as his thrusts grow harder.

He nuzzles my neck before trailing kisses down to my shoulders, leaving tiny bites along the sensitive flesh. Fuck, I love that. My husband is such an amazing lover, and knowing how hot he gets at the idea of sharing me is the icing on the cake of our marriage.

As I near my orgasm, Ian pounds into me, speeding up, and I can tell he's fighting to hold back his release. The pressure builds, and my climax rushes over me like a dam bursting free, taking away every thought as the pleasure rips through me. I shudder through my orgasm, my pussy clamping around him.

He thrusts one last time before he erupts, moaning into the purple lace covering my breasts. We're panting for air when he collapses on top of me, his cock still twitching inside of me.

Ian mutters against my shoulder, "Christ, you drive me wild."

I run my fingers through his hair and giggle. "Just wait until the weekend. You haven't seen anything yet."

I'm too content after my orgasm to be worried about my lack of dancing skills. Ian's the most wonderful husband, and a quickie was just what I needed tonight.

Ian had invited Jace and Matt to come over Saturday evening, and I've been watching pole dancing tutorial videos online to prepare. Every day, I sneak into the spare room to practice when Ian isn't around. It helps me relieve some of the stress about my impending performance since I still don't feel graceful on the pole. It will be different with guys there, though, and hopefully the sexual energy from everyone will make me not feel as self-conscious.

By Saturday lunchtime, I'm nervous, but also crazy turned on. I can barely eat, but I know that my body needs the fuel because I'm hoping to get a nice workout tonight.

After I eat as much as I can get down, I spend a long time pampering myself with self-care. A warm bath with a peach-scented body scrub loosens my nerves. I let my mind drift, imagining how tonight will go. Are the guys going to just watch me dance and then fuck me? Will they make me choose between them, and are Matt and Jace going to both fuck my pussy, or will Matt just want my mouth again? I have no idea what the agenda is, but just thinking about them using me as their fucktoy has me flushed and turned on.

Wait. I jerk upright, causing water to splash over the side of the bathtub. Anxiety sets in as I realize I needed to have a serious conversation with

Ian about anal sex. Jace keeps saying he's going to use my ass, but Ian got possessive when I told him about Jace fingering my backdoor.

Yeah, fuck, I need to talk to him. I climb out of the bathtub, and force myself to slow down long enough to slather lotion all over my body. As much as I want to race out there to chat with Ian, the other guys won't be here until evening, so there's plenty of time.

Once I'm sufficiently moisturized, I put on my silk robe and hunt the house for my husband. I find him on the couch in the living room, watching a football game on TV.

I snuggle against him and give him my cutest, "Hi."

Ian pulls me into a sweet kiss before replying, "Hello, love. You smell good enough to eat. Did you enjoy your bath?"

"Mmm, yes. I'm nice and relaxed."

I'm only half fibbing. My body is relaxed, but my mind is keyed up about tonight and the conversation about anal sex.

Ian kisses the top of my head. "Good. I can tell you're still a little tense. Remember, it's only for a bit of fun tonight, no big deal. If you want to stop at any time, then let me know. I'll toss the guys out and we can watch a movie together."

Yeah, right, I don't think I'd ever stop for a movie when I have three guys willing to fuck my brains out.

I keep my voice light. "Um, we need to talk about what happens if one of them goes for my butt. I mean, I can say no, but you know how I get…"

He chuckles. "Babe, I already told them they can have any hole but that one."

Uh, he did? Fuck. Knowing he discussed what holes of mine they can use makes my head swim, but my stomach ties in knots from disappointment. Yeah, I'm totally a slut who wanted it in the ass tonight. I take a few seconds to get my thoughts sorted, and my words burst out in a heated whisper. "But what if I want it?"

He glances down at me with surprise. "Do you?"

My face warms as I shrug. Why is it so difficult to talk to my husband about my sexual needs? This should be the one guy who I can tell anything to, and yet I'm still embarrassed about my submissive urges and wanting to be treated like I'm just three holes to be used.

"How about this..." Ian kisses my head again before continuing. "Let's experiment with that ourselves first, and then I'll decide how I feel about someone else fucking your ass."

A thrill runs down my back and my nipples harden. Oh God, this is so damn dirty to be discussing. "Like today before they get here? Right now?"

He snickers softly. "No, before next time."

Oooh, next time! I sigh and snuggle closer to him. "That sounds good."

After a second of silence, he murmurs into my hair. "Erin, I want you to be happy with everything that happens, but just remember this is supposed to be fun for you, too."

"I know." I fiddle with the collar of his shirt as a warm feeling of being protected fills me.

He continues, "I love you so much, and you're my priority. So be honest and tell me if you need something different, okay?"

My heart squeezes with emotion, and I swear I'm the luckiest woman in the world to have a husband as thoughtful as Ian. "I will. Promise. I love you, too."

He plants another soft kiss on my head and wraps an arm around me as we settle into watching the rest of the game.

CHAPTER 3

My hands tremble as I stare at myself in the bedroom mirror. The black lace teddy that Ian bought me highlights my breasts and hugs my curves. It's thin lace, and if I bend over, Jace won't need to do a hole check tonight. He'll be able to see everything clearly. Thank God I took the time to tidy up the lawn down there. The ensemble is slutty as hell, and it makes me feel like I'm about to be served on a silver platter to three hungry lions. Mmm, not that I'd mind if the lions ate me.

I pull my long brown hair up into a ponytail and fasten a black choker around my neck. To complete my look, I slide on my sluttiest black spiked high heels. Luckily, I've been practicing dancing in them. The instructional videos were really helpful, and I've got a few moves down. It will be enough to please the crowd, and something tells me this is going to be an easy audience to win over.

As I adjust my breasts in the cups of the teddy, my heart skips in anticipation. Obviously, I've been the center of attention before in my banging sessions with the guys, but tonight is different. All eyes really will be on me from all angles with the mirrors on the wall, and I'm trying not to psych myself out.

The doorbell rings, and Ian calls down the hallway, "They're here."

I smooth my hands over the black lace, feeling nervous but eager. Ian and I meticulously planned out tonight's events. He'll greet our guests, get them drinks, and lead them to the spare room. He'll turn on some music and when the moment is right, I'll make a grand entrance and give them a performance they'll never forget. Easy, right?

Just thinking about it has my core tightening, and a surge of warmth rushes through me. Hopefully by the end of the night, I'll have a good story for my best friend Sasha. I promised to tell her all the slutty details. Oooh, I'll send her a picture while Ian gets the guys settled.

I grab my cell phone and snap a photo of myself in the mirror.

Erin:

The men are here and they are about to get the full stripper treatment.

Sasha:

#jealous. You better give me all the details tomor-row.

I giggle at her response.

Erin:

I will. Promise!

It really is too bad that her husband won't share her like mine will. At first, I didn't want to become a hotwife, but now that I am one, it's fucking fabulous. Sasha struggles with monogamy and she would have loved to have a husband as open as mine. I'll just make sure to tantalize Sasha with all the filthy parts so she can imagine it was her instead. Hopefully this doesn't include a sad tale of me ending up flat on my face as I try to twirl around the pole in these heels.

Oh God, why did I agree to do this? My anxiety bubbles up and before it turns into full-blown panic, I take a few deep breaths. Okay, stop it. I can do this. I shouldn't be worrying. This is just going to be some sexy fun with the men. I keep giving myself a pep talk as I leave the bedroom.

The nervousness fluttering in my stomach increases the closer I get to the spare room. I can hear upbeat music playing through the door. I don't pause to give myself time to worry. As I open it, I see Matt and Jace are sitting on the same couch, lounging comfortably, while Ian is on the other one. Their focus immediately shifts to me when I enter.

Jace is just as sexy as I remembered from my trip to the casino. He has a powerful, fit frame, and he's wearing blue jeans and a green T-shirt. His presence dominates any room he's in, and I can feel myself growing damp between the legs as I meet his deep blue eyes.

The men stare at me with undisguised hunger as desire simmers low in my stomach. My face grows warm, but I refuse to look away. I'm a sexy slut and I'm going to own it tonight.

I keep my head high as I saunter over to the pole with what I hope is a confident stride and give them my best seductive tone. "Hi, guys."

"Holy fuck, Erin, you're killing me in that outfit," Matt groans as he squirms in his seat.

I focus on Matt and my nipples harden when I see he's wearing a T-shirt that shows off his muscular arms with their full sleeve tattoos. My attraction to Matt always surprises me because he's in his mid 20s, which normally would be too young for me. But his enthusiasm when he fucks me is endearing, and I love being a super slut and worshipping his cock while Jace drills into me from behind. Mmm, yeah... I'll take some of that tonight.

When I peek at my husband, I see that Ian's eyes are dark pools of desire, and I can feel my pussy growing even wetter. I've been turned on all day, but his appreciation works me up even more.

Jace stands up and approaches me, and my body buzzes with neediness. I want his hands all over me. Or better yet, his cock inside me.

He steps behind me and wraps his arms around my waist. When he nuzzles my neck, I hold my breath and my nipples pucker. I press back against him and wiggle my ass as he presses his lips behind my ear in a gentle kiss.

He whispers softly, "You look stunning."

I remember to breathe again as I spin in his arms. His eyes burn with passion as his gaze bores into me, and I feel my heart race with a sexual hunger. The room fades away as I focus on his obvious desire for me, and I forget all about my fear of performing.

With one hand on my waist and the other on my lower back, he pulls me closer to him. His lips brush against mine softly before deepening the kiss, his tongue exploring every corner of my mouth. As I melt into his touch, the last of my worries and doubts disappear from my mind. I can feel his passion for me through every movement of his hands and lips, and it makes me feel alive. They really won't care what I do, and they'll love every minute of it. I have to trust this, and I want to have fun with them, too.

I moan as Jace cups my breast with his hand, and his thumb brushes against my nipple. I'm spellbound as the fingers of his other hand caress my inner thigh. Oh, fuck. I shiver with delight as he grazes my wet folds through the teddy. I wish the fabric wasn't between us. If he doesn't stop, I'm going to beg him to fuck me before I even dance for them.

I tear my mouth off his with reluctance. "Don't you want a show?"

Jace laughs. "Definitely. Work your magic." He gives my nipple one last tweak before stepping back.

I glance towards the couches as Jace sits back down. Matt grins enthusiastically, and his intense stare heats me up. Ian looks like he's already half out of his mind from lust, and I mentally smile. Yeah, Ian is enjoying watching me with other men in person instead of over video chat.

I turn and take a tentative grip on the pole as I survey my surroundings. The music pulses through me, my clit throbbing in time to the beat. A surge of power washes over me, and I push away the last of my reservations. I know what they want, and I want it too.

As soon as my hold on the pole tightens, my body sways in a sensual rhythm. I glance at my husband and admire how sexy he is as he sits back with a clear bulge in his pants. The show might be for all the guys, but Ian is the one I want to please the most. I'm going to fuck the pole the way I want to fuck my husband.

I dance in a slow, undulating wave around the pole, using my entire body for effect. Each time my face passes the guys' line of vision, I smile seductively and lick my lips.

Their expressions encourage me, and I tug down the strap on my right shoulder to tantalize them. Matt shifts, and I can tell he's trying to make more room in his pants for his growing erection. Feeling the lust emanating off the men makes me feel like a goddess, and I continue to move to the music, letting it flow through me. I was concerned I was going to be awkward the entire time, but I feel fluid and graceful. Dancing for them gives me an erotic high I didn't expect.

Jace smiles wickedly, and I can tell he wants to tear my teddy off and bury his cock deep inside me. But he just has to wait. I pull the strap on my arm down farther until it falls down, and I tease them by showing off the upper swell of my breasts.

I twirl and give the guys a view of my ass as I drop low to the ground and work my way up the pole. I throw them a little extra shimmy before I turn around and hook my leg around the pole as I lean my body against it. The music is inside me, pulsing through my veins, and there's no stopping me now. I thrust out my hip and give them a view of the sheer panel on the front of the teddy that barely hides my pussy.

All of them have huge grins, and I want to give them more. I focus on my dancing for a few moments as I rock to the beat and jiggle my ass at them. As I peer over my shoulder, I notice the men leaning forward slightly, enraptured, and I'm shocked at how powerful I feel. They're craving every little movement I make. I'm a sexual enchantress enslaving them with my body.

I hook my leg around the pole again and rotate around it. Every nerve ending in my body is alive and the music washes over me like a living thing. I rub my body against the pole as I let the song fill me.

Matt wipes the sweat from his forehead as he leans forward. "Christ, she's sexy."

My heart races as my face burns from the rush, but I need more. I want the men so crazed for me that they come over here and fuck me. It's time to show them more skin.

I slip my straps off my arms and turn my back to them as I roll the garment down far enough to expose my entire backside. Jace whistles as he gets a good eyeful. I bend over to remove my heels, and then I slide the teddy all the way off.

I pause a moment to compose myself, but when I look back, my pulse jumps as the intensity of their gazes sends a jolt of heat between my legs. I'm naked except for my black choker necklace.

Twirling slowly around the pole, I allow them to feast their eyes on my entire body. My clit throbs, driving me wild, and I let myself go completely. The erotic atmosphere intoxicates me, and it's like I'm a totally different person. The end of my ponytail tickles my shoulders as I dance, and I trace my hand lightly up my side before grabbing the pole and swinging my legs in front of me. I thrust out my chest and point my toes as I arch my back to give them a good look.

Jace leans forward and when he licks his lips, my confidence skyrockets. I love teasing him, and knowing he's thinking about fucking me hard sends a ripple of pleasure straight to my clit.

As the song ends, I position my back towards them, grab the pole and open my legs. When I bend over, I hope someone takes the hint. I'm ready to be fucked.

Another song starts, and I stay bent over and reach a hand between my legs to play with my clit. The guys have a full view of my fingers as I tease myself and dip two inside my pussy.

I hear a rustle as one of the men stands up, and I'm not surprised to look over my shoulder and see Jace behind me. He brushes my hand aside and takes over. I close my eyes as a delightful buzz zings through me. He expertly strokes my swollen nub while easing a finger into me, and I wiggle my hips against his hand in encouragement. I cry out when he slides a second finger into my wet pussy.

My lips part at the delicious sensation and I moan, "Yes."

Jace spanks my ass cheek while circling his thumb over my clit, and a jolt of pleasurable pain shoots up my spine. He moves his spanking hand to push on the small of my back and forces me to bend over more as he adds another finger, stretching my pussy lips open.

Ohhhh god. I whimper in ecstasy as I push against his fingers. Fuck, I need to come. My entire body is aching for release, and I thrust back on him, begging for more.

Jace's voice is gravelly with need. "You're so greedy for it. Tell me you're desperate to come for me, my sweet little slut. Tell me you want my cock buried so far into you that you can feel my balls slapping your ass."

Matt gives a sharp inhale of pleasure, and I look under and behind me to see Ian's reaction. Ian white-knuckles the arm of the couch and his chest is visibly rising and falling. The tent in his pants is bigger than I've ever seen before.

Knowing that my husband is turned on is all I need to allow myself to sink further into submission. I'm ready to be used, and surrender myself to the moment. Jace strokes his hand along my back as he waits for me to answer, his fingers inside me slowing down.

"Please don't stop," I whimper, then beg, "I want it. All of it. Please?"

He rewards me with fast circles around my clit, driving me mad and forcing me to hold onto the pole tightly for support. I pant as I lift my ass up for more.

Jace coos at me. "You're so lovely when you're desperate. Good girl."

Pleasure washes over me and I bite my lip to stifle my cries, but they escape anyway. Matt gets off the couch and drops to his knees right beside us as I tremble on the brink of orgasm.

Matt bends forward, grasping my chin with a strong grip, and demands, "Open your mouth."

My head swims at the command and my lips part automatically. As Matt pulls his cock out of his jeans, Jace pushes me onto my hands and knees. Matt aims his cock at my mouth, and I moan a second before he slides it inside. I try to swallow him all down, my lips stretched wide to accommodate his girth. He buries in deeper, pushing past my gag reflex, and I concentrate on licking and sucking on him.

Jace smacks my ass with a loud crack, and Matt hisses when I squeak from delight and my throat convulses around his shaft. The feeling of my wet mouth makes Matt go crazy, and he becomes rougher than he ever has before.

I shift my gaze upwards and lock onto Matt's dark eyes as he fucks my mouth. There's a wildness in his eyes that matches how I feel, and I welcome whatever they want to do to me. I'm focused on Matt, so I'm surprised when Jace slams into me from behind. The shock of pleasure is so intense, the room spins as I cry out around Matt's cock.

Jace hooks his elbow around the pole for leverage and sets a punishing pace, hammering into me relentlessly as his balls slap against my sensitive clit. He doesn't seem to be holding back. My body is overwhelmed by their combined force, and I give into the intoxicating feeling of being used for their satisfaction. It's pure bliss.

Matt holds my head in place and uses my throat, his cock thrusting in and out rapidly. I'm so busy being ping-ponged between the guys, I barely have time to wonder what Ian is doing. He knows he can stop this at any time, but I'm not expecting him to. He set this up tonight, and he's the one who wants the full experience of seeing me fucked by two men at once.

Matt's cock pulses in my throat a second before he blows his load. He groans loudly as spurts of hot cum coat my throat. I struggle to swallow it all down, and when he pulls out, some escapes and drips down my chin. Knowing I'm going to be a mess makes me feel like an even dirtier slut, and I revel in the sensation.

Jace grabs my ponytail and I yelp as he jerks my head back. The bliss spikes through me and the joy builds in layers. He drives into me, riding me, and my toes curl as ripples of pleasure wrack my body until I can't take it anymore. I cry out as I orgasm, and he fucks me through the waves of euphoria in an unrelenting rhythm.

I expect him to keep fucking me until he comes, but he suddenly stops and removes his cock, pulling me back against his chest until I'm upright on my knees. He kisses my neck as he holds me in place by my hair. I'm still shuddering from the aftershocks of my orgasm and my brain is mush.

"Does our little slut like being used?" Jace growls as he releases my hair.

I moan out, "Oh god, yes, please don't stop."

I'm still floating when Ian appears in front of me, dropping to his knees to pull me into a scorching kiss. Ooooh, god, yes! I'm desperate to suck my husband's cock and I claw at his jeans, trying to get to him, but he grabs my wrists and holds them between us.

Between deep kisses, he says, "Erin, baby, you're so gorgeous. But I just want to watch tonight."

Watch? My husband must be half crazy, but I know he'll fuck me later, so he'll still get to come. Jace drags the tip of his cock over my slick folds and teases my clit with the head.

I moan out, "Yes, my love."

Holy shit, having Ian in the room is more intense than I expected. Last time he was watching over video, and while that was hot, it's nothing compared to touching him while another guy's cock is poised to press into my pussy.

Ian breaks off the kiss and stares at me with lust-filled eyes. I can tell he's getting a major rush from viewing the show and my eyelids flicker from pleasure as Jace sinks his cock into my sopping wet hole. He feels even thicker than he did a few moments ago, and it's exquisite as he massages every nerve ending deep inside me. I'm drunk on pleasure, and I lean forward to grasp my husband's arms as Jace slams into me.

Jace's voice is rough when he starts in with the dirty talk. "Are you enjoying being used like a fucktoy?"

"Yes," I whimper, closing my eyes in ecstasy as he pumps into me, fucking me furiously.

He's brutal as his cock jackhammers me. I cling to Ian like I'm afraid he'll disappear if I let go. I need the connection, or I might shatter into a million pieces.

My breasts swing with every whack against my pussy, and Ian takes advantage and moves a hand down to play with my nipples. I cry out as he tugs on my nipple and the delicious thrill drives me higher and higher towards another orgasm.

Jace reaches in front of me and finds my clit with his fingers. Sparks of electricity travel down my thighs, and my pussy squeezes him hard. I'm almost at the peak of ecstasy and I just need a bit more. I ride out the building tension.

Just when I'm about to orgasm, Jace's voice is deep and commanding. "Come for us."

My pussy contracts with such force, it startles me, and my orgasm sweeps over me, short-circuiting my brain as I cry out. My pussy milks Jace's cock as he pounds into me until a rumble vibrates in his throat. He explodes, releasing ropes of sticky cum deep inside me.

As we shudder together, the pressure subsides, and my legs lose their strength. I'm shaking and clinging to Ian to keep myself from collapsing on the floor as Jace pulls out.

Ian scoops me up and carries me over to the couch. He lays me down on my back and sits by my head, stroking my hair.

"Are you done, baby? Have you had enough?"

My brain is fuzzy and it's difficult to answer, but as I look across at the other couch, Matt is sitting there stroking his cock. He's hard again.

I want him.

I need him inside me, filling me and using me as Jace did. I open my mouth to beg Matt to fuck me, but the words stick in my throat.

I manage to choke out, "Please, I need more."

My husband gives me a fierce, approving smile. "You heard her. She wants more."

Matt doesn't need any more prompting, and he gets up and Ian moves over to the other couch to watch. Matt settles between my legs, hikes one of my knees over his shoulder and drives into my cum-soaked pussy. He fucks me hard, hammering away at me, and I cry out as pleasure ripples from my fingers to my toes as he ravages me.

His speed picks up and I think he's about to blow his load when he slows down, edging me closer and closer to my orgasm again. I can feel each thrust hitting a wonderful spot inside me and it drives me crazier than the fast pounding did. I'm about to beg him to speed up when Jace kneels by my head, his cock hard again.

I open my mouth eagerly, and he guides the tip past my lips. I can taste myself on him, which almost shuts my brain off from how filthy it is. I'm sucking on a guy who just fucked me while my husband watched. What type of woman does this?

A slutty hotwife, apparently.

Me.

I love the freedom of letting go and taking pleasure. My body feels boneless as I let go, surrendering to them again, as Jace thrusts deeper. All I can think about is them fucking me in both holes. Maybe someday I'll get every hole filled at once. Would I then get a medal for being a total slut? I'd giggle if my mouth wasn't busy.

Matt shifts positions, pushing my knees close to my chest, and being curled up while the two guys fuck me sends me over the edge again. My throat is full of Jace's cock and it muffles my cries, but my body convulses from the intense pleasure. My juices explode around Matt's cock, and knowing I'm making a mess of everything makes this filthier in a wonderful way.

Fuck, this feels amazing. The high of having Jace's cock in my mouth and my pussy being used by Matt drives me wild. When Jace comes a second time, he pulls out of my mouth fast to paint stripes of his semen all over my face. I feel like a complete whore, and that's exactly what I craved tonight and didn't even know it.

Ian murmurs from the other couch, "Shit, that's sexy."

That comment unleashes Matt, and he slams into me hard enough that my tits bounce. My voice is hoarse as I beg him, "Just do it! Use my pussy. Come in me!"

Matt groans out, "Yessss," and his fingers dig into my hips so hard that I'm pretty sure he's going to leave marks. But I don't care, I want the visual reminder of tonight.

The thought tips me over the edge again and I spiral out of control once more, calling out, "Oh god, I'm coming...fuuuuuck..."

My pussy clenches on Matt's thick shaft, and he stills as his warmth floods me. We're locked together, and the aftershocks of my orgasms zip through me with mini-contractions. He sighs with satisfaction and slowly withdraws his softening cock, dropping my legs back to the couch.

Holy fuck, that was insane.

Ian gets up and comes over to my couch to sit down and pull me into his lap. I shiver as I feel cum leaking out of me. Yeah, I'm probably getting his jeans dirty, but I don't care. I rest my head against his shoulder and realize I'm getting cum on his shirt also. Oops.

Ian's voice holds a hint of amusement. "Now are you done?"

"For now," I tease him in a sing-song voice. I'm definitely not done with him, but I am done with the other two.

He strokes my hair as he murmurs into my ear, "I'm going to put you in bed and then talk with the guys, okay?"

I nod and wrap my arms around him, melting against him. He smells good, and the comforting scent of home and safety is like a blanket that wraps around me. My eyes drift shut, and I'm so exhausted, I think I could fall asleep on him.

Ian stands up with me in his arms and I feel cum-drunk as I call out to Jace and Matt, "Thank you both for the good fuck."

Jace's deep laughter is the last thing I remember.

CHAPTER 4

I must have fallen asleep, because when I wake up, I'm under the covers in the middle of our king-size bed with just Ian. I roll over to face him.

"They're gone?"

Ian strokes my cheek, smoothing wisps of hair that escaped my ponytail off my face. "Yes, we're alone now."

My heart expands in my chest with all the love I feel for him. He's the best husband in the world and I'm the luckiest woman on Earth. "Thanks for setting all this up, my love."

He cups the side of my face with his warm palm. "Of course."

When he leans forward to kiss me, my whole body tingles, and I coo with happiness. I deepen the kiss, telling Ian I want more without using words. He responds by wrapping his arms around me, rolling onto his back, and dragging me on top of him.

He's already naked, and I wiggle until my pussy is against his cock. I don't have the energy to reach between us, so he takes over and I shift just enough for him to hold his cock steady and guide it into me.

I moan as he fills me. My face is inches from his and he pulls me closer to him so he can kiss me. I love my husband, and there's nowhere else I'd rather be. The man knows me so well, and he supports every fantasy and desire I have. I'm grateful and I want to make him happy, too.

I rock against him as I whisper against his lips, "You take care of me better than anyone in the world and I love you, Ian."

"You deserve the best in the world. I would do anything for you. I love you, too."

As I lift my hips and start a gentle rhythm, I pepper his face with soft kisses. His hands find mine and we lace our fingers together as we make love. This is one of my favorite types of sex with Ian, and my body starts tingling from the delicious friction.

I'm so worked up that my orgasm comes quickly. I gasp out as the pleasure erupts and my pussy contracts around Ian's shaft. He wraps his arms around me and we cuddle for several minutes, neither one of us moving, as aftershocks quiver through me.

Ian trails kisses from my ear down to my collarbone, sending a wave of fresh desire through me. I pull up a little so I can feel him sliding into me, and my body lights up when he moves a nipple to his mouth, sucking on the sensitive bud. A bolt of pure bliss flashes through me as he nibbles the tip and then runs his tongue around the areola before taking my nipple fully into his mouth and sucking it. My hips buck against his and I moan out his name.

Ian gives my tits lavish attention as I continue riding him. It feels wonderful, but I know he needs to come. He deserves to come.

I can feel the heat building between us, his hands roaming all over me, igniting every inch of skin. Switching my movements, I sit up straight and grind down hard on him, feeling every inch of him filling me. He grasps my hips, guiding me with each thrust, his breathing becoming more ragged as he approaches his climax. His eyes roll into the back of his head from pleasure as I increase my tempo. I'm so wet, I can hear the slapping of my pussy against him as I ride him.

I can feel the tension building in Ian's body as he nears his climax. He's panting and muttering nonsense phrases. He's so far gone, anything is going to make him explode.

I slow down for a moment, and he looks up at me, startled. I grind my pussy into his groin and wiggle around on top of him before going back to bouncing on him. With a smirk, I toss my head back and brace my hands on his abs to give myself a little more leverage as I ride him faster and harder than before.

"Come for me...come for me...come for me," I chant.

With one final surge, Ian's moans reach a fever pitch and he loses control, exploding inside of me. His cock spasms and his cum mixes with the other two guys' as his leg muscles quiver from pleasure. I ride him a few more moments before collapsing onto his chest.

Ian sighs, "Christ, babe, you drive me nuts."

I snuggle on top of him and giggle. "Same thing, next weekend?"

He groans in mock protest. "Anything for you, my love. But before next time, there's an ass I need to claim."

I get a naughty surge of happiness and I tilt my head and smile at him. "I think that can be arranged."

We kiss softly before I scoot off of him. My body is worn out from tonight's activities and my eyes drift closed. I'm warm and content, but my mind fixates on next time. Is he really going to let Jace fuck my ass?

I really want it. I'm such a dirty slut, and I wouldn't have it any other way...and apparently, neither would Ian.

BONUS STORY

A First-Time Backdoor Experience with My Husband

When my husband gets off work on Monday, I'm prepped and ready for him. It's time for him to fuck my ass. I've been sending him dirty text messages all day to get him worked up, and he told me to be in bed when he gets home. I follow his directions, and I'm waiting for him when he arrives.

Well, okay, he might not be expecting this. I'm naked and in the middle of the bed, leaning back on a pile of pillows with my knees bent and my feet flat on the mattress. My hand is between my legs, and I'm circling my finger around my clit when he walks in. I'm horny and worked up enough that I could easily get myself off before he touches me. I can already feel my arousal dripping down the crack of my ass.

Ian stands by the door and locks eyes with me, and his smile makes my stomach flip. I can see he's hard under his slacks and I grin at him.

"Did you have a good day at work, my love?"

He starts taking his shirt off and almost growls at me. "If you consider being hard and trying to hide behind my desk all day a 'good day,' then, yes."

Oooh, nice. My pussy clenches and I give him a mock pout. "Oh, poor baby. That does sound rough."

The corner of his mouth twitches and I speed up the motion of my hand, enjoying the swirl of pleasure in my core.

Once he finishes removing all of his clothing, he opens the dresser drawer where we keep the lube and I can tell the moment he doesn't find it.

"Are you looking for this?" I hold it up for him to see. I want to giggle. Did he expect me not to get it out? "You wanted me ready."

Ian laughs and as he climbs onto the bed, I get onto all fours, presenting my ass to him. I'm a filthy girl who wants her husband to claim her ass. I've waited long enough.

Ian puts one hand on each ass cheek, caressing them. "You're sure you want this?"

"Less talking, more ass fucking," I demand.

He chuckles and leans forward to get the lube. Ian's touch sends a tingle of excitement to my clit, and I can't believe I'm so excited to let him take my ass. The thought of him possessing it turns me on more than I thought it would. It makes me feel like his dirty little slut, and I love it.

After spreading lube between my cheeks and working it in, he also adds some to himself. My husband kneels behind me as he rubs his lube-coated dick up and down my crevice, and I groan from pleasure. I push back against him.

When the head of his cock nudges my tight entrance, Ian says, "I don't want to hurt you."

I look at him over my shoulder, frustrated that he won't just shove it in. "Please. Please. Fuck my ass, Ian, and make me your little slut."

I never realized how much calling myself a slut could make me soaking wet, but it turns out, I really enjoy being called dirty names, even if I'm the one doing it.

He bites his bottom lip as he lines up the head of his cock again, and this time he presses in hard and keeps going. Fuck, it hurts for a second, but the pain is instantly replaced by a delightful fullness. A fiery heat races through me, and all I want to do is throw my ass back and take Ian's entire length.

I want Ian to really fuck me. My pussy aches with need and my arms shake. I need this.

Grabbing two pillows to support myself, I lower my chest to the bed and surrender my ass to him. The feeling of submission overwhelms me. Until the time I fucked my veterinarian and he called me a 'good girl,' I didn't realize how much I craved submission in the bedroom.

This moment with my husband sinks me further down into submission than I've ever gotten with just him. I'm giving my husband everything I have, and my brain shuts off as I embrace the animal instincts running through my body. I need my husband's cock. He said this hole was his. Now he needs to claim it.

He grasps my hips firmly to steady me as he sinks his cock into me. Once Ian is in up to the hilt, he stops and gives me a moment to adjust. His hands run all over my ass before he strokes my lower back in soothing patterns until the muscles in my butt unclench.

It feels different from him fucking my pussy, in a good way. The sensation is intense and new and a little scary. But with a little patience, I'm able to relax fully as Ian keeps stroking my lower back.

He must be able to sense the moment I fully give in and open myself to him, because he starts thrusting. I moan softly as the pleasure builds. Being this open and vulnerable has me crazed and desperate for him to give me relief.

"Rub your clit for me," he demands, and I snake my hand between my legs.

My clit is swollen and covered in wetness as I swirl my fingertips around it. The hunger builds fast and my clit throbs as the warmth in my core turns into an inferno as the overwhelming fullness spreads throughout me. The fire rages within me, consuming me from the inside out. I need this. I crave this. It's been a long time coming. I need his cock in my ass. I need it like a drug, and I've been starved of it too long.

But here it is. Here he is, claiming my ass so thoroughly, owning me like no other.

I cry out, "Yes! Yes! Give me more. Harder."

His fingers dig into my hip bones as my husband loses himself to the moment. He fucks me harder and my breasts sway beneath me, slapping against one another.

"Tell me I'm yours," I gasp out.

Ian sounds like he's almost growling as he fucks my ass hard. "You're mine. This ass belongs to me."

He picks up the pace and I stroke my clit faster, right on the edge of bursting into flames. "Take it! Take it, please, make me your good girl, ohhhh god."

Ian embraces the moment with me. "No one gets to use this hole unless I say so. It's mine."

"Yes, yours!"

A powerful climax explodes through me as I hear him affirm that I belong to him, that he owns my ass and controls me. My world focuses down to just Ian and the possessiveness of his powerful hands as he drives into me. I scream with my release as wave after wave of scorching pleasure erases everything outside of us.

The first pulse of Ian's seed blasts me as he cries out in triumph, "Fuck, fuck, you're mine."

Each hot rope of cum is like liquid love filling me, and I focus on his pleasure. It satisfies a deep part of my soul to submit myself fully to him. Tears trickle down my cheeks, and I collapse onto my stomach as he pulls out.

Holy fuck. I've never felt this level of intense connection with him before.

Ian rolls onto the bed next to me and our chests heave as we try to calm down. After a minute, he pulls himself off the bed and I can barely think enough to wonder what he's doing as he heads to the bathroom.

When he comes back, he has a wet washcloth, and I moan softly as he cleans me up. I'm still floating in my post-orgasmic bliss.

He discards the cloth in the laundry basket and lies down on the bed again before pulling me against him.

"Fuck, that was good," he murmurs as he kisses my head.

I can only hum in response as my eyes close. As I mentally drift, his fingers caress my shoulder, and a slight smile tugs at the corners of my lips. My ass is a little sore, but in a delicious way that reminds me I was claimed by my husband.

This means that when the time is right, he might let Jace fuck my ass...maybe.

I'm such a lucky, slutty wife.

Slutty Wife on Edge

Book 4

Lacey Cross

Chapter 1

My heart pounds as my husband, Ian, maneuvers our car into the empty parking lot of the veterinary clinic. Ian isn't giving me many details about why we're here, but he promised me a Saturday afternoon I'd never forget. What fantasies await behind those shuttered windows? Ever since my first visit to the clinic where my best friend told me to ask about "special services," my life has taken a wild, thrilling turn. I fucked my cat's vet Jace and his technician Matt multiple times, so a trip to the clinic while they are closed only means one thing…I'm getting another shot at their gorgeous cocks.

A shiver runs down my spine as I remember the last time I fucked them. Ian installed a stripper pole in our spare room, and I gave the three men a private dance. Jace and Matt's strong hands gliding over my skin as I danced for them was erotic as all fuck. The pole still stands ready in our spare bedroom, but today isn't a dancing day. I have a feeling this playtime will lead us somewhere entirely new and deliciously taboo—hopefully with a cock in my ass by the time we're finished.

Since that first day with Jace, he's been teasing me about fucking my ass, but he's never tried. This past week, Ian laid claim to my ass in the most wonderful way. The feeling of him filling my ass was completely different from anything else I've experienced. I've never felt so loved and wanted.

Ian turns off the car and grins. "Are you ready, baby?"

I nod, breathless with excitement and unable to find my voice. Is it bad for me to hope that Jace is finally going to fuck my ass today? I'm new to anal sex, and I've only done it once, but with Jace's continual teasing about it, I'm turning into a wanton slut over the idea.

Since Ian lovingly and sexily claimed my ass for his own...there's a chance he'll be willing to share it. I've been wet all day just thinking about it, and I almost touched myself earlier today to take the edge off. But I was a good girl and held back. I'm so worked up, I bet whatever orgasms I have today are going to be amazing. I'm ready for the men to use me any way they want to and the ache between my legs as I get out of the car proves how much of a slut I am. Thank God my husband loves the slut he married.

As we walk across the parking lot, Ian surveys my chosen outfit approvingly. After a lot of debate this morning, I picked out a sea green skirt and simple matching tank top. Lots of easy access.

He steps behind me and rests his hands on my hips, pulling me back against him and making me stop walking. "I love that color on you."

I can feel his hardness against my ass, and I shimmy my hips to torment him. He makes a happy sound deep in his throat and holds onto me and grinds against my ass. Hell, at the rate he's going, do we even need to go into the vet's office? He could push me up against the side of the building and fuck me right here.

"You know," I say, "if you had told me what was happening today, I could have made sure I was dressed correctly."

He kisses my neck. "What you have on is perfect. You look beautiful."

I laugh and wiggle my ass again. "Thank you. But I want to look more than beautiful."

"Oh?"

"Mmm hmm." I press my ass against him harder. "I want to look like your slutty wife."

He laughs. "Don't worry, Erin. You always look like that because that's what you are."

Oh fuck, why is that so hot? I know he only means it in the most loving way. He and I both enjoy my newfound wild side. I whimper and lean into him. He's so hard against me, and all I want to do is grind on his cock. I think of how he felt in my ass again, how full and new it felt, and my clit aches.

He pushes my legs apart far enough that he can slip his hand down the front of my skirt and finger my pussy. What the hell? We're in the parking lot! I glance around and relax when I realize the side of the building is hiding us from the main street.

He makes a little growling sound against my ear. "You're so wet already. You're looking forward to this, aren't you?"

I rock against his hand as his fingers circle my clit. I'm already in a little bit of a submissive headspace just from the thought of what Jace and Matt are going to do to me, and the tone of Ian's voice makes me slip a little farther. "Mmm, yes. I've been thinking about it all morning."

"Good," he says, his fingers stroking me faster. I whimper and move my hips with him. Just feeling his hardness against me makes me think of being on all fours on our bed while he fucked my ass for the first time earlier this week. Everything is making me think of a cock buried into my ass. It would feel so good if he did that again—or if he decides to let Jace do it. I can't stop hoping that his whole plan today is to let Jace use whatever hole he wants.

He nips at my earlobe. "You're going to love what we have planned for you."

When he pulls my skirt up over my hips, I'm aware of the cold air on my ass, and I get lightheaded thinking of how it felt to have him filling me up. I really should protest that we're in the parking lot, but my head is too fuzzy and everything feels too good. His fingers keep moving on my clit while his thumb presses softly against the fabric of my panties, as if he's trying to rub my asshole.

It's such a good tease, and I whimper again. "Ian. I want you so much, are you sure you don't want to just go home and fuck me?"

I don't really want that, and I know he doesn't either, but he's making me desperate.

"I'm just making sure you're ready for all our cocks."

"Fuck, you know I am." The swirling of his fingers is hypnotic as heat grows in my core and my pussy clenches. If he keeps going like this, I'm going to come all over his fingers.

He pulls his hand away. "I guess we better get in there and see what happens."

I whimper at the loss of his fingers. I know he has to stop toying with me or else I won't get to fuck Jace and Matt, but I still wish he would have pushed me against the building and taken me right here. I want all three of the guys to use me today, and that includes my husband. I want to be the slutty wife of his dreams.

"Please," I say, wiggling my ass at him again, but he laughs and gives me just the lightest, most playful swat before pulling my skirt down.

"Patience," he says, shaking his finger at me.

I sigh. "Fine."

When Ian makes up his mind about something, there's no changing it. That's why I haven't tried to beg him to let Jace fuck my ass. If he decides to share me, he will. But if he does decide to...I'll give him a private dance on that stripper pole every night I live.

CHAPTER 2

We walk into the double glass doors together. My entire body is buzzing, and after Ian's little stint in the parking lot, I'm even more ready to beg for someone's cock. Ian's been delighting me with surprises ever since I became a hotwife, and all my experiences with Jace and Matt have been amazing. Whatever they have planned for me, I want it.

Matt greets us at the door as we walk up. He gives me a long, appreciative look, his gaze tracing all my curves. His greeting is warm and makes me melt. "Hi, Erin."

He's younger than Jace. His short blond hair and deep-set grey eyes are almost cute, but the full sleeve tattoos he has on both arms make me shiver. It gives him a raw and very male energy that makes me appreciate his stamina and strength. I'm not usually attracted to younger guys, but Matt is sexy enough that his age doesn't matter. Slut Erin just likes smoking hot guys.

Matt closes and locks the door behind us and starts pulling down the window shades as Ian and I move to the center of the waiting room. Just being back here at the veterinarian clinic makes my breasts tingle. Shit, am I going to get turned on every time I bring my cat to the vet now? Just being here and knowing that the guys are going to use me makes me sink down into my submissive headspace even more. I feel pliant and ready to be used.

I'm going to do whatever they want, like the dirty slut I am. Let's get this party started.

When Jace walks into the waiting room from one of the back offices, I take a moment to admire him. I'm very aware of how his tall, well-built body can make me feel. He has a commanding presence, and he exudes a strength that makes my whole body respond...and I love it when he calls me a good girl.

Both Jace and Matt are wearing blue scrubs, but Jace has a white lab coat on over his. There's nothing about their clothing that should be sexy, but they're so hot it makes saliva pool in my mouth. Maybe I'm Pavlov's dog and trained to want them now. I'll do all sorts of tricks for a long, hard treat.

I want Jace to call me a good girl.

And I really want him to fuck my ass.

Jace gives me a long look that takes in all of my curves. I pose a little and push my hip out, trying to show off. I bet he's remembering how sexy I looked twirling on that stripper pole. That was the night where his teasing about taking my ass inspired Ian to finally claim that hole for his own.

Fuck, I really hope Ian is ready to share.

"Hello, Erin."

Jace's deep, velvet voice makes my head swim in the best way. I want him and Matt to use me and make me their mindless slut.

"Hi, guys." Butterflies swirl in my stomach, but I'm more turned on than nervous. Even though I don't know what's going to happen next, a part of me is loving the suspense. This is the best way to drive me wild with desire.

"Are you trying to look innocent in that modest outfit?" Jace gestures at my skirt and t-shirt. "Because it isn't going to work. I remember the black lace teddy you were wearing last time I saw you."

I flash a flirty smile at Jace. "Nope, that would be silly. We all know what I want."

He moves closer to me, smiling so warmly. "Yes, we do."

When he pulls me against him, his scrubs can't hide how hard he is against my thigh. "We all know you want to be spit roasted again while your husband watches." He pushes a strand of my long, brown hair behind my ear gently. "Are you ready to be a good little slut and do as you're told?"

My knees go a little weak as I imagine sucking on his cock, and I purr a lusty, "Yes."

"Good girl." He gives me a long, passionate kiss. As our tongues twine together, I throw myself into the kiss and plaster my body against his. The longer he kisses me, the more needy I get.

Right when I'm about ready to try to ride his thigh, he steps back. "Get on your knees like a good fucktoy."

Jace's words are sharp without being mean, and I kneel immediately. The tiles are cold, but I don't care. All I want is to be a good girl so they will give me their cocks and fill me full of cum.

Matt and Jace don't waste any time. They push their scrubs down just enough to free their gorgeous cocks. Both men are huge, thick, and veiny. Matt is longer than Jace, but Jace is so thick it makes me salivate. I want to suck on them and get fucked by them both. This is the fourth time I've played with them, and I know how wonderfully full I feel when I'm stretched out by them, both in my mouth and pussy.

I can feel how wet my panties are, and it almost makes me laugh. Thank god I wore them today. I'd be a mess already without them.

Jace takes control. "Open your mouth like a good fucktoy and suck on our cocks."

His command makes me dizzy as I part my lips and stick out my tongue. Am I going to suck on them both at the same time? Jace and Matt step close, and I wrap a hand around each of their shafts. It's show time.

Leaning forward, I stretch my mouth as wide as it can go so I can engulf the head of Jace's cock. He gives me just long enough to swirl my tongue around the bulbous tip before he thrusts forward, filling my throat. He pushes past my gag reflex and holds me there. I groan, my throat working around his cock. He tastes different from Ian, and that turns me on even more. It's a dirty reminder that someone's cock is in my mouth and it's not my husband's. I know Ian wants this for me—for both of us. He loves me, and that's why he shares me. He gets hot watching me with other guys, and I get to be a dirty slut and get multiple orgasms. It's a win/win.

I bob on the cock in my throat and stroke Matt's shaft in the same rhythm.

"Fuck." Jace's voice is strained, and I feel a sense of pride. I'm a good cocksucker if he sounds like that.

He puts his hand on the back of my head, forcing me to move faster. I stroke Matt to match the rhythm, and Matt's breathing gets heavy as he jerks against my palm.

When Jace pulls back and his cock slips from my mouth, I immediately turn to lick the head of Matt's cock. It's salty with pre-cum, and Matt shoves his cock into my mouth harder than Jace did. I have to work to keep up with him while Jace continues to control the movement of my head. There's no chance to pull back and catch my breath.

Matt groans as he slams into my throat. I can feel how tense he is, and I try to push down harder, eager for his cum, but Jace pulls me off Matt's cock. Fine, take away my treat! I get my hand back around Matt and continue stroking both of them.

I expect Jace to shove his cock back into my mouth, but instead, Matt steps to the side and Ian moves in front of me. His cock is out, leaking at the swollen tip. Oooh, what's this? I didn't know Ian was going to participate today. This is slut wife heaven.

My pussy clenches from desire as I suck on my husband. Having a third cock in my mouth within minutes pings the naughtiest side of my brain. I want to be the ultimate slut for them.

I sink onto Ian's cock with just as much joy as I took the other men's. Jace holds onto my head and pushes me down fast and hard. I can barely breathe, and I don't care. My brain shuts off, and I become just a hole for them to use. Ian's cock is leaking on my tongue, and I want to keep sucking mindlessly until he blows his load down my throat.

Jace keeps a hold of my head, moving me from one cock to the other like a filthy slut who's just there to get them off. The longer it goes on, the more I want to be that. All I want is for them to explode in my mouth as their ropes of cum mix together and become too much for me to swallow. I want it dripping out of my mouth and running down my chin until I'm covered in cum.

Before any of them come, Jace forces me to stop. He pulls me off, and I gasp, filling my lungs with air. I put on makeup this morning, but when I see a smudge of pink on Jace's cock, it tells me that my face is probably a messy disaster. I love it.

Jace hums low in his throat as his thumb brushes my bottom lip, smearing my lipstick even more. "Such a gorgeous fucktoy."

A bolt of lust zips through my core as I stare up at the men. If Ian preplanned this all with them, my wonderful husband knows me better than I thought.

CHAPTER 3

Jace's grip is firm on my upper arms as he hauls me to my feet. My nipples harden in response to his commanding voice.

"Strip for us," he orders.

I reach for the hem of my shirt without thinking, ready to pull it off as quickly as I can. The sooner I'm naked, the faster I can get their cocks in me.

"No," he says in a firm tone that startles me.

I pause with my arms crossed over my body and look at him, waiting.

"Strip like you're getting ready to swing around a pole for us. Give us a show."

Pleasure pulses in my veins. Now I know what he wants. I give all three of them my sexiest smile before pulling my top up slowly. Matt makes happy sounds as each inch of skin is revealed. Their eyes on me sends lightning bolts of delight through my body. It reminds me of the other weekend when I really was dancing on the pole for them and how powerful I felt knowing I had them all under my spell. When I get my tank top off, I give it a little twirl and let it fly across the room.

I'm a little showier when I remove my skirt. Turning around so my ass is facing them, I rotate my hips in a slow circle. My firm ass is one of my best assets, and the extra exercise with the stripper pole only accentuates my curves. I want all the men thinking about my ass.

God, this is so filthy.

I hook my fingers in the waistband of my skirt and drag it slowly down my hips as I continue to bounce and jiggle my ass. When my skirt and shirt are off, I turn around, striking a little pose. My arms are behind my head, elbows out, and my hip is cocked to one side. The bra and panties I'm wearing are a matching set in lavender. The balconette lace bra barely covers my nipples, and the bottom is a wisp of silk that has me hyperaware of my ass.

Jace's eyes sizzle with heat as he looks at me while Matt groans, "God, Erin. You're so fucking hot."

Jace and Matt exchange glances, and Matt nods before heading towards a back room. Those two seem to be up to something, but the way my pussy is buzzing, I enjoy the mystery of everything today.

Jace gives me a speculative glance. "We're moving. Follow me."

When I take a step, he holds his hand up. "On your hands and knees."

A blush works its way up my body. "On my..."

He nods and his voice is like steel. "Now."

I do as he says, dropping down and getting on all fours, ready to follow him. The cold tiles bite into my knees, giving me a perverse pleasure.

"Good girl. Now crawl."

He takes a few steps towards the room Matt disappeared in. I slowly follow him, knowing that Ian is behind me and watching my ass. Why is this hot? The floor looks clean, but this is a veterinarian clinic so is it really? Crawling on a potentially dirty floor is degrading...which makes me even wetter. This is what it means to be their fucktoy—to obey.

My panties are damp and I bet Ian can see the wet patch. Just knowing I'm being watched has my pussy begging for one of their cocks inside me. They better not make me wait much longer.

Jace stops at the door to a small office and steps aside, gesturing me in first. "Go on. I want to appreciate the view."

As I crawl past him, I put a little extra shimmy in my hips. I want his eyes on my ass. I want him thinking about fucking me. About taking control of the hole he hasn't shoved his cock in yet.

"Mmm, so sexy," he says, and I shake my ass again.

He gives it a tiny smack, just enough to make me jump. I'm on my hands and knees in what looks like Jace's personal office. Matt is sitting in the desk chair, and Jace hovers behind me. I hear Ian come into the office, and when I glance over my shoulder, Ian leans against the wall and crosses his arms. I can tell he's prepared to enjoy whatever is coming next.

"Now, we're going to play a game," Jace says, and my eyes snap back to him. He strokes my ass, and I whimper before he continues. "We're going to use you."

His fingers slip down, dodging the hole I want the most and teasing the opening of my pussy through my panties. I moan and push back against him, but he doesn't press his fingers into me.

"We're going to take everything we want."

Lower, and he's teasing my aching clit. If someone was in my mouth while Jace was rubbing my clit, I bet I could come in two minutes.

"But one thing. You don't get to come without permission."

That startles me. I glance back at him, confused.

"You heard me," he says. "You're a greedy little fucktoy who is here for our pleasure."

My head is spinning. Oh god, I need his cock, and I'll beg as much as I have to.

Jace moves my panties aside, pushes two fingers into my aching pussy, and I moan from the pleasure. I'm not sure how much more of this teasing I can take without a cock inside me.

He finger fucks me slowly. "What are you thinking about, Erin?"

"What?" It's difficult to talk when my mind is fuzzy.

"Are you thinking about how good this feels?"

I'm shivering with need, and every stroke of his fingers is a shock to my clit. "Yes."

"Are you thinking how desperate you are for my cock?"

When he rams his fingers into my soft flesh roughly, I cry out. "Yes—fuck, yes."

He spins his fingers around so that his thumb is pressed against my clit. "You better be ready to beg, and you better hope I'm in a giving mood. I might just fuck you and leave you a desperate, wet mess."

I don't know if he expects an answer to that, so I stay quiet as his fingers quickly bring me close to coming. I push back harder, desperate to feel him inside me as deep as he can go. I just need a little more…

He pulls his fingers out, and I whimper as the swirling pleasure fades. Jesus, that's mean. The ache in my pussy doesn't go away, and I wiggle my ass. "Jace…"

"Before you get more, you're going to make Matt feel good," he orders me.

My brain parrots it back to me. Make Matt feel good. Okay. I crawl towards Matt, and all I can think about is being a good fucktoy and making him come.

While I was distracted with Jace's finger in my pussy, Matt stripped naked. His cock protrudes from his lap, thick and heavy. He's stroking it lightly, and it's fully erect for me.

I settle between his knees and take him into my mouth. I've given him a blowjob so many times I'm starting to know what he likes. Swirling my tongue around the tip, I clean up the pre-cum leaking out of him before applying just the right amount of suction as I slide his full length into my throat.

He groans and starts to fuck my mouth, his hips moving fast. I don't get to control the pace. I try to relax my throat and stay open for him as he holds onto my head and takes control. Every stroke is a lightning bolt of delight straight to my clit.

When Jace pushes my panties aside again, it's the only warning I get before he slams balls deep into my pussy. I cry out from the pleasure, but the sound is muffled by Matt's cock.

"Does that feel good, my sweet little fucktoy?" Jace's voice is a little strained, and I revel in knowing I'm giving him pleasure. I try to moan that yes, it does feel good, but my words are garbled. Matt hisses from the vibrations against his shaft, and I give up on talking as I throw myself into giving Matt the best blowjob of his life.

Jace hammers into me, and being trapped between their cocks switches something off in my brain. I really am their fucktoy right now. The only thing that would make this better is if Jace was fucking my ass, but this is close to perfect.

The pleasure builds in layers as I ping pong between the men's cocks. Every thrust from Jace shoves Matt's cock deep into my throat. I imagine both of them coming at the same time, and it almost tips me over the edge.

A stinging spank jolts me back to the moment as Jace growls, "You better not come without permission."

Heat swirls in my core as Jace drills into me, riding my pussy like he's in a competition. Every slam of his hips shoves Matt's cock so far down my throat, it's impossible for me to speak. I'm taking both of them deeper than I ever thought I could. I'm going to come, I know I am, I want to.

Before the pleasure erupts, Jace pulls out of me. I hate the immediate empty feeling, and I push back without thinking. I'm a greedy slut who needs more. My body is throbbing, and I'll do anything to come all over his cock.

"Focus," Jace says. "I haven't decided yet if you're coming today, and we're not done with you."

Fuuuuck. I want to protest, but Matt's cock in my mouth makes it impossible. Matt grips my hair, fucking my mouth vigorously while my brain keeps focusing on my ass and how much I want Jace's cock inside it.

Matt's voice is tight. "I want a turn with that pussy."

Jace must have agreed because Matt pulls out of my mouth. The men help me to my feet and then bend me over the desk. I don't get any warning before Matt's cock plunges into my pussy. I cry out from the pleasure. Matt is longer than Jace, and he's immediately knocking against a pleasurable spot deep inside me. Each thrust from Matt sends sparks of electricity to my toes, and I'm already close to coming.

"How does that pussy feel, Matt?"

Jace is talking like I'm not even here. Like I'm just an object. A toy for them to use. I groan at the thought and grip the edge of the desk harder. Each whack against my pussy is scraping my nipples against the wood and compounding my pleasure. I want to play with my clit and come for them.

"So warm and tight," Matt pants out as he jackhammers into me.

The friction in my pussy is more than I can take. Laying my head on the desk, I surrender to them and give up on coming. The desk smells of lemon cleaner, and it's almost as if I'm watching from above my body as the men use me. This is better than anything they've done to me before, and suddenly it doesn't matter if I don't come. I just want to make them happy.

I can feel my body tense as if I'm going to orgasm and then remember I'm not supposed to. Taking slow and steady breaths, I try to force my muscles to relax. I can't risk being a bad girl and them not fucking me. I've never felt like this before. I'm just a dirty slut craving cock.

"Uh oh, I think our fucktoy is going to come without permission."

Jace's voice holds a hint of amusement, and I cry out as Matt laughs. "You're right."

I'm doing everything I can to avoid coming, but it's not working. I can't stop it. I'm going to—

Matt pulls out of me an instant before the pleasure breaks and my pussy clenches around nothing. Nooooo. I mewl out in frustration. Oh holy shit. I'm so desperate to come. Why won't they let me come?

Matt presses his hand on my shoulder, so I can't stand up. "You know what I think?" His voice is teasing, and I can tell his question is directed towards Jace. "I think she's waiting for someone to fuck her ass."

I groan. Yes. God, yes, I want Jace to take my ass, but at this point, anyone's cock would do. I bet I'd come as soon as someone stretched me out. I want to orgasm like that, full and screaming.

"Too bad that she doesn't get to choose," Jace says. "Bring her here."

Matt takes a fistful of my hair and uses it to force me up. The pressure on my scalp is a painful pleasure, and I'm careful not to pull away from him. Matt makes me kneel again in front of Jace. I lick my lips as I stare at Jace's hard cock. The head is swollen and shiny, and I'm desperate to run my tongue over his veins.

Jace holds onto the base, aiming it at my mouth. "Suck it."

I open my mouth and glance over at my husband to make sure he's enjoying this. He's watching us intensely and rubbing his cock through his jeans. When he gives me a little smile and a nod, I engulf the tip of Jace's cock. My husband wants to see me be a slut, and I'm more than willing to play my part.

Jace barely needs to push me down, and I greedily suck on his cock. I can taste and smell myself on him, and I love how filthy it makes me feel. Licking my own wetness off someone's cock who isn't my husband is the right kind of dirty for me.

He groans as I deep throat him. "That's it. Just like that. Such a good little cocksucker."

Yes, I am. His praise makes me suck harder. This is as good as being a good girl. Maybe better. He's fucking my face steadily, and all I can do is kneel here and take it like a good cocksleeve.

"Now suck on Matt." His voice is tight, and I wish he had come, but I move over to Matt's cock like an obedient fucktoy.

I lick and clean my juices off Matt's cock, and the heady mixture makes my head spin. Jesus, this is so damn dirty and so fabulous. Jace kneels behind me and pulls my panties down to my knees. I'm so close to coming I really might explode as soon as he sinks into me.

Jace teases the head of his cock against the opening of my ass, and I groan. Oh god, what is he doing to me? He needs to just push it in. Do I have to beg?

I try to stay focused on Matt's cock in my mouth, but all I want to do is cry out and plead for Jace to fuck my ass.

Jace puts more pressure on my forbidden hole and growls, "Do you want my cock?"

"Yes." I struggle to get the words out around Matt's cock because right at that moment, Matt speeds up. His body is tensing, and I know he's close. I'm desperate to taste his cum, and I try to beg between thrusts in my throat. "Yes, please!"

"Tell us what you want," Jace demands, and I have to pull back from Matt for a moment to get the words out. "I want you to fuck my ass, Jace. Please? Fill me."

He presses harder, and I mewl from desire and slide my lips around Matt's cock again. Matt swears and pulls my head down firmly until my nose bumps against his pelvis. I'm so soaking wet I'm not sure Jace would even need lube to fuck my ass. He could just gather some moisture from my pussy and go for it. I'm such a slut, and I want to come with Jace slamming into my ass while Matt face fucks me.

Matt's thigh muscles quiver a second before he loses control. He comes violently, thick ropes of cum spurting down my throat as he keeps fucking my mouth and his entire body spasms. I lap it up as fast as I can, but there's so much that it's running down my chin.

As Matt sags back into the office chair, I grind on Jace's cock and try to think fast. "Please. You've been teasing me about using my ass since the day we met. I know you want it. Please? Fuck my ass."

"Greedy fucktoy," Jace says. "What do you say?"

It takes me a moment to realize that he's not talking to me. I look over my shoulder. Ian is sitting in a chair, stroking his cock through his jeans and watching these two guys turn me into a mindless fucktoy. He set all of this up for me, and the decision is up to my husband.

I could beg him, but I don't want to. The decision has to come from him. I'm a greedy, dirty slut. And I wait for him to choose.

After what seems like forever, Ian says, "No," and I moan loudly. Fuck.

Ian rubs his hardness under his jeans faster. "Her ass belongs to me. I'm not ready to share my toy yet."

When he calls me a toy, a warmth of love for my husband washes over me. I know he can't be a hard dom, which is why both of us enjoy what we do with Jace and Matt. Ian gets to see me turned into a desperate slut, and Jace gives me the harshness I crave. In a crazy way, Ian not sharing my ass today makes me feel loved and cared for.

When Jace hammers into my pussy, all other thoughts drain from my head. He drills into me, brutal and fast, and I'm crying out "Oh god," with every whack against my pussy. It's a glorious roughness, and I try to match his thrusts, forcing him to fuck me harder.

Jace's voice comes out in a puff between each thrust. "If you're a good girl and thank me afterwards, you can come."

My body lights up with pleasure, and I gasp as he continues. "But you better be quick. I'm about to fill this tight pussy, and then it's all over."

The thought of him filling me is all I need to come. My orgasm bursts through me, and stars twinkle along the corners of my vision as waves of ecstasy assault me. Jace fucks me through my orgasm, and I chant, "Thank you, thank you, thank you!" as the pleasure keeps going. My entire body shudders, and my pussy milks his cock, trying to get his cum.

He grunts, and right when I think I won and I'm about to get the payoff, he pulls out and yanks me up on my feet. He pushes me back onto his desk and removes my panties before he's between my thighs, lifting my knees with his forearms. I barely have time to get used to the new position before he's balls deep in my pussy again. The first thrust makes me scream as another orgasm rips through me like wildfire, sizzling all my nerve endings from my fingers to my toes.

He hooks one of my ankles up on his shoulder to free his hand and starts rubbing my clit. "After all that," he groans, "you think you're just going to get two?"

His hips slam into me, and the fingers on my clit speed up. My back arches as the pleasure is so intense I almost shatter to pieces. I'm filthy, this is filthy. Rapture tears through me without warning, and I cry out as I writhe from the pleasurable pain. It's almost too much.

"Fuuuuck," he grunts and explodes. His cum surges into me, thick and heavy. There's so much it's leaking out of me before he's even done. He fucks his cum into me as he spasms and jerks until he's done unloading. I'm full of cum from two different men and feeling completely satisfied.

I can barely think as the men move around me, kissing me and touching me softly. I'm not sure who is doing what, and I don't care. I feel amazing, and I'm floating in my happy place. The men clean me up and thank me for being such a good fucktoy. I'm mentally fuzzy, and all I can do is grin at them. When I'm tidy and dressed and clean, Ian takes my hand and leads me out to the car to head home.

CHAPTER 4

By the time we get back to the house, my brain is working again. I feel the best kind of filthy. That was a crazy experience, and I can't believe how much keeping me on the edge of coming would turn me into a desperate slut. Thinking about how I was willing to debase myself gets me wet and needy all over again. Fuck, that was hot.

We're barely inside the front door before Ian pushes me against the wall. Well, hello. I guess he's just as turned on as I am. Not that I'm surprised. He just watched me get used over and over again.

His mouth covers mine, and he lifts my tank top to play with my nipples. I whimper and groan, trying to push against him. I want him so much.

"You were a good little slut today," Ian says between kisses. "But I told you. Your ass is mine until I say someone else can have it."

"Oh god, please fuck me," I moan and beg. All those orgasms weren't enough, and I won't feel complete until Ian comes as well. "Please? I want you inside me."

Ian grins as he shoves my skirt and my panties down my hips. He helps me step out of them, then opens his jeans to pull his dick out. When he lifts my leg and hooks it around his waist, his cock slides into my pussy easily since I'm wet with Jace's cum still.

"Fuck, Erin. You're so hot."

My back is against the wall, and he slams against me for a moment before pulling out and dragging me to the living room. Jesus, the position changes are making my head spin. He sits on the couch and pulls me into his lap. I follow his lead and straddle him, sliding down onto his cock.

As I start to move and rock in his lap, he pulls my shirt off, then scoops my breasts out of my bra, playing with both nipples with his thumbs. I grind on him, feeling my body tense as he pumps up into me. Oh god, I think I'm going to come again.

I moan when he pulls on my nipples and says, "You were desperate to have it in the ass. Admit it."

"Yes. Fuck yes. It felt so good when you did it. I want more of it."

"Mmmm, nice. I'll give you more," he says as he tweaks my nipples roughly. His words sizzle my brain as I cry out with another orgasm. I drive down onto his cock as he slams up into me, fucking me through my orgasm. My pussy pulses and my body shakes as I ride him through the pleasure.

When the rapture dies down, he pushes me to my feet and bends me over the arm of the couch. Holy fuck, this is insane. I lay my cheek on the couch cushion while I hear his clothes rustle. The sound of plastic ripping and a pop top is the only warning I get before I feel the cool lube between my ass cheeks. Ooooh, yes!

"You were ready, just in case?" I giggle as his fingers stroke me, working gently into my ass to spread the lube around. The feeling is glorious, and my clit throbs from the pleasure.

"Of course," he says. Like it's the most obvious thing. "I wasn't sure if I was willing to share you yet, but I wanted to be prepared in case I was."

That's just like my man to think of everything. His fingers work more lube into my ass, and I groan, grinding back against him as he opens me up. When he's satisfied, he lines his cock up, and I feel the tip pressing against me. My body tightens in anticipation.

His hand strokes down my spine, calming me. "Breathe."

I do, but it's hard to relax when I want this so much. He pushes forward, and the burn is just as immense this time. But now I know how good it's going to feel in a moment—how dirty and delicious. It's easier to be calm and not tense up when you know how glorious everything is about to feel.

His head pops past the rim, and I groan at the sudden sense of being so beautifully full. I try to push back, to take him all, but he keeps my hips still. He sinks into me so slowly that it's driving me crazy after this afternoon. All I want is for him to fuck me, fill my ass up, and he's taking so long with it.

"Your ass is so tight," he says. "And it's mine. Remember?"

"Yes." How could I forget?

He keeps a slow, gentle pace until he's buried fully. I groan and shift, encouraging him to fuck me the way I want.

"So eager," he says, laughing a little. "You love my cock in your ass."

"I do," I mewl out. "So, fuck me already. Please?"

He keeps going slow, and it's killing me. I try to get leverage and shove my hips back to make him move faster, and he responds by giving me what I want as he drills into me.

"This hole is mine." His voice is strained. "Say it."

"It's yours! God, it's yours."

My body is singing as my breasts drag against the fabric of the couch with every slap of his hips against mine. I'm not sure I've ever felt this good.

"What's mine?" He growls, and I can tell he's feeling territorial.

"My ass." I'm close to screaming with pleasure. "My ass is yours."

"Rub your clit," he demands. "I want to feel you come while my cock is in your ass."

He doesn't have to tell me twice. I move a hand between my legs. My clit is sensitive and throbbing. It only takes a few strokes before I'm ready to explode.

"You're mine," he says again. "And I'll share my good fucktoy when I'm ready to."

That's all it takes. My husband's possessiveness sets off a chain reaction, and my body undulates as the pleasure overwhelms me. My entire body is clenching around his cock as I'm assaulted with sharp peaks of pleasure.

He keeps fucking me while the joy transcends me to a higher plane. The second I relax a little, he groans my name and shoots thick jets of cum into my ass, over and over.

He pulls his cock out and wraps me up into his arms. "You're so fucking sexy," he says, stroking my back. "I love you so much."

"God, Ian. I love you too." I mash my body against his, not wanting to break the connection.

We stay that way, just enjoying the moment, until we're both ready to clean up. We take a shower together and then cuddle up in bed, still naked. Ian pets my hair while our legs tangle together and I play footsie with him. My head is tucked under his chin, and I can't remember the last time I felt this relaxed.

"You're amazing," he says, kissing the top of my head.

I'm satisfied and feeling loved. I tighten my arms around him. "You're pretty great, too."

We're quiet for a moment, and I can't help but tease him. "Are you ever going to let Jace fuck my ass?" I make my voice all high and pouty, and he laughs.

"How about next time we get together with Jace and Matt?" He kisses the top of my head again. My heart starts to pound, and even as tired and sated as I am, my pussy gives a little whimper of pleasure as he continues. "Next time, I'll share your ass."

I give his chest tons of little kisses. "You, sir, have just earned yourself a private pole dance."

He chuckles, and I feel it rumble through his chest as I melt into him. I really am the luckiest slut in the world, and I can't wait to see Jace and Matt again.

The Slutty Wife's Desires

Book 5

Lacey Cross

CHAPTER 1

I'm nestled in bed, cocooned under the blankets, when Ian joins me after brushing his teeth. This is my favorite time of the day. I get to snuggle with my man and enjoy a few minutes of connection, even on our busiest days.

I rest my head on his chest as he caresses my back. My mind begins to wander, reflecting on how much my life has changed since embracing my desires and becoming a hotwife. It's been an exhilarating journey of self-discovery. Who knew I would be so hot for backdoor action? Not this girl.

The experiences have been intoxicating—all orchestrated by my wonderful husband. That first day when I offered myself to Jace and Matt at the veterinarian clinic, I had no idea that becoming a hotwife would strengthen my marriage...but it has. Having a husband who loves watching me with other guys is pretty fucking fabulous. This really is the life.

I sigh contentedly and snuggle closer into the warmth of his chest, lightly tracing my fingertips around his nipples.

"Babe?" I whisper softly. "I've been thinking a lot lately...about us. About this whole hotwife thing."

"Mmm, is that so?" Ian's voice is a deep, soothing rumble as he gently strokes my back.

I tilt my head to look up at him and grin. "Is it weird that I feel closer to you after fucking other men?"

Ian laughs. "That's because you're my sexy slut who likes being naughty."

A flush of pleasure warms me. "You're really okay with it, though? You don't want to stop?"

"Sweetheart, I'm more than okay with it," he assures me, his eyes glimmering with mischief. "In fact...I may have a little surprise planned for this weekend."

My heart skips a beat, and I want to squeal in excitement. Is he finally going to let Jace fuck my ass? I try to play it cool and keep my voice flirty as I walk my fingers up his chest. "A surprise? What is it? You know I hate waiting."

Ian chuckles, capturing my hand and bringing it to his lips for a kiss. "Sorry, love. You'll have to wait and see. But trust me, you're going to love it," he promises with a wink.

I pout dramatically, giving him my best puppy dog eyes. "Oooh, you're such a tease! Not even a tiny hint?"

"Nope!" He grins, tapping my nose playfully. "But have I ever disappointed you before?"

"No, your surprises are always amazing," I admit, snuggling closer. "You just get me. I suppose I can wait."

Just because I'm waiting doesn't mean I won't fantasize. It's going to be a week of raunchy daydreams.

Ian tenderly cups my face, his expression adoring as he gazes into my eyes. "I'm the luckiest man alive."

"Mmm, and don't you forget it, mister." I give him a slow, sensual kiss, savoring his familiar taste and the scrape of his stubble against my skin.

Ian pulls me on top of him, and my knees rest on the mattress on either side of him. I can feel his hard cock through his pajama pants as I fit my pussy against it and gently rotate my hips. I guess we're not going straight to sleep.

His fingers trace circles on my lower back before they trail down to cradle my butt. "I love your ass," he murmurs. "And it's all mine."

His words make me squirm in delight. He recently installed a stripper pole in the spare room for me because he knew I wanted one, and I've been taking pole dancing lessons. My ass is firmer than it's been in years, and even I enjoy admiring myself in the mirror.

He grips my buttcheeks and forces me to rock against his hardness. A pleasurable tingle swirls in my core as I try to be cute. "But maybe you want to share my ass sometime...like this weekend?"

He's been teasing me about letting Jace, our cat's veterinarian, fuck my ass, and I'm really, really hoping that's the surprise this weekend. I've had several hotwife encounters, but Jace and his technician Matt are my two main play partners.

"Maybe," he says with a grin as he moves a hand between us. I lift up slightly so he can pull his cock from his pajamas. He pushes aside my panties, and I sigh in pleasure as he slides inside me.

"Hmm, someone is nice and wet at the thought of getting their ass used," he groans.

"It's all for you, babe," I whisper as I slowly ride him.

He and I both know that the thought of Jace fucking my ass makes me instantly wet, but this is the game we play. He teases me about that hole being only his, and I try to pretend I don't want anyone else.

I kiss him again, our tongues swirling together as I imagine Ian really letting Jace fuck my ass. I've only ever done anal with Ian and I'm new to it, but I'm quickly turning into a slut at the thought of Jace's thick cock sliding inside my ass.

Keeping my movements slow, it's not long before Ian has his hands on my hips and tries to make me grind faster against his cock. When I don't speed up, he rolls us over until he's on top.

I moan and wrap my legs around him as he fucks me hard. He pants out, "If you want Jace to fuck your ass, you're going to have to beg for it."

His words turn me on even more. I whimper and writhe, desperately grinding against him as he keeps plunging deep into my pussy. God, I love this man. He gets me so fucking hot.

We move together as I shamelessly plead. "Please, baby. Please! I want Jace to fuck my ass!"

He looks pleased, and he rewards me by lifting my legs higher and fucking me harder. I continue to chant, "Please," while he pumps into me and my eyes roll back in my head. Fuck, yes! I think I'm going to get what I want.

Ian kisses me again as we move faster. I whine against his lips in desperation. My pussy aches, clenching tightly around him, as the pleasure builds.

His voice is thick with lust as he asks, "You want another man to use my hole?"

I nod frantically as the bliss spirals in my core. I'm going to come any moment. "I need it. Please. I want him to fill my ass with his cum."

Hearing my own filthy words come out of my mouth almost tips me over the edge.

"That's my dirty slut," Ian groans.

When he gives a sharp thrust, I cry out and explode with pleasure. Delight rushes through me, and my pussy clamps around him. Ian jackhammers against me and erupts, filling me with his seed.

I arch my back and sob in rapture, gasping from aftershocks of pleasure. I tremble as I come down from the euphoric high. Holy shit, that was intense.

When he collapses beside me, I cuddle up against him, sighing contentedly. Ian kisses me softly, and when he speaks, the tone of his voice is amused. "I guess you really want it. We'll see how I feel on Saturday."

I want to protest that I did a good enough job begging that I deserve my reward, but I'm too content. "Okay, love. We'll just see on Saturday."

The workout has exhausted me, and within a few minutes, I'm out like a light, dreaming about being filled up by Jace and having every hole used.

CHAPTER 2

Ian is awake and out of bed before me on Saturday, and I'm so excited I practically dance into the kitchen. He's leaning against the counter, sipping his coffee, looking unfairly handsome in a simple t-shirt and jeans.

I greet him in a sing-song voice. "Good morning, my love."

He raises his eyebrows at me while he takes a sip of his coffee. After I pour myself a cup, I sidle up to him with a mischievous grin. "So...about tonight. Can't you give me a little clue? A tiny hint about what you've got planned?"

Ian chuckles, setting down his mug and looping an arm around my waist. "Well, well, someone's certainly eager. But my insatiable wife is going to have to wait. Patience is a virtue, remember? All will be revealed in due time."

I pout playfully, batting my lashes. "But I'm no good at patience, you know that. Come on, babe. Just a little morsel to tide me over? I can make it worth your time?"

I run a hand over his cock and feel it twitch underneath his jeans. When he pulls away, I pout again while he grins affectionately.

"Nice try, but I'm not spoiling the surprise. Trust me, you'll like it."

My mind races with possibilities. Jace and Matt must be coming over—and if Ian is really considering letting someone else fuck my ass, it would be Jace.

Ian finishes his coffee and sets his mug in the sink before kissing my forehead. "All right, I need to run an errand. There's something I need to get for tonight's festivities."

"Ooh, intriguing." I tilt my face up for a proper kiss goodbye. "Hurry back to me. I'll just be here, you know, slowly dying of curiosity."

"So dramatic," he teases, smacking my ass playfully as he heads out. "Don't get into too much trouble while I'm gone."

The second the door closes behind him, I bolt for our bedroom, tearing through my closet with single-minded determination. What to wear, what to wear...I need an ensemble that screams "irresistible sex goddess."

When I can't decide, I call my best friend, Sasha.

She answers with a yawn. "Yo, what's up?"

Sasha grew up only being allowed to watch 80s re-runs, and the way she talks always makes me smile.

"Hey, wake up. I need your help. Ian invited a guy over tonight to fuck me, and I need to know what to wear."

Or at least I assume he invited someone over...he better have.

She groans, and it sounds like she's pulling covers over her head. "You woke me up to brag about all the cock you're getting when you know my husband won't share?"

She likes to grumble good-naturedly about my sexcapades, but she also loves hearing about them.

"Fine, I won't tell you the details..."

That makes her giggle. "Now, now...don't be hasty. What're the options?"

I describe five outfits, but before she can tell me her opinion, she swears. "Shit, I gotta go. I just heard the garage door open, and I've got to help unload groceries."

I laugh. "Fine, I'll figure this out myself!"

She hangs up with a, "Love ya!" and I survey my choices again. Well shit, she was no help.

I mull over what I'm going to wear as I think about Sasha's situation and how lucky I am. Ian really is the best husband.

Sighing, I look at my lingerie again and give up. I'll take a shower and think about it.

By the time Ian returns, shopping bag in hand, I'm fresh from the shower and wrapped in a towel, agonizing over two different sets of lingerie.

He clears his throat from the doorway. "I see you've been productive," he observes wryly.

I stick my tongue out at him. "Hush, just trust the process. Wait, what's in the bag? Gimme!"

"So demanding, too." Ian shakes his head with a smile, handing over the goods. "I picked up a little something for you. For tonight."

I reach into the bag eagerly, pulling out a stunning pink negligee. It's sheer lace, and I can tell that the low cut is going to give everyone a tantalizing view while still leaving something to the imagination. It's sinfully sexy and utterly perfect.

"Ohhh..." I breathe, running my fingers over the delicate fabric. "It's beautiful."

He looks pleased with himself. "I'm glad you like it. But I want to tell you the plan for tonight because you have a choice to make."

"Oh?" Hopefully, this plan includes whether I want Jace's cock in my ass. The answer is 'yes.'

Ian takes my hand, rubbing his thumb over my knuckles soothingly. "Mack is coming over."

"Mack?" Surprise floods through me, followed by a pleasurable thrill. I haven't seen Mack since that afternoon at his place when Ian watched him ravish me in the backyard. God, that was fun. I can't be unhappy about getting another shot at his monster cock, even if it means I don't get Jace in my ass tonight.

"I think we could get up to some sexy trouble together."

Ian pulls me against him and gives me a quick kiss. "Perfect. Mack mentioned he'd love to see you twirling around the stripper pole if you're up for it…"

The idea sends liquid heat pulsing through my veins. "I think I can manage that," I reply coyly. "You know how much I love putting on a show."

Ian's eyes darken with desire. "Mmm, that I do. Have I mentioned lately how incredible you are? How much I adore you?"

"You're not so bad yourself, stud." I wink, looping my arms around his neck. "But you know what they say—show, don't tell."

He growls playfully, pulling me flush against him. "Oh, I'll show you all right. Later. When I have you all to myself again."

I shiver at the promise in his voice. "Can't wait, but I want at least four orgasms tonight, so if Mack doesn't deliver, you better be prepared to bring your A game."

He laughs. "Deal."

I reluctantly disentangle myself and shoo him out so I can finish getting ready. I put my hair in a high ponytail so it doesn't get messy when I dance, and as I shimmy into the negligee, I study my reflection in the mirror. The lace clings to my curves, the sheerness hinting at the bare skin beneath. I look daring. Sensual. Desirable. Like a woman ready to embrace whatever happens.

Mack isn't Jace and Matt, but variety is the spice of life, right? And novelty can be its own aphrodisiac. My ass might not get fucked tonight, but that just means I'll want it all the more when it actually happens.

Besides, I'll be too busy trying to stuff Mack's enormous cock in me to even think about Jace.

Drawing in a deep, steadying breath, I smooth the negligee over my hips and psych myself up to shake my booty for the love of my life and his best friend from college. Maybe Ian will get so horny he'll want me to suck on him while Mack fucks me. Mmm, I love being spit roasted. A girl can dream, right?

CHAPTER 3

The doorbell's chime echoes through the house, sending my heart leaping into my throat. Mack's here! This is really happening.

Ian pops his head into the bedroom, his expression a mix of excitement and reassurance. "Stay put, love. I'll get the door and text you when we're ready for your grand entrance."

I nod, and right as he turns to leave, he pauses. "You look absolutely incredible." His eyes shine with adoration and undisguised hunger. When the doorbell rings again, he winks. "See you soon, baby."

He leaves, and I'm suddenly a bundle of nervous energy. Ian converted our spare room into a sensual playground for us, with a pole and two couches, plus mood lighting and a sound system. I've only danced for a few people other than Ian, and I'm always worried I'll look awkward and unsexy. Logically, I know the feeling is unfounded because I'm hot—becoming a hotwife has given me a fuckton more confidence. Plus, Ian isn't going to invite anyone over who isn't enthusiastic about watching me dance. But I still get a tiny bit of stage fright every time.

I pace my bedroom, checking my hair, my makeup, the drape of the negligee for the hundredth time. The waiting is always the hardest part, anticipation building until I'm ready to crawl out of my skin.

After what feels like an eternity, my phone dings with a text from Ian. It's time.

Slipping on a pair of black high heels, I hurry down the hall, pausing outside the spare room. The music mix that I made for dancing is on, and I can hear it through the door. It helps to calm my nerves as memories rush back, snapshots of the first time I danced for an audience—Ian, Jace, and Matt, their appreciative eyes fueling my confidence, my desire...

I'm ready.

I open the door and freeze, mouth falling open in shock. Four pairs of eyes meet mine—Ian, Mack, Jace, and Matt. They're all here. All of them, wearing matching grins.

Surprise gives way to pure, incandescent delight. They came. They all came for me. I almost giggle at the thought—well, they haven't all come yet. But hopefully soon.

As if on cue, the music changes to my favorite song, and the beat gives me an electrical charge. These guys are here to fuck me. I feel powerful. A goddess in the flesh.

Hips swaying, I step into the room, letting the door fall shut behind me. "Hi, guys."

I lock eyes with Ian, his face glowing with fierce pride and unconditional love. It fills me up, gives me the strength to embrace the wild, wanton side of myself.

Looking at each man in turn, I give them all a smile, saving Jace for last. When I meet his gaze, a shiver of longing tingles along my spine. Oh, the things he could do to me...the things I hope he does to me tonight...

The guys all murmur hello, and I can tell they're already entranced. Jace's deep, velvety voice stands out when he says, "Are you going to be a good girl and dance for us?"

His 'good girl' fries my brain, and it's difficult to answer. My entire body tingles, and I sound breathy when I finally say, "Yes."

With the room feeling like it's spinning, I stand in front of the stripper pole and let the music pulse through me. Closing my eyes, I start slowly, my arms above my head as my hips undulate to the music. The beat vibrates through my body, guiding my movements as I lose myself to the rhythm. My fingers splay across my stomach, moving up to my breasts. Even though my eyes are closed, I know everyone is watching me...wanting me. I can feel myself getting wetter, and I want to give these men everything.

I dance for my men—for the one who holds my heart and the ones who set my body on fire. There's no thought beyond this moment and the sensual glide of the silk on my skin and the heat of their gazes following my every move.

Each appreciative murmur spurs me on, every low groan igniting me. I've never felt sexier, more powerful, more alive. I'm embracing the moment, and anything feels possible tonight.

As I dance, the negligee gives them brief peeks of the skin underneath. I'm an inferno of lust as time becomes meaningless. The world narrows to the sway of my hips, the arch of my back, the simmering hunger building in the room.

I hook a leg around the gleaming pole, letting my head fall back. This is my element, where I'm utterly confident, completely free—a goddess of desire, reveling in her own allure.

When the song ends and a slower one starts, I pause and look at the men. My chest heaves, and I can feel my skin flush with arousal. I'm ready for someone to fuck me.

Ian and Jace are on one couch, and Matt and Mack are on the other. I focus on Ian, swaying my hips as I move to stand in front of him. I'm desperate for someone to touch me, to quench this thirst I have for all their cocks.

Ian leans forward, sliding a finger under a strap of the negligee and drawing it off my shoulder slowly. He drops it and moves the other off. The front dips down, and my nipples peek out. He slips the straps over my arms, and the garment falls to the floor to puddle at my feet. All I'm wearing now are my panties and the high heels.

To the side of me, I hear someone suck in a breath. I tilt my head towards Matt and Mack, and both are staring at me with unbridled lust. I feel it to my very core.

Ian's voice is rough when he speaks. "Who's going to take her first?"

Jace stands, leaving no doubts about his intention to make the first move. My heart races as I feel the desire humming between Jace and me as Jace steps closer.

"You look so tempting," Jace murmurs, his voice low and dangerous. His fingers trail along my jaw, tilting my head up to meet his eyes.

I glance over at Ian and see the raw desire burning in his eyes. He nods slightly, silently giving me permission to surrender to Jace.

Jace's lips clash with mine, his tongue delving into my mouth, and I feel my insides melt. I'm ready to wrap my legs around him and beg him to fuck me right when he breaks off the kiss.

"Are you ready to be a dirty little slut and take all our cocks?"

"Yes."

Mmmm, hell yes, I am.

Jace pushes me to my knees before taking his cock out of his jeans. It's thick and long, and I lick my lips as I remember how he feels in my mouth. I lean towards him and part my lips, looking at him in case he stops me. He doesn't.

His shaft slides into my mouth, and I moan in pleasure as I taste his pre-cum. Knowing the other guys are watching me give Jace a blowjob makes me want to do a good job of it, so they wish it was them—especially my husband. I trail my tongue along his shaft, savoring the taste of him as my tongue explores the contours of his thick veins.

As I bob my head up and down, he slides his hands around the back of my head to control my movements. He pulls me closer as he thrusts into my mouth. The base of his cock smacks against my chin, coating it with a sheen of spit as I deep throat him. It's messy and I'm getting saliva around my mouth, but I don't care. I want to see if I can make him come.

I relax my throat as he face fucks me, allowing him to speed up his thrusts. The more aggressive he becomes, the wetter my pussy gets. The next time I take him in fully, he holds me there, my throat working around his shaft. He groans and pulls out right before he comes.

Jesus, this is hot. I wanted to taste him, but I love feeling like a toy that the men can use however they want, so letting him decide what happens makes this better.

Jace pulls me up to my feet, his lips crashing against mine in a bruising kiss. He plunders my mouth, and I wish his cock was inside me while he was doing it. I don't know what it is about Jace, but everything about him just does it for me. I lucked out when I decided to see if he offered extra services that day weeks ago at the veterinarian clinic. If I had been looking for a regular play partner, I couldn't have found someone who turns me on more. He seems to know exactly what I like.

When he finally pulls away, I'm panting, my lips swollen and wet. He cups my chin and brushes his thumb across my lips. I want to suck on his thumb, but his next words stop me.

"You're such a good little cocksucker. I think it's time you shared that pretty mouth of yours with the others."

Oooh, I couldn't agree more. When he presses on my shoulders, I sink to the floor again and look up at him, waiting for instructions.

"Crawl over to Matt and Mack," Jace commands. "And suck on their cocks too. Show them how much of a cock-greedy slut you are."

I practically purr as I glance over and see Matt and Mack still sitting on the couch. But now they both have their cocks out. Yeah, this is dirty. I can't wait to get my hands and mouth on them.

Slowly, I crawl across the floor, wiggling my ass for Jace and Ian's enjoyment. I want them both thinking of Jace sinking his thick cock into my ass.

If that doesn't happen tonight, I better get lots of orgasms to make up for it.

When I reach the couch, I pause and sit up on my knees. I'm uncertain who I'm supposed to suck on first.

Mack chuckles as if he can see my uncertainty. He holds the base of his thick shaft and motions me over. "Well, don't just stare, slut. Get to work."

Mmm, guess it's Mack first. I crawl between his legs and hesitate as I wrap my hand around the base of his monstrous cock. Mack has the biggest cock in the room, and the one time I fucked him, I thought he was splitting me in two. How am I going to get that all in my mouth?

Fuck it, I'm going to try. I lean in, wrapping my lips around the head of his cock and relaxing my jaw so I can take as much as I can into my mouth. It doesn't seem like I've got much in there, but Mack groans so I can tell he's enjoying it. To give him more pleasure, I make the blow job super messy. Saliva drips down his shaft, and I use my hands to massage the half of his shaft that won't fit in my mouth. Sucking on a guy who is too big to fully take inside my mouth gives me a nice slutty feeling, like I'm just a mouth hole for this guy to use.

Movement next to us makes me peek over at Matt. He's stroking his cock while he watches me try my best on the enormous shaft in my mouth.

"Switch," Jace's voice rings out.

When I pull up off of Mack's cock, I give him my best cutesy smile. "Sorry, that's all you get. Duty calls."

He grins and rubs the saliva off my lips with his thumb. "I'll get more of what I want later."

Oh, I bet he will. Crawling between Matt's legs, I turn my attention to him. I've given Matt multiple blowjobs over the last few months, so I know what he likes. I lick and kiss up and down his length before opening my mouth wide to take him in. This is the third cock in my mouth tonight, and I love how each guy has a unique taste and feel against my tongue.

Matt has always been an enthusiastic lover, and as I suck on him, I enjoy his moans and harsh breathing. He doesn't seem to be in any danger of coming, so I throw myself on his cock, hollowing my cheeks and applying suction. Even though I'm sucking on him, my arousal builds with each passing moment, until I'm a trembling, needy mess, aching to be used.

Suddenly, Ian's voice breaks through the haze. "Erin, my love, I think it's time we take this to the bedroom." His words are laced with a mixture of tenderness and arousal.

I reluctantly pop up off of Matt's cock and give him a cheeky grin. Matt's eyes are dark with lust, and I get a thrill from knowing I did a good job. I bet I could have made Matt come if I had more time.

Ian moves to me and gently helps me to my feet. His strong arms steady me as my head spins.

"Easy there, love," he murmurs, guiding me towards the bedroom. I lean into him, my body trembling with lust. I need a cock inside me—maybe two.

CHAPTER 4

The guys follow us into the bedroom. The room is dimly lit, casting a warm, sensual glow over everything. Ian leads me to the bed and gently lowers me down. I kick off my high heels, and as I sit on the edge, I watch Jace carry in a chair. He positions it facing the bed. When Ian sits down in it, I get a jolt of pleasure. Well, that's nice and dirty. He's getting comfortable to watch three guys fuck me.

Jace moves in front of me and brushes a stray lock of hair from my face. "Erin," he says softly, "do you trust me?"

I don't hesitate before answering. "Yes, I trust you."

And I do trust him. I've fucked Jace and Matt multiple times, and even when they're being rough, they are careful with me. It's what makes them such good play partners.

The sound of the drawer of the nightstand opening makes me glance over. Ian gets something out and hands it to Jace. It's a silk blindfold that I've never seen before. Huh, looks like someone bought more than just lingerie for tonight.

Jace holds it up in front of me. "You good with this?"

"Oh god, please."

Like I'm going to say no to being blindfolded and ravished by multiple men? This is one of my top five fantasies, and I've told Ian that before.

This isn't a coincidence, and it's another example of my incredible husband making sure I get my fantasies fulfilled.

Jace places the blindfold over my eyes, plunging me into darkness while he secures it in the back of my head. The loss of my sight heightens my other senses, and I become acutely aware of the sounds and sensations around me. I can hear the men breathing, the rustle of fabric as someone undresses, and the creak of the chair as Ian shifts his weight. My skin tingles with anticipation, every nerve ending alive.

Suddenly, I feel lips on mine, and I know it's Jace. He kisses me deeply as his hands caress my body, igniting sparks of pleasure wherever he touches. I melt into his embrace, my body responding to his every move.

I feel the bed dip as someone else joins us. This person's hands are strong and confident, and from the feel of him, I'd guess it's Mack. He explores my curves, and whenever he hits a ticklish spot, I gasp in pleasure.

The sensations are overwhelming, and I feel myself being pulled more and more deeply into the erotic haze. I'm completely at the mercy of these two men, and the thought thrills me to my core.

They push me down until I'm lying on my back. My heart races as I realize I don't know what to expect since I can't see them. Hands roam over my body, and it's three sets. I shiver as unknown fingers trail down my sides, electrifying every nerve in my body.

One man grabs my thighs, gently parting them. I feel exposed and vulnerable, but the trust I have in these men keeps me pliant. Another man settles between my legs, his breath hot against my pussy. Holy hell, someone is holding me open for someone else? That's filthy and hot.

I moan as his tongue darts out, teasing my clit and tasting me. For some reason, I expected them to go straight to the fucking. I didn't imagine anyone would go down on me. Not knowing who it is makes this dirtier, and I can feel my orgasm building. My toes curl and I arch my back as the pleasure threatens to consume me.

Before I come, another man captures my mouth in a searing kiss that steals my breath away. I think that's Mack? The sensations are overwhelming, yet I have no idea which man is doing what to me. My mind is lost in a haze of lust, my body alive with sensation. Their skilled hands and tongues have me teetering on the edge while I rock my hips against the mouth on my pussy.

"Ohhhh god," I moan, almost feeling crazed by how amazing this all is.

Just as I think I can't take anymore, they switch places. A new guy is between my legs, this one licking and sucking harder. Jesus, maybe that's Matt? He seems less skilled and more eager, and my pussy loves the attention. When the person slides a finger inside me, the digit seems thicker than I remember Matt's being, and I give up on trying to figure out who is doing what.

I surrender myself completely to them as my inhibitions are stripped away. A third guy takes his turn at my pussy, and this time, I can't hold back my orgasm.

I cry out as my muscles spasm and pleasure floods my system. I buck my hips as ripples of ecstasy turn my mind to mush. When I come down, I'm panting, my body tingling.

"That's the first one," Ian says from his chair, and I giggle, remembering how I told him I wanted four orgasms. With three other men, plus Ian, somehow, I don't think this is going to be a problem.

Someone lies next to me on the bed. It's Matt who speaks. "Get on top of me."

My heart races as I carefully straddle his hips, his firm hands helping me. Slowly, I lower myself down, gasping as his cock slides into me. The sensation is exquisite, made even more intense by the blindfold.

With my sight blocked and my other senses heightened, I can feel every inch of him filling me. It's a delicious friction as I begin to move my hips. The scent of our mingled arousal fills the air, spurring me on. Matt's hands grip my waist, helping me find a steady rhythm. Each time I sink down onto him, a shudder of pleasure ripples through me.

"That's it," Matt groans, his voice husky from desire. "Ride me."

I lose myself in the sensations as his cock massages me every time I sink down on it. I can hear the wet sound of us slapping together as I ride him. It's obscene and wonderful. Waves of ecstasy build within me, my movements becoming more frantic as I chase the pleasure.

Matt meets each of my thrusts, driving himself deeper. The tension coils more and more tightly until finally, it shatters. My body convulses around him, stars bursting behind the darkness of the blindfold.

"That's two," Ian says, and I can't do anything but moan.

I hear the telltale sound of the lube bottle opening, and I grind against Matt's cock in anticipation. Oh god, I know what this means. It means Ian is the most wonderful husband on the planet and he's agreed to share my ass.

A strong hand presses firmly between my shoulder blades, pushing my upper body down towards Matt. I'm completely exposed, and slick fingers glide along my ass crack, circling my puckered hole. I moan softly, my body trembling with arousal. The fingers probe gently, working the lube in until I feel completely slick and open. Just the thought of what's about to happen makes my pussy clench around Matt's shaft.

Suddenly, I feel the blunt head of a cock pressing against my well-lubricated opening. My breath catches as it slowly sinks inside, stretching me deliciously. I bite my lip, trying to stay still as, inch by inch, I'm filled.

A groan rumbles from behind me, and powerful hands grasp my hips, pulling me back onto the thick shaft. I cry out, the sensation of two cocks in me at once bordering on too much, yet it's somehow perfect. Based on the size of the cock, I'm assuming it's Jace behind me. He begins to move, withdrawing almost completely before driving back in.

Each thrust into my ass forces me down onto Matt's cock. The dual pleasure makes me moan continuously. I can feel every inch of them massaging me, and it feels like I'm going to explode from pleasure.

The pace builds, each thrust into my ass harder and deeper than the last. I'm lost in a haze of ecstasy. I'm just a mindless doll being used by both these men. All I can do is rock back to meet every punishing plunge.

"Fuck, you feel amazing," a deep voice rasps, and I know I was right. It's Jace fucking my ass. Finally.

Just knowing it really is him almost tips me over the edge. The guys have been teasing me for weeks about Jace fucking my ass, and being double stuffed is even better than I imagined. I'm going to remember this night forever.

Jace hammers into me relentlessly, and the pleasure builds. I'm like a toy being wound up more and more tightly until I'm trembling, on the edge of release. When Matt plays with my nipples and pulls on them, the sensation is too much. I cry out as another orgasm hits, my inner muscles clenching around him as waves of pleasure crash through me.

I'm chanting, "Fuck, fuck, fuck," as the bliss spikes and recedes and the men continue to fuck me.

When the pleasure finally dies down, I collapse, boneless, into Matt. Jace withdraws slowly, a soft whimper escaping my lips at the loss. I feel so wonderfully full, so thoroughly used.

A hand caresses my flushed cheek.

"Good girl," Jace murmurs. "But we're not done with you."

My husband's voice sounds thick with lust when he says, "Three."

This time my head is too mushy to giggle. When Jace slides his cock back into my ass, I moan loudly from pleasure. Holy fuck, this is crazy in the best of ways.

I'm overwhelmed with sensations, my body still trembling from the orgasm. The bed dips as someone settles next to me—I'm assuming Mack. His strong hand guides my head towards his cock. I open my mouth eagerly, thrilling at the idea of becoming the ultimate slut servicing three men at once.

Mack's cock brushes against my lips, and I part them, letting him slide into my waiting mouth. Due to his massive size, I can't take him all down and he doesn't try to force it. The familiar salty taste of him sends a shiver through me. As I begin to suck and lick, I hear Ian's voice, low and approving. He better be loving this show. It's not often his wife is going to get three holes stuffed at once.

The thought sends a fresh wave of arousal through me. My body feels like it's on fire, hyper-sensitive to every touch and sensation. Jace and Matt continue to fuck me, their thrusts deep and relentless. I moan around Mack's cock, the vibrations eliciting a groan from him.

I'm completely surrounded, utterly possessed by the men. Every inch of me is filled, used, claimed. I've never felt so wanton, so thoroughly debased. And yet, I've never felt sexier.

The pleasure builds until I'm trembling on the edge of ecstasy once more. I redouble my efforts, sucking Mack harder and rocking between the two cocks in me.

"That's it, slut. Take it all," Mack growls, his fingers tangling in my hair.

I'm drowning in the sensation of being so thoroughly and deliciously stuffed. I hope this moment lasts forever, that I can stay like this, a writhing, moaning mess of pure bliss.

Jace's tone is dominant. "You're such a dirty slut, taking all of us at once." His words send a shiver of pleasure down my spine. "But you love it, don't you? You love having all your holes filled."

My mouth is too full to respond, so all I can do is mumble around Mack's cock. Mack groans, "Fuck, yeah, that's it, baby. Suck me harder."

Jace's grasp on my hips tightens as he drives into me. "Look at you, getting off on being our shared slut. You were born for this, weren't you?"

His words send a buzz through my body. Having all these men inside me while Ian watches does feel right, like this is what I was meant to do. I know it sounds crazy, but right now my brain is foggy from so much pleasure, I want everything. Just thinking about how much of a slut I am pushes me closer to another orgasm.

"You're gonna come for us, aren't you?" Jace growls. "Because good girls come when they're told to."

Mmm, I am a good girl, and I enjoy doing what I'm told. I can't tell him that, because of Mack's cock stuffed in my mouth, so I try to show him I'm a good girl by rotating my hips faster.

Jace demands, "Come for us."

His words, combined with the pounding rhythms of their thrusts, sky-rocket me into another plane of existence. My orgasm rips through me, wave after wave of blinding ecstasy. I cry out around Mack's cock, my body convulsing as I shatter into a million pieces.

"Four," Ian calls out, his voice strained with his own arousal as he watches the depraved scene unfold before him.

Mack groans, "Fuck, her mouth feels so good, I'm not going to last much longer."

Jace yanks on my hair, pulling me off Mack's cock, as he asks, "Are you a greedy cum slut who wants us to come in all your holes?"

I whimper at the thought, my pussy clenching in anticipation. "Yes, please," I say breathlessly. "Please fill me up."

Jace chuckles darkly. "Then beg for it. Beg us to use you and fill you so full of cum that it's dripping out of you."

I don't hesitate, the words spilling from me in a desperate plea. "Please, please come inside me. I want all your cum. I want it all over me, in every hole. Use me, own me, make me come over and over again. I'll do anything, just please don't stop. Need all the cum!"

I'm trembling with desire, my body aching to be filled by them. Jace's grip on my hair tightens as he laughs. "What do you think, Ian? Does your slut wife want it enough?"

Oh god, don't ask him. He might say no!

"Oh, I think she wants it more than anything," he says, his voice low and ragged. "Look at her, begging for it. She deserves to get every last drop."

My heart races at Ian's words, relief washing over me. Jace pushes my head back towards Mack's cock, and Mack guides his shaft between my lips.

Jace growls, "You heard your husband, slut. You're about to get exactly what you asked for."

My body is on fire as the three men ravage me. Jace's thick shaft pulses deep in my ass, stretching and filling me. Matt's cock strokes my sensitive inner walls, hitting all the right spots. And Mack's huge member fills my mouth, hitting the back of my throat with each thrust.

The sensations are overwhelming, and with the blindfold on, everything is surreal. I moan around Mack's shaft, and he grips the back of my head, holding me in place as he fucks my mouth.

Jace's fingers dig into my hips, his pace becoming erratic as he chases his climax. "Fuck, you feel so good," he growls. "Taking all of us like the greedy slut you are."

Matt leans forward, his breath hot on my ear. "That's it, baby. Squeeze my cock with that needy little pussy." He reaches down to furiously rub my swollen clit, sending me spiraling towards the edge.

The men are relentless as they pound into me. When another orgasm hits me, my body convulses around the thrusting cocks. Wave after wave of mind-numbing pleasure washes over me, leaving me trembling and breathless.

Through the fog of my climax, I vaguely hear my husband's voice. His tone is a mix of pride and awe. "Five."

The ecstasy seems to go on forever as the men continue pounding into me. I feel completely overwhelmed by the sensations, my body quivering with pleasure.

The combination of these three powerful men using my body is beyond anything I could have imagined. I'm drowning in a sea of carnal bliss, my senses overloaded with the sounds and smells of our depraved union.

Suddenly, the men let out groans, and their bodies stiffen. I feel Matt come first as he coats my pussy walls. Then Jace spasms and pumps his hot seed deep into my ass while Mack floods my mouth with his thick, salty release.

My mind is blown, and another massive orgasm hits me. I can feel their cum spurting and pulsing, coating my insides. I swallow Mack's load greedily as the other two men finish emptying themselves into my needy holes.

It feels like it goes on forever, wave after wave of pure bliss. I'm completely lost in a haze of satisfaction. When they finally finish, I'm trembling, my body buzzing with the aftershocks of the most intense orgasm of my life.

Slowly, the men pull out of me, and Jace gently helps me lie down. He removes my blindfold, and I blink, adjusting to the soft light. Jace looks down at me, his eyes filled with satisfaction.

"Are you okay?" he asks softly.

I nod, still trying to catch my breath. "Yes, I'm...I'm amazing," I manage to get out, my voice barely above a whisper.

Jace smiles, and I feel a deep sense of contentment wash over me. I got what I wanted. My husband finally shared my ass with Jace.

I close my eyes and mentally drift, allowing the afterglow to envelop me. I can hear the men moving around, getting dressed to leave.

Ian comes over to me and caresses my cheek. When I open my eyes, he says, "I'm going to show them out. I'll be back."

There's a tenderness in his eyes, but also something else...my husband needs me.

"Okay, love. I'll be here." I giggle at my words. Where else would I be?

CHAPTER 5

I'm not sure how long Ian is gone, but when he comes back, he's naked. The bed dips as he climbs in beside me. His strong, warm hands gently caress my skin as he leans in close. I can smell the faint scent of the other men still lingering on me, and it sends a shiver of excitement through my body.

"You were amazing," he murmurs, his lips brushing against my neck. "So beautiful, taking them all like that." His fingers glide slowly down my arms, tracing patterns on my flesh. "I love watching you come undone, seeing and hearing your pleasure."

I sigh contentedly, melting into his touch. "I love you," I whisper, my eyes fluttering closed.

His hand drifts lower, caressing the sticky wetness between my thighs. I gasp at the sensation, my hips arching up to meet his exploring fingers. "That's it, my love," he croons. "Let me take care of you."

He rubs the mixture of Matt's cum and my wetness into my skin, as if he's fascinated with me being full of another guy's cum.

"You're so incredible," Ian murmurs, his voice thick with emotion. "I'm the luckiest man alive."

I want to tell him that I'm the luckiest woman in the world to have a husband as thoughtful as him, but he kisses me before I can. I sigh from the pleasure as he caresses every inch of my body. His touch is reverent, worshipping every curve. I feel utterly cherished.

Ian's fingers brush circles around my clit, and I shiver from delight. He knows my body so intimately, every sensitive spot that drives me wild. As he strokes me, I can feel the familiar coil of pleasure building deep within me again. Holy fuck, how can I have another orgasm in me?

"That's it," he murmurs, his voice thick with desire. "Just let go."

His thumb presses down on my clit, and I cry out as the delicious waves of another climax wash over me.

Ian holds me close as I tremble in his arms. His eyes shine with raw emotion. "I love you so much. You're my everything."

My heart overflows with the depth of my love for this incredible man as he kisses me softly and settles over me.

His muscular frame presses against me, and I can feel the heat of his body as he slides his cock between my sensitive folds. He moves slowly, letting me feel every inch of him as he fills me completely.

A shudder of pleasure ripples through me, and I gasp at the exquisite sensation. Ian's eyes lock onto mine, his gaze smoldering with barely contained desire. "You feel so good," he murmurs, his voice low and ragged. "So wet for me."

He begins to thrust, his movements agonizingly slow and deliberate. Each drag of his thick shaft sends electric jolts of pleasure coursing through my body. I moan and arch into him, craving more.

Ian lowers his head, trailing hot, open-mouthed kisses along my neck. His stubble scrapes deliciously against my sensitive skin, making me whimper. I hold onto his shoulders as he picks up the pace. The wet sound of our bodies slapping together fills the air. Every thrust makes me moan with delight.

"That's it, baby," Ian encourages, his voice strained with the effort of maintaining his control. "Come for me. I want to feel you come."

Ian's thrusts become deeper and more powerful, hitting a magical spot inside me that makes me see stars. The tension builds until I'm teetering on the edge and desperate.

"Oh god" I cry out, my voice breaking. "I'm so close, please don't stop!"

He moves one hand down to where we're joined, his fingers finding my swollen clit. The dual sensations of his cock filling me and his skillful touch on my most sensitive spot push me over the edge.

My orgasm crashes through me, waves of bliss pummeling me. He comes with me, and I convulse around his shaft, milking him as he groans and unloads ropes of cum deep inside me. My vision goes white and stars explode behind my eyelids as I ride out the incredible high.

When I finally come down, I collapse bonelessly against the mattress. Ian peppers my face with tender kisses, murmuring words of praise and adoration.

"How many times did I come?" I ask breathlessly, looking up at him with hooded eyes.

Ian chuckles, brushing a damp strand of hair from my forehead. "Honestly, I lost count."

He wraps me in his arms, and we snuggle together, basking in the afterglow. "So, does this mean you still want to share me?" I tease, tracing patterns on his chest.

Ian grins wolfishly. "Absolutely. Though, I think I'll be keeping your gorgeous ass all to myself. I'll only let the others play with it on special occasions."

I laugh and kiss him as a feeling of utter contentment envelops me. I float on a cloud of blissful satisfaction, my body humming with the memory of pleasure.

"That was incredible," I murmur, nuzzling into the warmth of Ian's neck. "I can't believe how lucky I am. To have you, to have this."

Ian presses a kiss to my hair. "I'm the luckiest man, baby."

We lapse into contented silence, basking in the afterglow until I have a thought and almost giggle. Oh god, poor Sasha is never going to believe the night I just had. Yeah, I think I'll keep this experience to myself. I'm the perfect, slutty wife who just took on four cocks and lost count of how many times I came.

Ian kisses my head again, and a rush of love for him makes me smile. In this moment, I feel closer to him than ever before. This is exactly where I want to be—wrapped up in his arms, completely and utterly satisfied.

Best. Life. Ever.

The End of Erin's Stories

Making Me a Naughty Hotwife

Book 6

Lacey Cross

CHAPTER 1

I yawn and stretch as I walk into the kitchen to make coffee. As soon as I open the canister, I'm already feeling more awake from the smell. I hear the sound of power tools coming from our backyard, and I smile as I recall my husband reminding me that a contractor named Devon would be here today with his apprentice to start building our new deck.

As the coffee percolates, I peer out the window at the workers. My breath catches in my throat as I see the two guys who are working on our deck. Oh wow, they're hot. Devon is a striking man that I'd estimate to be in his late 40s. His sexy 3-day stubble beard adds to his silver fox appeal, and he has tattoos peeking out from under the sleeves of his work shirt. He exudes a dominant and confident presence that makes me think he knows exactly what a woman needs...and I'm pretty sure it's not just a sturdy deck.

His apprentice is probably in his mid-20s and impressively fit and buff. He moves with an athletic grace that comes from spending a lot of time working out. When he laughs at something Devon says, his charming smile could melt any woman's panties. This guy also has tattoos, and it adds to the sexy vibe they both give off. They're laughing together as they work, and I'm distracted by their muscular frames. Mmm, I can just imagine the things they could do to me with their strong, capable hands.

My body aches with yearning, and I imagine stroking their hard stomachs. Ugh, I shouldn't be thinking like this. I've been married to Michael for 12 years, and while I'm incredibly happy, I can't shake the feeling that I missed out on something during my college years...mostly my chance at being a slut.

I've always struggled with monogamy. Not that I don't love my husband, but I never thought I'd want to fuck only one man for the rest of my life. Meeting Michael changed my mind, but it hasn't stopped my gangbang fantasies.

But really, it's all my best friend Erin's fault that I'm drooling over the guys in the backyard. She's been living the hotwife lifestyle and is having the time of her life. Her first time as a hotwife was being spit-roasted between her cat's veterinarian and his technician....talk about a purr-fect experience.

If she can have her vet, why can't I have a carpenter and his assistant? I shake my head at myself, feeling a little silly, but my chest flutters in excitement at the thought. Sadly, my husband won't share. As soon as Erin fucked the veterinarian, I joked to Michael that maybe I needed to be a hotwife. He claimed he'd never share me...I mean, I really can't complain since I'm not interested in sharing him either. Oh well, a girl can watch and dream.

As I stare out at the sexy guys, desire pulses in my core as I imagine being sandwiched between these two delicious specimens. We could have a contest to see who could nail me the hardest. No matter which one got first place, I'd be the real winner in the competition. Maybe I should go out and inspect their work. You know, for quality control purposes.

I giggle at the thought of what Michael is going to say when he comes home to find me in such a playful mood. I'm off work all week for a staycation, and it's going to my head. My only plan is to binge watch trashy TV shows and relax. Besides, someone needs to be around in case the workers need anything. Not that I'll be able to satisfy ALL their needs...

Shit, with how turned on I am just by seeing a couple of attractive guys, Michael better be ready for some action when he gets home tonight. After daydreaming of getting drilled by sexy construction workers all day, I'm going to need some attention. I'll tell Michael I've got a hole that needs to be repaired with his specialized tool.

I smile and take a sip of my coffee, already feeling more happy and relaxed than I have in a long time. Staycations are the best.

After lunch and daydreaming about various holes being reamed by muscular men, I'm worked up enough that I decide it's time to send some flirty messages to my husband. Michael is going to laugh his ass off at me drooling over the workers, and hopefully I can get him horny.

Sasha:

> When you hired the deck guys, did you know they were super hot?

Michael:

> Sorry, I didn't think about their appearance when I hired them.

I snort at his reply.

Sasha:

> You sure? They're suuuuper sexy. I've been watching them all morning. I thought maybe you hired them for me.

Michael:

> You wish. Someone's in a slutty mood today.

I laugh when I read his message. My husband knows me so well. I am a little slut, but I'm *his* little slut.

Sasha:

> Damn right I am. So when you get home, I have expectations.

Michael replies quickly, and I buzz with a restless neediness.

Michael:

> I don't know. Do you deserve my cock?

I enjoy playing hard to get when we both know I'm willing to do anything to get his cock when I'm this turned on.

Sasha:

> LOL, or maybe the question is…do YOU deserve my pussy?

Michael :

> No, it's definitely whether you deserve my cock. You might have to tell me what you're offering to get it. I don't just give this magnificent rod of flesh to anyone.

Oh god, he's going to make me beg. I bite my bottom lip, and when Devon walks past the window, he catches my eye and distracts me. Oh my, it's hot out. I hope those two are staying hydrated. Hmmm, I have some drinks in the fridge I could offer them…but first, I need to secure some cock for tonight.

Sasha:

> If I'm naked and on the bed when you get home, will I deserve it?

Michael:

> Lucky for you, my cock is hard, and HE thinks you deserve it. Now go watch the workers some more and think about what I'm going to do to you when I get home.

Yes, sir!

See, he wants me to ogle them. I have my husband's permission.

I spend the next twenty minutes sipping a glass of cold water in the kitchen and watching the guys while they take a break, sitting in the shade and chatting. I can't hear what they're saying, but their laughter is loud enough to come through the window. The deep tone makes my pussy tingle and I daydream about being spit-roasted between them. Erin claims it's heaven on earth to have multiple guys filling your holes at once. I want to experience heaven on earth...I'm assuming it's just a fantastic orgasm.

My phone dings again with a text from my husband.

What're you thinking about right now?

I try to decide what to tell him, but then smile. Yeah, I'll have fun with this.

I'm picturing taking both of them to our bedroom.
One fucking my pussy, the other in my mouth.

I rub my thighs together as warmth spreads through my belly from admitting I'm such a slut. Thank god the air conditioner is on in the house. I'd be burning up with lust otherwise.

What else would you want them to do?

Is my husband trying to turn me into a nympho or something?

Well, I would want them to call me filthy names as they hammer into me. They'd fuck me until I came so hard, I'd forget what day it was, and then they'd fill my mouth and pussy.

Oh god, I can't believe I just typed all of that to him while he's at work. He doesn't reply immediately and I get concerned he's shocked or upset. When he finally texts back, my eyes widen as I read the message.

Michael:
All right, you've convinced me.

Sasha:
What? Convinced you?

Is he telling me to do it? My heart races, but I can't believe he means it the way I'm taking it. I hold my breath until his reply appears.

Michael:
I want you to seduce them. If you get them to fuck you, I want all the details when I get home. But either way, you're getting my cock as soon as I walk in the door, so be ready.

Whoa...did one of his work friends take his phone? I have to double-check before I get my hopes up.

I dial his number and as soon as he says hello, I blurt out, "Really?"

He chuckles. "Yes, really. I've been thinking about you being a hotwife for a few weeks and was going to talk to you about it. My meeting is about to start and I can't miss it, but call me and let me know how it goes. This is going to be the longest meeting ever. I love you, and trust you."

I whisper, "Love you," while my entire body lights up with desire.

He hangs up the phone and leaves me reeling for a few moments until a huge grin crosses my face. I squeal so loud that the two guys in the backyard look over towards the house and I have to duck quickly to avoid them seeing me through the kitchen window.

Oh my god! He means it! I'm going to take this opportunity and see what happens. Shit, I hope I still remember how to flirt.

Chapter 2

After a quick shower, I slip on my sexiest bikini. I adjust the cups of the hot pink top to try to contain my boobs. I've put on a few pounds since last summer and it made my bikini almost too small at the top, since most of the added weight went to my tits.

I admire myself in the mirror from behind and shimmy my hips. Well, okay, it all went to my tits *and* ass. My husband loves my curves and seeing how hot I am in the mirror makes me feel like a sexual goddess—one who's going to seduce two men today.

I wrap my long, blonde hair in a messy bun and head to the kitchen. It's warm outside, so I decided to offer the hard-working men some water and a snack...well, I'm the snack, so hopefully they're wanting a nibble of me.

Butterflies beat against my stomach and I'm terrified they're going to say no. If they don't take the bait, this could get super awkward. I'd have to avoid them all week. My skimpy two-piece suddenly makes me feel exposed, and I debate whether I really should do this as I grab two bottles of water from the fridge. The confidence I felt is quickly waning, and I try to give myself a pep talk. The worst that can happen is they say no, and it's not like I'm going to ask them outright to fuck me. I'll be subtle...smooth.

I almost change my mind and turn around when I get to the patio door, but when I glance outside, the younger guy is wiping sweat from his brow with the bottom of his shirt, exposing his stomach and chest. The ripple of his abs distracts me.

I want him. Them. Both.

When I walk out the sliding glass door, their conversation comes to a screeching halt and Devon gives me a slow smile as his eyes rake up my body. I don't mind the obvious appreciation since I came out here wanting it. The younger guy follows suit, his gaze moving to my cleavage.

Okay, I can do this. I strut up to them, not stopping until I'm barely a foot away, and I notice Devon's eyes are dilated. His reaction is all the encouragement I need.

I use my sultriest voice. "I wanted to see if you guys needed some water in case you get dehydrated in the sun. It's so hot today."

I smile suggestively at the younger guy because he's the closest to me. He gulps before stuttering out, "I'd appreciate that. Thank you, ma'am."

"You can call me Sasha. No need to be formal," I purr. "You guys have been working so hard, you deserve a break."

"Hi, I'm Chris," he croaks out and ducks his head as if he's shy. I can tell I'm making him nervous, and it's adorable. The ball is officially rolling in the right direction.

I turn to Devon. "Is there anything I can get you? Or help with?"

He looks me up and down again, as if he understands my true intentions. "I'd appreciate something to drink, especially since I'm suddenly very thirsty."

Oh, Devon isn't shy like Chris. I like that. I like it a lot. I can feel the wetness between my legs, and I'm already imagining myself being the water they both need.

A grin spreads across my face as a flush warms my core. "Well, if you come inside, I might have something to quench that thirst."

I head back inside. I know that sounded like a cheesy pickup line come to life, but when I glance back at them over my shoulder, they're both eyeing my ass like it's a juicy peach. Mmm, nice. I suppress a victorious cheer. It's game time, and I'm pretty sure I'm already winning.

They trail behind me as I sashay into the kitchen, and when I open the fridge, I make sure to bend over and give my ass a little wiggle. I'm a naughty minx, and I'm loving every second of it. "We have soda, and my husband has some beers if you're allowed to drink on the job."

I'm still bent over when I feel the heat of someone right behind me. I look back and Devon is standing close enough that he's almost touching me.

"Is your husband going to be okay if we...sample his goods?" Devon asks, his deep voice brimming with unspoken promise.

Mmm, he wants to play. I twitch my backside at him again. "Oh, he insists that you've both been working so hard, you deserve a reward. He wants me to...feel good. You wouldn't want me to be unsatisfied, would you?"

"Just making sure," he murmurs, placing a hand on my bikini-clad buttock. I swear I can feel sparks flying as he traces his fingers down to my covered mound, gently massaging me through the thin fabric.

Holy hell, how did things turn this raunchy so quickly? I figured I'd have to bust out some serious seduction moves, but all I had to do was strut outside in a bikini, and now here I am with a man's hand between my legs.

Devon pushes my bathing suit bottom aside and slips two fingers inside my pussy, groaning when he finds out how soaked I am. I brace myself against the fridge shelf, clinging to it for support. A tingling sensation zips through me, and I whimper. Mmm, he could do this all day if he wanted. He pumps his fingers in and out and I rock against his hand as the pleasure builds.

His voice is rough as gravel when he finally speaks. "We should discuss your expectations for the job. My company has a strict policy of ensuring that every customer walks away fully satisfied." He continues to fuck me, and it's all I can do not to scream with ecstasy as he keeps talking. "So why don't you tell me exactly what it is you need, and we'll make sure it's taken care of."

Oh my god. He wants me to tell them what I want? Can't they just use me for their pleasure? My head is woozy, and it's difficult to gather my thoughts. Suddenly, I realize that I'm holding the keys to the kingdom. He's literally asking me to tell him what to do. I could say anything...

For a split second, I debate what I want to say. My husband and I've had many talks about me wanting a little roughness in the bedroom. Michael might be dominant, but he was honest about not being able to give me any pain. I never really imagined I might get it from someone else. I close my eyes, grateful that I'm not looking at him when I utter my darkest desire. "I want you both to fuck me senseless, talk dirty to me, call me filthy names, and spank me until I'm begging for more...I want it rough."

As soon as the words leave my lips, I panic. Have I gone too far? But Devon responds by hooking his finger and stroking a spot that sends fireworks exploding through me. I buck against his touch, losing myself in the pleasure.

He slides a third finger inside me, and I push against his hand as my orgasm builds. Holy fuck, this is crazy. I'm half in the fridge while getting fingered by the guy building our deck...one who is definitely talented with his hands. Thank god we cleaned the fridge recently.

Devon picks up the pace, his fingers performing a symphony that has me yearning for the main act. He slaps my ass and growls, "Your pussy is so fucking wet."

The sting of the spank gives me a jolt of pleasure, and I clench around his fingers. I'm teetering on the edge of ecstasy when he withdraws his fingers, leaving me hanging. Seriously? He's pulling out before the grand finale?

With a firm grip on my upper arms, he hoists me out of the fridge like a rag doll and closes the door before pressing my back against it. I crane my neck to meet his gaze, finding a hunger in his eyes that rivals a starving man at a buffet.

His voice is husky. "Say it again. I want to hear what a dirty little slut you are and what you want us to do to you."

Oh. My. God. My entire body trembles from desire and my voice sounds breathy. "I want you both to take turns fucking my pussy."

He runs his wet fingers along my lips. "What else?"

I flick my tongue out, tasting myself as I answer. "Fuck my mouth. Make me choke on your cock."

"Mmm hmm," he murmurs encouragingly, pinning me to the fridge. "Keep going."

"Use me," I moan. "Call me a whore. Fuck me hard, spank me. Pull my hair. I need it all. I need you to do every depraved thing to me."

I don't recognize the slut begging for them to fuck her senseless, and I feel like I'm going to hyperventilate from admitting what I want. This is one of the hottest things I've ever done, and I can't wait to tell Michael about it.

I reach to try and touch his cock through his jeans, but he swats my hand away. "Did I say you could touch me?"

Oh. He tips my chin up, so I'm looking at him as he continues. "I'm the one in charge. Now, crawl over to Chris and kneel in front of him like a good girl so you can suck on his cock. If we're satisfied with your work, you'll get a treat."

His bossy tone turns me on even more, and I do like treats. I let out a soft groan before sliding out of his grip and down to the floor. The linoleum is unforgiving on my knees as I crawl towards Chris, but I keep stealing looks back to see if Devon is watching me.

He is. His eyes are dark and lust filled as he focuses on my ass. Yeah, he definitely seems like the type who appreciates my curves.

It's not very far, but I put an extra swing in my ass since I know Devon is watching. Right before I stop, Devon says, "We're going to use you hard, but if you need to stop, say 'red light' or tap our legs."

Ooooh, he's giving me a safe word? Michael has never been rough enough with me for us to consider having a safe word. There's no way I'm going to use it, but an unexpected spark ignites inside me at the thought.

As I kneel in front of Chris, I can see the outline of his hard cock through his jeans, but he looks uncertain of what he should do. For a guy who is sculpted like Adonis, he sure seems nervous. I would've thought he had a lot of experience with girls lining up for a taste of him. But maybe he's never been in a situation like this—not that I have either.

Despite my need to devour his cock, I flash him a flirtatious grin. "What would you like me to do?"

Chris's lips quirk, and his voice is richer and deeper than I expect. "Take it out and give it a good lick."

Well, well, isn't he full of delicious surprises? I can feel my pussy growing wetter as I reach up and unzip his pants, freeing his thick, mouth-watering cock. I push his pants and boxers down to his knees, licking my lips as I gaze up at him while massaging his balls. They're heavy and full.

"Suck it," he murmurs, tangling a hand in my hair and giving my bun a tug.

His roughness makes my core quiver. I'm practically drooling at this point. Today's tasting menu is beyond tantalizing. I run my tongue up the length of his shaft, swirling around the head. His dick throbs, and I slide the tip inside my mouth, teasing the slit with my tongue. Since he's been working hard outside, he has a manly musk, but it's not unpleasant. It makes me notice how different he is from my husband, which makes what I'm doing dirtier.

I want to savor him, but he has other ideas. He shoves his cock into my mouth until it hits the back of my throat. Yeah, I don't think he's shy after all. I think he just needed to warm up. I try not to gag around him as my pussy pulses with arousal. I told them I wanted it rough, and it looks like they're taking me at my word.

Chris takes his time fucking my face, using me like I'm just a hole for his pleasure. There's a wildness to his actions, and his moans make me feel like I'm about to win an award for the best blow job. He's controlling my every movement with his fist in my hair, and I relax my jaw and accept it. This is exactly what I needed, and I didn't even know it. I want to be just a hole for them to use.

Saliva drips down my chin while I clutch the base of his shaft with one hand and massage his balls with the other. He curses softly and bucks, and I taste pre-cum pooling on my tongue. He's close to exploding, and suddenly I want it. I want to make him come.

He drags my mouth back and forth on his cock as fast as he can, and I brace for his orgasm. He lets out a deep moan and shoves his cock as deep as it will go into my throat. It triggers my gag reflex as his cock explodes. Thick ropes of hot, salty cum spurt into my throat. My mouth fills to overflowing and the excess dribbles out of my mouth, coating my chin as I suck and swallow all of it. My brain is foggy from being used as he slides out of my mouth. I give his cock a tender kiss as I'm filled with a deep satisfaction. I make a good slut.

He collapses against the kitchen counter. "Holy shit, that was amazing."

I giggle and wipe the side of my face with my hand. "Thanks," I say cheekily. I love turning guys on so much that they lose control. It makes me feel sexy as hell.

Before I can wonder what's next, Devon reaches under my arms and picks me up. I gasp, startled, and he chuckles at my reaction as he carries me, bridal style, into the living room.

His voice rumbles through his chest. "It's time for me to use that filthy mouth."

Delight ripples through me at his words. He's really taking my request for dirty talk to heart, and I love it. He puts me down and points to the carpet in front of the couch. I scramble to where he gestured and settle myself on my hands and knees.

He sits on the couch within reach. "You're going to suck me like you did for Chris, understand? If you can't handle all of me, tap my thigh, but otherwise, I'm going to use that mouth of yours hard."

Ooooh, yes, please. I nod as he leans back and unzips his jeans. His cock is possibly the most beautiful cock I've ever seen. It's thick with a slight curve towards his stomach. Saliva pools in my mouth as I think about him using me. My husband couldn't have picked a better contractor for our deck if he tried. Everything about Devon turns me on.

Devon holds the base of his cock and strokes it slowly as my eyes follow his hand. Just when I'm about to ask him if I can touch it, he growls, "Open wide and show me that sexy tongue."

I do as I'm told and extend my tongue as I look up at him. Devon stares at my mouth as he strokes himself, and the longer he makes me wait, the more turned on I get. Jesus, is he ever going to let me suck on him or is he going to just imagine what it feels like as he masturbates? His choosing to stroke with his hand instead of using my mouth is torture. What kind of guy does this?

I know the answer. One who likes to be in control.

Finally, he spreads his legs, and warmth swirls in my core in anticipation. His eyes are still trained on my mouth when he asks, "How badly do you want to suck my cock?"

I can't help but smile because it's so sexy how he's drawing this out. I trace my tongue across my bottom lip before responding. "Very badly, please can I have it?"

"Beg for it," he demands, still stroking his shaft.

My face flushes from how naughty this is. I'm about to beg to suck a cock that isn't my husband's. I can feel myself sinking down into the deepest recess of my mind and turning into the sluttiest version of myself as I get ready to beg. Michael better enjoy the retelling of my adventure later, because I'm about to do whatever Devon wants.

I place my palms flat on his thighs and stare up into his eyes. "Can I suck on your cock? Please? I need it. I want you to face fuck me and make me choke...use my mouth."

"Damn," he growls as I beg. "Fuck, yes. Give it your best try. If you do a good enough job, I'll fuck you and let you orgasm."

Wait, what happens if I don't do a good job? I keep my thoughts to myself as I move between his legs. I don't intend to find out. As soon as my head is close to his cock, he grabs my bun with one hand, guiding me towards him as I open my mouth, sticking out my tongue. Instead of forcing me onto his cock, he drags it across my tongue and my lips.

He smears pre-cum along my mouth, and I can taste the saltiness of his cock, and smell the scent of his musk. He's all man, and knowing he's been working half the day makes this filthier. Cumsluts who want to be used don't care when or where. My pussy clenches and I can tell my bikini is soaked. I better make this the best blow job he's ever gotten. I really want to come.

He rests the head of his cock on my tongue as I flick my eyes up. When we make eye contact, I close my lips over the head of his shaft, gently sucking on it. I tease the underside with my tongue while pushing down, making him sink slowly inside. I take as much of his cock as I can without gagging before pausing with his cock stretching my throat.

He gently pets the side of my face and tugs on my hair, urging me back up. As soon as I release his cock from my mouth, I take a deep breath and smile at his satisfied moan. I guess my husband wasn't just being nice when he said I give great blow jobs.

Knowing Devon is enjoying this gives me more confidence, and I lick from the base all the way to the tip, before sucking the head inside my mouth. I feel his cock swell as he hardens even more.

"Fuck, that feels good," he murmurs and reaches for my right breast.

I whimper when he tweaks my nipple through the fabric of my bikini, and I throw myself into the blow job. I suck on his cock harder as he massages my breast and keeps his other hand on my head to force me down farther on his shaft.

"You have great tits and such a hot mouth. Your husband is a lucky guy. He gets to use you all he wants," he groans as he thrusts his hips up, driving his cock down my throat.

Deep down I know my husband can't really use me all he wants because we don't have that type of dynamic, but the fantasy Devon's words evoke turns me on even more. The way he's talking to me stirs up a craving I didn't even know I had. I want to experience what it would be like to just be a toy for someone to use.

As if he knows my thoughts, Devon groans, and his movements become harsher as he pumps in and out of me. He bumps against the back of my throat, and I fight the urge to gag. When he stops playing with my breast so he can put both hands on my head, I surrender myself to the face fucking. This is what I wanted and I revel in the debasement of being a mouth he can use. His grip on my bun tightens as he forces me up and down his shaft. I try not to choke, but it's pointless. I whimper around his shaft and drool drips down his length. This is glorious.

Devon pulls me up until just the tip is still inside my mouth and he tilts my head back so I'm looking into his eyes. "You love being a fucktoy, don't you?"

I want to respond that I do, but before I can say anything, he presses me back down on his cock. As I bob my head up and down, my mind goes fuzzy and I know that I really am a fucktoy. He could use me like this all night long and I would beg for more.

When he finally pulls me off his cock, I'm gasping for breath while he looks at me as if I'm the hottest thing in the universe. "Do you want me to come in your mouth?"

Oh god, I really do. "Yes, please."

He smirks. "Too bad. Fucktoys don't get to choose."

Before I can fully comprehend what's going on, he pushes me aside and gets off the couch. When he picks me up and hoists me over his shoulder with my ass in the air, I get a glimpse of Chris watching us with wide eyes. I give Chris a little wave as Devon carries me down the hall towards the bedroom. Since the door is open, it isn't hard for him to find. He throws me onto the bed, and I giggle as I bounce.

Chris follows us into the room and looks uncertain, as if he's not sure he's supposed to be in here. Devon points at the chair by my vanity table and barks at him, "Take off your clothes and sit. You're going to watch me fuck our toy."

Chris scrambles to do as he's told. When he peels off his shirt, my brain turns to mush at the sight of his six-pack. Yeah, I'd love to run my tongue all over that.

"Hands and knees," Devon growls at me, and I stop drooling over Chris and get in position.

My ass is in the air facing the guys as I steady myself on all fours. Devon slips my bikini bottoms down to my knees, and I lift each leg so he can peel them off. The cool breeze on my pussy from the air conditioner makes me feel exposed and vulnerable. I can feel their eyes devouring me, and knowing how wet I am from their rough treatment almost embarrasses me. I didn't know how much I was going to enjoy this, but it's so much better than any fantasy. Michael wins the Husband of the Year award for letting me experience this. I'm going to give him twenty imaginary tokens for blow jobs when he gets home tonight, and I won't even give them an expiration date.

Devon brings me back to the moment by smacking my right ass cheek, and the sting makes me moan. He slaps the other side, and when the pain turns to pleasure, my clit throbs.

His voice is gruff with appreciation. "You have such a great ass."

I arch my back and jiggle my butt at him, giving him more to look at as he teases a finger around my clit. I'm so turned on, my inner thighs are damp and I'm desperate for him to fill me up. Is he going to make me beg for his cock?

Instead of fucking me, he starts spanking me again...hard. My head spins from delight as he alternates ass cheeks. Holy fuck, I'm going to be sore tomorrow when I sit down.

He stops spanking me and I lower my elbows to the bed, resting my forehead on the backs of my hands to spread myself wider for him, offering up whatever he wants to take. He rubs the head of his cock up and down my slit, gathering my wetness before rubbing my pussy juices on my asshole.

"Ooooh," I moan at how naughty it feels. Am I going to let some guy I've never met before today fuck my ass? Mmm, yes, I will...if he wants to.

He probes my tight hole with a finger before applying pressure and pushing past the resistance. It burns for a few seconds and then I relax. I never considered getting it in the ass today, and I probably should have when I offered myself up.

He plays with my ass for a minute before withdrawing his finger, leaving me aching and empty. When the tip of his cock presses against my pussy, I groan. Am I disappointed that he's not taking my ass, or am I just desperate for any hole to be filled?

Devon slides in slowly, stretching me wide with his massive girth. I cry out in pleasure as he fills me completely. He reaches under me to push up my bikini top, pinching and pulling on my sensitive nipples as he sets a steady rhythm. I could easily lose myself in this slow, deliberate pace, but the sound of his groans tells me that he's nearing his limit.

He starts pounding me harder and faster, the slap of skin against skin echoing in the room. The sensation is overwhelming, pushing me closer and closer to the edge. I'm on the brink of ecstasy and my toes curl as I barrel towards my orgasm.

He smacks my ass again, the sting only heightening my pleasure as he relentlessly drives into me. He grasps my hips and yanks me towards him with every thrust. "Such a tight little cunt," he mutters, and I revel in his filthy praise. The knowledge that one of the hottest men I've ever laid eyes on is currently ravaging my pussy thrills me. I can't wait to share every dirty detail with my husband later.

I cry out as my pussy flutters around Devon's cock, my orgasm washing over me. I desperately grind against him, craving more of the delicious friction. When the bed dips in front of me, I'm greeted by Chris's hard cock, already slick with desire. I eagerly open my mouth, savoring the taste of his pre-cum as he guides my head up and down his shaft. The contrast between his flavor and Devon's is intoxicating, and I greedily devour every inch of him.

As both of them ravage me, driving me back and forth between their hips, my mind dissolves into a haze of pure ecstasy. I'm reduced to a moaning, writhing mess as they use me. It's exhilarating, and I almost wish it would never end.

Devon grunts as he jackhammers into me and unleashes a torrent of filthy words. "You're such a good fucktoy, taking both our cocks down that pretty little throat. I can't fucking wait until you're covered in our cum, a sticky, dripping mess."

"Mmm," I moan, the sound vibrating around Chris's cock.

"That's right, you dirty little slut," Devon groans, slamming into me with renewed vigor. His crude words make me shiver, and I crave more of it. He can call me his good little slut all night long, as long as he keeps fucking me like this.

He spanks me and growls, "Fuck, you're going to be so full of my cum, it's going to be leaking out of you for hours. Is that what you want, you greedy cumslut?"

I whimper a muffled, "Yes," and he spanks me again, the sharp sting only heightening my pleasure. I'm completely lost in the moment, my sole focus pleasing these two men. The bedframe groans in protest as Devon picks up the pace, the wet slap of our bodies getting louder.

He starts raining spanks on my ass with every thrust as he pants, "You.
..are...such...a slut. Admit it."

I pull my mouth off Chris's cock just long enough to scream, "Fuck yes!"
before he shoves it back in. I hum and moan, savoring the taste of him as I
writhe in pleasure.

"You like this, you filthy whore?" Devon growls, slapping my ass with
such force that the sting lingers.

Devon pounds into me relentlessly, each thrust pushing me further into
ecstasy. I whimper, desperate for more. Suddenly, I know deep down I
really am a filthy whore. Everything they are doing to me is spectacular, and
I wanted to fuck them before my husband even told me to seduce them. I
was daydreaming about all the cocks I wanted inside me for months, ever
since Erin became a hotwife. I'm a slut who is desperate to be used like this.

My thoughts spiral me into another orgasm. My pussy clenches around
Devon's cock as I come, my orgasm tearing through me like wildfire. I
scream and shake uncontrollably as they continue to use me for their
pleasure.

"Your husband has a greedy slut for a wife. I love it." Devon's voice is
strained, and I can tell he's on the edge. I redouble my efforts with my
mouth, desperate to bring Chris to the brink as well.

Devon jerks a few times and then stiffens and roars as he comes. His ropes
of hot cum spurting inside me make me cry out in bliss. The feeling of his
seed coating my walls sets me off again, and I ride the waves of pleasure.
Chris's eyes are glazed over with lust, and I almost giggle. I bet I have that
same look.

As soon as Devon finishes unloading, he moves away. "Chris, it's your
turn. You need to feel this tight cunt."

Oh god, yes. I need it.

Chris pulls out of my mouth and Devon gives my ass a sharp slap. "Now
be a good girl and tell Chris you want his load in your cunt."

A dirty zing lights up a pleasure response in my brain as I say, "Please, I want you to fill my cunt with your cum."

"Good girl," Devon says as he rolls me onto my back.

Mmm, yes. I spread my legs wide, eager for Chris to fuck me. I raise my knees as Chris climbs between them, and I urge him on. "Use me, please? I need it."

Begging for more cum amplifies the filthiness. Chris drives into me, and I moan with pleasure. The new position heightens every sensation. I secure my legs around his waist and hold onto his shoulders, urging him to fuck me harder. He latches onto a nipple with his mouth. As he sucks greedily, the delight makes me lose control. I mindlessly rock against him as another orgasm builds, but right before it hits, Chris explodes. I shiver in delight as the warmth of his cum makes me feel slutty and fulfilled.

Devon collapses on the bed next to me. He kisses my forehead and whispers, "Fucking hell, you're wonderful."

Exhausted, I lean into him while Chris slumps down and rests his head on my stomach. They both pant as I caress Chris's head and Devon tenderly strokes my shoulder. Their affection makes me feel floaty and happy. This might be the craziest sexual encounter of my life. I had no idea what was going to happen when I woke up today.

The guys both press against me, our sweat-slicked skin sticking together as we come down from our high. My pussy still throbs with unsatisfied desire, wishing for another release, but I know Michael will give it to me when he gets home. Fuck, Michael is going to lose his mind when he hears about this.

As my skin cools, Devon speaks. "That was an unexpected treat. Thank you. Is there anything you need before we get back to work? Water? A snack? I don't usually just fuck someone and leave like this, so I want to make sure you're all right."

I'm so relaxed I can barely speak, but I manage to smile at him and say, "I'll be fine. This was so perfect, and I really enjoyed it."

Devon raises an eyebrow and chuckles, "Just enjoyed?"

I laugh in return. "Okay, okay. I fucking loved it. It was everything I wanted and more. Thank you."

Chris murmurs his gratitude as he climbs off me, and the guys get dressed quickly. Both of them smile and we exchange quiet goodbyes. Once they're gone, I stare at the ceiling while my thoughts whirl. Did I actually do that? Yes. I fucking did.

As I feel cum leaking out of my pussy, I smile and force myself into a sitting position. Oh god, I need to find my phone and tell Michael what happened.

CHAPTER 3

When I'm ready to call Michael at work, I'm sprawled on the couch, wearing panties and my cotton robe. I'm munching on almonds and sipping water as my body buzzes with anticipation. I dial his number, and he picks up on the second ring and doesn't give me a chance to speak. "Tell me about the filthy things you did with those two men."

I let out a giggle. "So impatient! Maybe I did nothing, or maybe I've changed my mind and decided not to tell you anything."

"Sasha..." His tone has a warning, and a shiver runs down my spine, making my pussy ache.

"Well..." I whisper, dragging out the word. "I might have fucked two men today...but are you sure you want to hear about it while you're at work?"

He groans. "Shit, you're right. Don't tell me anything. It's going to be torture wondering what happened until I get home."

I'm enjoying how his voice is strained with desire. I take a moment to consider my next words. "Do you want me to shower and be waiting for you in bed when you get home?"

He inhales sharply. "No, don't shower. I want you on the bed, on all fours, ass in the air, waiting for me to take you."

I'm grateful that I'm already sitting down, or my legs might give out on me. Oh fuck. I love how he's being so commanding.

"Yes, sir!"

Michael says goodbye, and the yearning in his voice sends a wave of pleasure through me and I can feel my panties growing wet. After we hang up, I toss my phone aside and lay my head back, a grin spreading across my face as I replay today's events. My pussy throbs as I slide my hand under my robe, teasing my clit through the soaked fabric of my panties. I think about how it would feel if Devon and Chris took turns fucking my mouth again. What if they didn't come inside me and just came wherever they wanted? They could glaze my tits and ass, or come on my face.

I spend a few moments imagining Michael taking a video of the men using me so I could watch it later. The thought almost pushes me over the edge, and I have to stop touching myself before I come. I whimper from the stolen orgasm, desperate for release. Michael didn't tell me not to come, but I really want to wait for him. Ugh, how much longer until he gets home? I check the time on my phone, willing the minutes to pass more quickly. Michael was right. The wait IS going to be torture. With a sigh, I close my eyes and let my mind drift back to the filthy things those men did to me.

When Michael arrives home, I'm exactly where he instructed me to be. My knees are at the edge of the bed, and I'm totally naked, spread open for him. I have two pillows under my chest to help me stay comfortable, and I glance over my shoulder at him and greet him with a playful, "Hi, love. Welcome home."

He remains silent, quickly shedding his clothes and standing behind me. Why isn't he speaking? I'm practically quivering with lust as he explores my slick pussy with his fingers. I'm still a wet mess from all the cum inside me and being turned on all day.

"You're such a slut, eager to be used like this. You're sopping." He pinches my tender ass with his free hand, and I let out a gasp as pleasure and pain intertwine.

My reaction makes him growl, "What? Did you think you'd earn some reward after what you did? I bet you have no idea how badly I want to fuck you right now."

As he removes his hand from between my legs, I whine in disappointment. Why isn't he thrusting into me?

He delivers a light slap to my ass cheek. "Did you think you'd be treated kindly because you allowed those two guys to use you? No. I'm going to fuck you hard and take my pleasure from you. Tonight, you're mine to use."

My eyes widen in surprise. Oh fuck, he's never talked to me like this before. I moan out, "Yes, whatever you want."

This is awesome. I might have found a new kink of his that I wasn't expecting. I peek back over my shoulder at him once more, and he's stroking my wetness onto his cock to lubricate himself. Mmm, I want him to fuck me. I close my eyes and let the pleasure consume me as he sinks into me. This is precisely what I've been craving ever since the guys finished fucking me earlier.

When he bottoms out, he pauses for a moment before withdrawing and slamming back into me. I moan from the painful pleasure and gyrate my hips to match his rhythm as he fucks me hard and fast. He's not holding back, and I don't want him to. All I want is to be his fucktoy.

He grabs my shoulders and forces me to rise up onto my knees as he relentlessly drives into me. He roughly massages my breasts as he slams his hips against my tender ass with each powerful thrust. I moan when he twists my nipples between his fingers. My body is electrified, humming with a pleasure I've never experienced before. Every touch, every movement sends jolts of rapture straight to my core, making me feel like a toy...a sensual goddess fucktoy.

He releases one of my breasts and his hand travels down my stomach. When he reaches my pussy, he teases my clit while continuing to fuck me. I pant as a slow, intense orgasm builds deep within me.

He whispers into my ear, "Are you ready to come?"

"Yes!" I cry out, pushing back against him while meeting his every thrust.

He groans, "Come on my cock while I fill you with my cum."

As soon as he commands me to come, I detonate. White-hot pleasure surges through me and my vision blurs as my orgasm obliterates every thought. My entire body convulses from the sheer ecstasy as he slows down and tries to prolong my orgasm as he explodes. As I begin to recover, I can feel him pulsing inside of me as he paints my insides with his seed. I've experienced so much pleasure today, I feel like I'm floating on another plane of existence.

His movements gradually come to a halt, and we both collapse onto the bed, a sweaty, panting mess. We lie there in silence, catching our breath, until he chuckles. "Well, that was..."

I finish his sentence. "Fun?"

"And dirty. Very, very dirty. I should be appalled at myself."

I giggle, but quickly sober up. "But you're okay with what I did?"

He draws small circles on my hip. "I'm more than okay. I didn't realize I would enjoy that so much."

Relief floods through me. He enjoyed himself. Thank god.

He pulls me close, capturing my lips in a passionate kiss. "Now tell me everything."

Oooh, this is going to be fun. I trace my fingers up his chest and lock eyes with him, whispering, "Well, first off, Devon fingered me while I was bent over with my head in the fridge..."

He groans and kisses me again, hungry for more details. When I finish recounting the story, he's silent for a few moments. I'm about to ask him what he's thinking when he finally speaks.

"Do you want to do it again? I'd like to watch next time."

A rush of love washes over me, and I shiver in pleasure. This is coming from the man who claimed he didn't want to share me.

I give him my most radiant smile. "Yes, I want to do it again."

He murmurs, "Good," and my mind reels with the possibilities now open to us. Who will I fuck next?

Life just got incredibly interesting.

THE NAUGHTY HOTWIFE'S STAYCATION

Book 7

Lacey Cross

Chapter 1

As I sip my morning coffee, I look out into the backyard from the kitchen window and watch the two guys building a deck for us. Devon and Chris are already hard at work, their muscular forms moving with purpose. The sight of them stirs memories of yesterday's escapade when I first become a hotwife, and it sends a delicious shiver down my spine. My wonderful husband had given me permission to flirt with them...and do whatever else I wanted...as long as I told him all about it afterward. I took him up on the offer and had a wonderful time with Chris and Devon.

God, yesterday was amazing. My body still hums with satisfaction, but there's an insatiable craving growing within me. I want more. I imagine having them both again, feeling their strong hands all over me, their heat enveloping me. The intensity of my desire surprises me. Yep, I'm definitely a slut. And you know what? It's wonderful.

My gaze drifts to my phone on the counter, and I'm tempted to text Michael about my dirty fantasies and see if I can get him worked up. As if summoned by my thoughts, the phone dings and a message from him pops up on the screen.

I blush, feeling both excited and curious. What does he mean by 'good girl?' Smiling, I type my reply.

Sasha:

> **What if I want to be bad?**

My pulse quickens when he replies right away.

Michael:

> I know you're still thinking about yesterday. I want you to touch yourself for five minutes and then tell me how you feel.

Ohhh, I like where this is going.

Sasha:

> **Yes, sir!**

My fingers slip beneath the soft fabric of my pajamas, skimming over the sensitive skin of my lower abdomen before settling at the waistband of my shorts and panties. With closed eyes, I gently rub circles around my clit, my mind immediately painting vivid pictures of Devon and Chris pleasuring me as Michael looks on. The familiar stirrings of desire coil tightly within me, my breath catching as pleasure sparks along my nerves. All too soon, the phone interrupts with a ding, signaling another message has arrived.

Michael:

> Time's up. Still want to be bad?

I groan in frustration. Ugh, now I'm even more turned on.

Sasha:

> **Do good girls get to play with toys and come? I don't think I'll make it through the day without an orgasm.**

WHAT? I know my husband, and once he says something like that, he's not going to give in, no matter how much I beg. Oh god, this is going to be torture.

I send him a text with a pouty face in response before setting my phone down. Well shit, now what am I going to do all day? Am I supposed to just daydream about fucking Devon and Chris again? Michael said to imagine a bunch of guys...mmm, that's more than two. The gangbang fantasy that pops into my head gives me a naughty zing that heads straight to my clit, and I rub my thighs together, trying to ease the ache.

Unable to resist temptation, I peek out the window to the backyard again. I watch Devon and Chris working, the sinewy muscles of their arms flexing as they hammer and saw. I imagine what it would be like to fuck them again, their strong hands exploring my body, their lips trailing fire across my skin.

You know, Michael only said I can't touch myself. Does rubbing against something count? A quick glance around the room has me considering the corner of the kitchen table, but I quickly discard the idea. No...I better not risk whatever fun plan Michael has for me tonight. I have a habit of getting turned on and blabbing all my secrets when he asks if I've been good. I'm likely to tell him I was a slut and pleasured myself with the table.

The day drags by slowly, each minute feeling like an hour. I try to watch some daytime talk shows to distract myself, but it seems like every show is talking about sex. The universe is clearly conspiring against me. By the time Michael is due home, I'm showered and ready to pounce on him, my body vibrating with pent-up desire.

He's chatting with Chris and Devon as they wrap up their work-day. They're laughing about something, clearly enjoying the conversation. What is my man up to?

When he finally comes inside, he's grinning mischievously. I stalk to-wards him, intending to kiss him so thoroughly that he drags me to the bedroom before dinner.

He speaks before I reach him. "I have a challenge for you." His tone holds a sexy note of promise, and it stops me in my tracks. "If you're a good girl the rest of the week, once the deck is finished, I'll let you fuck Devon and Chris again while I watch."

Oooh, what's this? My heart races at the thought of Michael watching me with the other men. I can feel my pussy growing wet, and my inner slut wants to grab pom poms and do a cheer. But I need to know the specifics of this challenge first.

With a coy smile, I wrap my arms around his waist and tilt my chin up. I gaze at him through fluttering lashes, the picture of feigned innocence. "What exactly do you mean by 'good girl'?"

"There's rules." I'm already nodding, ready to agree to anything, when he continues. "No solo play. You have to flirt with Devon and Chris every day, and finally, I get to use you for my enjoyment whenever I want. You'll be my freeuse wife for the next three days."

I blink at him, my mind racing. I can see where this is leading. My husband loves to edge me, but he's never done it for three days before because he enjoys watching me come too much. I doubt he'd even do it for two days...god, I really hope not.

My mind teeters between the choices, and the desire for Devon and Chris's cocks tip the scales. The chance to fuck them again wins out. I just hope he really won't edge me.

"Deal," I whisper, sealing my fate.

Michael's eyes darken with lust. "Then it starts now."

Now? My thoughts are cut short as he pushes me down, bending me over the arm of the couch. Oooh, hell yes! I wiggle my ass as he yanks my shorts and panties down to my knees. I'm so turned on I might orgasm in two thrusts. This is great!

He's got his cock out within moments, and I gasp as he slams into me. The sudden invasion sends a jolt of pleasure straight to my toes, and I moan in delight as he pounds against my ass.

His hands grasp my hips tightly, pulling me against him with each thrust. The sound of our bodies colliding fills the room, and I can feel myself getting closer and closer to the edge. I'm moaning, "Yes...yes...yes," as the pleasure builds.

Right when I'm about to come, Michael's groan signals he's close. He gives one last powerful thrust and unloads his warm cum deep inside me. His cock twitches and spasms as he fills me with his seed, unloading everything he's got.

Oh no, I didn't come! My body vibrates from the stolen orgasm as he pulls out and slaps my ass. "I'm hungry. I'm going to get the grill started for our chicken. You're in charge of the salad."

"Okay," I peep out, my brain woolly-headed from the lack of orgasm.

"Good girl," he murmurs, and I practically melt. Michael adjusts his clothing and heads to the kitchen while I lie there, still bent over the couch and trying to catch my breath. Every nerve ending in my body cries for the release I know isn't coming. Devon and Chris's cocks better be worth this...

I giggle. Shit, they will be. Yesterday with Devon and Chris was so amazing, even if my husband uses me for three days and leaves me hanging, it will be worth it.

Chapter 2

Day three of our deck-building adventure kicks off with a bang, and I mean that quite literally. I wake up to gentle caresses, my mind slowly drifting into consciousness. It takes me a moment to realize Michael is rubbing my back. When he can tell I'm awake, he kisses my shoulder while his exploring hand takes a decidedly more sensual path. As he slides it between my legs and brushes his fingers against my clit, shivers run down my spine.

His eyes are dark with desire as he gently pushes me onto my back and hovers above me. "Good morning, gorgeous,"

"Morning," I murmur.

His hard cock presses against me, and I instinctively arch my back, silently begging for more. He enters me with a slow, purposeful thrust that makes me gasp. The rhythm he sets is both torturous and pleasurable. Each thrust pushes me closer to the brink, but it's never quite enough to send me over. It's a delicious agony, and I can feel the familiar tension building, my body pleading for release.

I cling to his shoulders, grinding against him with desperation, my hips bucking uncontrollably. Just as the waves of pleasure begin to crest, Michael lets out a deep, primal groan and fills me full of cum. I writhe beneath him, trying to come as well, but it's too late.

A wicked grin spreads across his face as he gives me a quick kiss and gets out of bed. "Something to keep you thinking about me today."

"Thanks..." I try to keep the pout from my voice as I watch him gather his work clothes. The sight of his toned body, glistening with a light sheen of sweat, doesn't help. I'm quivering with unfulfilled need, and I want to pull him back into bed for round two. Shit, I need to be good. I really, really want that reward.

After he leaves for work, I force myself out of bed and make my way to the kitchen. As I prepare breakfast, my mind keeps wandering to the sex toy drawer in the bedroom. Why did I agree to this stupid game? Yeah, yeah, I know why. Michael's promise is enough to keep my hands off myself...for now.

The sound of a truck pulling up outside snaps me out of my reverie. Oooh, the guys are here. I spend the rest of the morning watching Devon and Chris out the window and replaying Michael's morning wake-up call in my mind. Between the sexy guys outside, my memories, and my husband edging me, I'm so turned on I could burst.

My husband needs to feel some sexual frustration, so I text him.

Sasha:

> Hey, when the guys fuck me, can I have one in my ass and one in my pussy at the same time?

I snicker when I see the chat bubbles pop up that say he's replying immediately.

Michael:

> You want that?

Oh wow, he didn't say no. Do I want that? I imagine having two holes filled at once and realize I really do want that...and I don't think it's just because I'm sex crazed at the moment. Who knows if I will ever get a chance with two guys again.

Sasha:

Yes.

Michael:

Your wish is my command.

Wait, who says they even want to fuck me?

Sasha:

What if you edge me for three days and they don't want me?

Michael:

They want you. They already said yes when I asked.

Whoa. I blink at his message. Yeah, I think I just fell a little more in love with my husband.

We send filthy texts back and forth for a while until Michael tells me he has to do actual work. Boo, work sucks. He should have taken vacation days with me.

After lunch, I decide to have some fun with Devon and Chris. I mean, I'm supposed to flirt with them every day. I didn't make up these rules.

Slipping into the bedroom, I trade my pajamas for a skimpy sundress that accentuates my curves in all the right places. The soft blue fabric clings to me, leaving little to the imagination. I give myself a once-over in the mirror as I wrap my blonde curls into a top knot. The dress is sexy but not overtly revealing—perfect for my plans.

As I make my way outside, I can feel the gaze of the guys on me, and it's like a shot of adrenaline. Devon's eyes, a stunning blue that always takes my breath away, lock onto me, and lust simmers beneath the surface. Chris swallows hard, his Adam's apple bobbing noticeably. I try to hide my smirk. I love knowing I can make them react like this. I hope they are remembering how it felt to fuck me.

"Good afternoon, gentlemen. I see you're working *hard*." My voice is laced with innuendo as I glance down at Chris's growing bulge in his pants.

Devon is the first to reply. "Afternoon, Sasha. You're looking...radiant today."

Chris just nods, seemingly at a loss for words. I suppress a chuckle, enjoying his discomfort and the palpable tension in the air.

We spend the afternoon engaged in playful banter while they work. Devon's a bit of a flirt, always ready with a clever comeback or a suggestive double entendre. The sexual tension is like a live wire, crackling with energy. I'm so aroused, I can barely think straight. Every movement and every word spoken seems charged with erotic potential.

"You know, Sasha," Devon says at one point, wiping sweat from his brow, "I never thought building a deck could be so...stimulating."

I arch an eyebrow at him, playing along with his game. "Oh? And what exactly are you finding stimulating?"

He grins, his eyes twinkling. "The company, of course. Nothing quite like working up a sweat with a beautiful woman around."

Chris, on the other hand, is adorably shy again today, but when he does speak, his voice is smooth and makes my heart patter. "The deck's coming along nicely," he comments during a water break. "Strong, sturdy. Built to withstand a lot of activity."

The meaning isn't lost on me, and I feel a blush creeping up my neck as I imagine being fucked against the railing. "I'm sure it'll hold up just fine," I respond, my voice huskier than I intended.

As the day wears on, I clean up a little around the inground pool, inventing reasons to bend over, to stretch, to do anything that might draw their attention. Each lingering look sends electricity through me. I know I'm just working myself up even more, but I can't seem to stop.

By the time Michael comes home, I'm vibrating with need. The day's teasing and flirtation have left me in a state of near-constant arousal, and I'm desperate for release.

I all but pounce on him as soon as he walks through the door. "I've been good," I report. "So, so good."

I can feel the heat in Michael's eyes as he studies me. Without a word, he pulls me into a scorching kiss, his hands rough and insistent as they explore every inch of my body. In the blink of an eye, he has me pressed against the wall, my legs wrapped tightly around him as he thrusts into me. It's fast and frenzied, just like this morning, and he leaves me hanging once again. Somehow, despite the frustration, I find myself not wanting it to end. It's a strange, twisted kind of pleasure, and I can't get enough.

As I lie in bed that night, my body hums with unfulfilled desire. The deck is going to be finished soon. I can make it...right? The reward will be worth it. I just have to hold on a little longer.

I close my eyes, and my mind fills with images of strong hands, heated glances, and the promise of two cocks. It's a long time before I'm able to sleep.

CHAPTER 3

The next day begins with a sense of anticipation because I know the deck is almost finished. I wake up after Michael has already left for work, my body yearning for release. The empty space beside me only intensifies my longing, and I giggle at myself. I'm so desperate I wanted him to wake me up and fuck me before work again, even knowing it might not end with me having an orgasm.

In the bathroom, I grin at myself in the mirror, taking in my flushed cheeks and bright eyes. My skin feels electric, hypersensitive to even the lightest touch. Today, I'm going to turn up the heat even more with my flirting.

I decide to wear a sexy pink bikini, knowing full well the effect it'll have on Devon and Chris. As I slip into the bikini, I feel the fabric gently embracing my curves. The top is generously sized, allowing me to easily adjust it to accommodate my ample breasts. I can almost hear the appreciative whistles from Devon and Chris when they see me in it. To complete the ensemble, I add a light, sheer cover-up, just enough to tease them with hints of what's underneath. The fabric whispers against my skin as I move, a constant reminder of how turned on I am.

I hear the sound of their truck pulling up outside. My heart races as I make my way to the back patio door to greet Devon and Chris. As they approach, I make sure to give them a good view, pretending to stretch. The sunlight streams through the sheer fabric of my cover-up, silhouetting my body beneath. They both give me a hungry glance, and a thrill runs through me. This is going to be one hell of a day.

"Morning, guys," I call out, my voice deliberately light and teasing. "Ready for another day of hard work?"

Devon laughs. "I'm always ready for hard labor."

Mmm hmm, I bet you are. I don't voice my thoughts.

Chris tries to keep his eyes on my face, but I can see the effort it's costing him. "Good morning, Sasha. You look refreshed."

I laugh, plucking at my neckline to force his eyes down to my cleavage. "Why, thank you, Chris."

As the morning progresses, the temperature rises, matching the heat building between us. After lunch, I decide it's time to cool off in the pool. Making a show of removing my cover-up, I can feel Devon and Chris's eyes on me as I dive in. The water feels heavenly against my heated skin.

While swimming, I'm acutely aware of Devon and Chris stealing glances at me. I make sure to give them a show, arching my back as I float on the surface, letting my hands trail sensually over my body as I pretend to adjust my bikini. I hope I'm driving them crazy as much as I'm turning myself on.

The temptation to touch myself is almost unbearable. As I float in the water, I let my mind wander, imagining Devon's strong hands caressing my thighs, Chris's gentle touch on my breasts. It's all I can do not to give in right there in the pool.

Other than the promise to be a good girl, the other thing stopping me from touching myself is that our neighbors can look out their back window and see our pool. I'm not so sure I want them to see me with my hand between my legs. We're not that friendly of neighbors.

Finally, when I can't take the self-imposed torture any longer, I decide to get out of the pool. I don't bother to dry off, instead heading towards the house, water droplets cascading down my body. As I pass the patio table, Devon calls out, his voice strained, "Hey, Sasha, could you pass me my water bottle?"

I retrieve the bottle from the table, and as I hand it to him, our fingers brush, sending a jolt of electricity through me. Our eyes lock, and for a moment, the air between us crackles with tension.

"Thanks," he murmurs, and I wish I could beg him to fuck me right here, right now.

Inside the house, I find myself drawn to the bedroom, as if pulled there. Before I know it, I'm standing in front of the full-length mirror, my hand hovering over my bikini bottoms. I can see the flush on my face, my stiff nipples showing through the wet fabric of my top. I can almost feel the relief that an orgasm would bring, imagining my fingers sliding beneath the fabric, finding that sweet spot...

Shit. I stop myself. This payoff better be worth the wait. I take a deep, shuddering breath, trying to regain control.

Needing a distraction, I call my best friend Erin. I've yet to tell her what I'm doing this week. She's going to love it.

Her cheerful voice is a welcome relief. "Hey, how's staycation treating you?"

"Yo, you're never going to believe the week I'm having." I spill every-thing—the challenge, how turned on I am, how much I want to fuck Devon and Chris again.

Erin laughs, the sound warm and understanding. "I don't know whether to be impressed or concerned. Why would you agree to let him edge you all week?"

"Um...duh, for some cock. But it's so hard," I whine, flopping back on the bed. "I'm so wound up. I feel like I might explode."

Erin's voice takes on a teasing tone. "Just think about how amazing it'll be when you finally get to come. I'm sure it will be worth the wait, and if not, Michael will make it so."

Yeah, she's right. We chat for a while longer, and by the time we hang up, I feel more centered, more in control. I can do this. I can resist.

Feeling refreshed, I decide to bring some cold water out to the guys. As I step outside, it's like my composure of a few minutes ago disappears. I immediately want to climb on top of one of them and ride their cock to glory.

"You know, Sasha," Devon says as he bends to pick up a tool, his muscles flexing enticingly, "You're making it very hard to concentrate on work."

I give him a slow, seductive smile. "Oh, I'm sorry. I had no idea."

"I'm sure you didn't," Chris chimes in, his voice low and husky.

Jesus, this isn't helping. I need to get out of here. "Well, I better go do some housework. Have fun!"

I sashay inside, making sure to sway my hips in case they are watching. By the time Michael gets home, I'm a bundle of nerves and pent-up desire. I practically corner him as he walks through the door, pressing my body against his.

"How was your day, sweetheart?" he asks, a knowing glint in his eye.

I tell him everything I did today, including how hard it was not to touch myself. As I speak, I can see his eyes fill with lust.

"Good girl," he says, pulling me into a searing kiss that leaves me breathless. "Just one more day."

I moan, my body pressing even closer to his. I can feel his arousal against my stomach, and it takes every ounce of willpower not to beg him to take me right there.

"Just one more day," I repeat, my voice barely a whisper.

Later, after Michael fucks me on the couch while we're watching a show and doesn't let me come, we head upstairs to bed. How in the hell am I going to make it through tomorrow? Devon and Chris are putting the finishing touches on the deck and then maybe Michael will tell me when I can come. Just one more day of exquisite torture, and then...bliss. I can make it. I hope.

The next morning I'm immediately excited. The deck should be done today, and soon I'll get my reward! Michael has already left for work, and there's nothing I need to do except flirt with Devon and Chris.

I get out of bed, and as I rifle through my swimsuit drawer, I debate which bikini to wear. After a moment's hesitation, I settle on a cherry red number that I know will catch their attention. Pairing it with a gauzy white cover-up and sunglasses, I head downstairs, grabbing a book from the living room before going straight out to the backyard.

Devon and Chris are already hard at work. I settle into a lounge chair by the pool, pulling out the book I have no intention of reading. My eyes are drawn to the men, watching their fluid movements and the play of sunlight on their hair.

"You guys really think you'll be done today?" I call out, pushing my sunglasses up on top of my head.

Devon straightens up, wiping a bead of sweat from his brow. The simple action draws my attention to the strong lines of his arms. "Oh yeah, it's coming along nicely."

Chris nods enthusiastically. "You're going to love it when it's finished."

I stand up, sauntering over to inspect their progress. Michael is going to stain it himself, so I can tell they really are almost finished. The wood is smooth under my fingertips as I run my hand along the partially completed railing. "It looks amazing already. You two are so talented."

As I lean over to get a better look, I feel eyes on me. "Well," I say, stretching languidly, "I think it's time for a little sun. Don't work too hard, now."

I make a show of removing my cover-up, feeling a thrill as I hear Chris's sharp intake of breath behind me. The sun feels warm on my skin as I settle back into my lounge chair. I reach for the sunscreen, taking my time applying it to my arms and legs, aware of the occasional glances thrown my way.

"Hey, Chris," I call out, my voice honey-sweet, "would you mind getting my back? I can't quite reach."

Chris nearly drops the hammer he's holding. "Uh, sure," he stammers, looking to Devon for...permission? Guidance? I can't quite tell. The dynamic between them fascinates me.

Devon nods almost imperceptibly. "Go ahead."

As Chris approaches, I can practically feel the nervous energy radiating off him. I hand him the sunscreen bottle, rolling onto my stomach and sweeping my hair to one side, exposing the nape of my neck. My skin tingles in anticipation of his touch.

"Just make sure you get everywhere," I say, my voice low and teasing. "We wouldn't want any sensitive areas to burn."

Chris's hands are shaking slightly as he squeezes some sunscreen onto his palm. The moment his fingers touch my skin, I have to bite back a moan. His touch is tentative at first, but as he works the lotion into my shoulders and back, he grows more confident.

"Is this okay?" he asks, his voice husky.

I hum contentedly. "Perfect. You've got magic hands, Chris."

From the corner of my eye, I see Devon's intense gaze on us. Fuck, I wish I was getting more than just a back rub out of this.

As Chris finishes up, I roll over, smiling up at him. "Thanks, handsome. I owe you one."

He mumbles something unintelligible and practically flees back to the safety of the deck. Devon claps him on the shoulder, saying something too low for me to hear, but Chris's blush deepens. I get the feeling that Devon is having fun teasing him.

The day passes quickly with me "supervising" from my lounge chair and the men working diligently to finish the deck. I make sure to keep the guys well-supplied with water, using every opportunity to bend over or stretch in ways that show off my assets. The sexual tension continues to build, like a rubber band stretched to its limit. As the sun begins to dip lower in the sky, Devon calls out, "That's it! We're done!"

Despite having watched them build it, I jump up, eager to see the finished product. "It's perfect," I breathe, running my hand along the smooth railing. I can already imagine the dinners Michael and I will have out on the deck.

Chris beams with pride. "Glad you like it. It was a pleasure working for you."

As Devon and Chris pack up their tools, Michael appears in the doorway. "Great job, guys. It looks fantastic."

Devon nods, a satisfied smile on his face. "We aim to please."

As they prepare to leave, Michael calls out, "Hey, why don't you both come back later tonight? We could have a little celebration, break in the new deck properly."

I feel a thrill of excitement run through me. This is unexpected but oh, so welcome. Devon and Chris exchange a look, then nod in unison. The anticipation in the air is almost tangible.

"Sounds great," Devon says.

The guys chat for a moment, organizing what time they will come over while I imagine how tonight will go. I thought I was going to have to wait at least one more day, so this is fabulous.

As we watch them drive away, I turn to Michael, my eyes sparkling with excitement. "Well, that's quite the invitation."

He pulls me close. "What can I say? I'm just as impatient as you are."

I laugh, my mind already racing with possibilities for the evening ahead. "I'm glad."

"Also..." He kisses me deeply and my toes curl before he breaks it off and continues. "You aren't allowed to wear panties tonight."

"Mmm, yes, sir."

As we head inside to get ready for the evening, I want to dance in excitement. I finally get to come tonight!

CHAPTER 4

I'm still getting ready when the guys arrive, and Michael goes out to greet them. Butterflies swirl in my stomach as I put the finishing touches on my outfit and join them. Stepping into the backyard, my sundress swings around my legs. I can feel the breeze teasing the bare skin beneath, a reminder of Michael's instruction to not wear panties. My heart races with the thrill of being so exposed, knowing that only the thin fabric of my dress separates me from the hungry eyes of the men.

Devon and Chris lounge against the railing of the deck, their eyes roaming over my body like predators sizing up their prey. Michael sits at the patio table he moved onto the newly finished deck for tonight. A small smile plays on his lips as he takes in the scene. I can feel the weight of all three pairs of eyes on me, and my body responds, a flush creeping up my chest as my nipples harden.

Devon's eyes travel down my bare legs, taking in my sandals and my red painted toes. I feel myself growing wetter with each passing second. I can practically taste the sexual tension in the air. If I don't get a cock inside me soon, I'm going to burst.

"The deck really is gorgeous." I sound breathy, and I struggle to keep my voice even.

Devon's eyes seem to shimmer in the dim light. "Glad you like it."

"I'm surprised we got it done in time, especially with the added distractions," Chris chimes in, his voice teasing.

Devon's gaze lingers on me, sending a shiver down my spine. "Why don't we give Sasha a tour of the deck?" he suggests, pushing off from the railing and moving towards me.

Michael's eyes meet mine, and he nods, giving me a subtle smile that sends a jolt of electricity straight to my core. The deck isn't that big, and I don't really need a tour, but I stay quiet as Devon takes the lead. He points out the intricate details of the woodwork and the custom-built railing, but all I can focus on is the strength of his body and the fabric of my sundress brushing against my bare skin, reminding me of how close I am to getting their cocks again. Chris follows closely behind, his presence adding to the mounting tension. Someone really needs to fuck me.

"You know what I think would make this deck even better?" Devon murmurs.

His voice scrambles my brain, and I swallow hard, my mouth dry. "What's that?"

He leans close to me and whispers, "You, bent over the railing, screaming my name while I fuck you senseless."

My body responds instantly, and I can feel my inner thighs growing slick with desire. I glance at Michael and get a jolt of pleasure when I see his hand massaging the bulge in his jeans. Oh, heck yeah. He's already getting started. Suddenly, I know the guys planned this.

Devon pushes my back against the railing, the wood digging into my skin briefly before he flips me around and bends me over it. I grip the edge, and the cool night air washes over my skin as Devon pushes my dress up, exposing my bare ass. I moan softly, lust clouding my mind.

Devon's fingers trace the curve of my ass, his touch igniting the barely contained fire within me. "You're such a naughty girl. You want us to fuck you, don't you? You want to feel our cocks inside you, stretching you wide and making you come until you can't take it anymore."

I whimper, my body aching for their cocks. "Yes, I want you—both of you."

Devon uses his knee to force my legs apart, and I moan as Chris moves close to get a better look at my wet pussy. This is exactly what I wanted...what I was craving since I fucked them a few days ago. I'm their plaything, and I love every second of it.

Devon traces my soaked slit with his fingertips, teasing my entrance. "Fuck, you're dripping," he rasps, his voice thick with lust. "You want this, don't you? You want us to use you, to make you come until you're begging for mercy."

"Yes. Please, I need it," I pant, desperate for release.

Devon plunges two fingers into me, and I cry out, my grip tightening on the railing. Holy hell, this is wonderful. He mercilessly fingerfucks me, his thumb circling my clit, sending me spiraling toward orgasm. I've been so close to coming for days I can tell it's going to happen fast.

I glance over my shoulder at Michael, and he's still rubbing his bulge through his jeans. Knowing he's aroused enough to touch himself in front of other people tells me he's enjoying this.

Devon pistons his fingers inside me and growls, "Do you like being a filthy little slut in front of your husband?"

Oh god, I do love my husband seeing my sluttiest side. I nod, my body aflame, and I cry out, "Yes, I'm just a filthy slut. Don't stop, please."

When Devon chuckles and withdraws his fingers, I whimper in protest. What the hell, I just told him not to stop! I hear the sound of a belt buckle, the rustle of fabric, and my heart races in anticipation. A quick glance at Devon shows him pulling his cock out of his jeans. Mmm, never mind. This is about to get good.

He strokes himself as he steps closer to me. "You want me to fill your desperate cunt while your husband watches?"

"Yes," I beg, pushing back against him. "Fill me. Just please, fuck me. I'll do anything you want."

Devon chuckles again, the sound sending a shiver down my spine. "Oh, I know you will," he murmurs, his voice dark and dangerous. "I'll fuck you until you're screaming in ecstasy, until you can't take it anymore. I'll make you come so hard you'll see stars."

Holy shit, he's so great at the dirty talk...but the house next to ours isn't that far away. I really shouldn't scream.

"We have neighbors..."

He presses the tip of his cock against my opening, coating it with my wetness. "Then I guess you better be a good slut and stay quiet."

A second later, he slams into me and I throw my hand over my mouth to muffle my cry of pleasure as he stretches me wide. He sets a brutal pace, his hips slapping against mine, and I can hear Chris unzipping his pants. When I glance over at Chris, he's stroking his cock as he watches us.

Devon's grasp on my hips tightens as he pounds into me, his thrusts becoming erratic. "Fuck, you're such a good little slut. Such a tight, wet pussy. I can feel you clenching around my cock, begging for more. You want me to fill you up, don't you? You want to feel my cum dripping out of you."

I've been needing to come so badly, and his filthy words send me over the edge. I explode, crying out as waves of delight crash over me. My hand mostly muffles my cries as my body convulses, my pussy clenching around his cock.

Devon pulls out and slides two fingers inside me again, massaging the pleasure point while my head spins. "You want Chris to fuck you too, don't you? You want all our cum."

Gripping the railing with both hands again, my body trembles with need and I pant, "Yes...all the cum."

Devon withdraws his fingers, and I whimper in protest. He guides Chris towards me, positioning him between my legs. Chris's cock brushes against my entrance, and I moan, my body aching for him.

"Fuck her," Devon growls. "Fuck her while we watch."

Chris thrusts into me, and I'm so sensitive from my last orgasm I cry out as he fills me up. I buck my hips as he bottoms out. If our neighbor looked out their bedroom window, they might be able to see what's happening. Just imagining them knowing what a complete slut I am sends an illicit thrill straight to my clit.

He hammers into me hard, and I welcome the painful pleasure. I can feel myself getting closer to the edge again as my body trembles. Fuck, this is intense.

I start to squirm, the sounds I'm making growing louder and more desperate. Chris reaches around and puts his hand over my mouth to silence me as he fucks me harder. Between his hand in front of me and him fucking me from behind, I feel like I'm trapped, completely at their mercy. And I love it.

He shifts his angle and massages new pleasure points. I lose control and groan into his hand, my eyes rolling back in my head as a tsunami of pleasure hits me. I ride the waves of my orgasm, becoming mindless with pleasure as my body convulses while Chris continues to fuck me. All I know is I want to feel these guys use me over and over again.

Chris suddenly removes his hand from my mouth and pulls out, leaving me feeling empty and desperate for more. But before I can wonder what's next, Devon lifts me off the railing, his arms wrapped around me. "You're ours tonight. Ours to fuck, ours to use. And we're not done with you yet."

Devon hauls me over to the table, pushing me onto my back right in front of my husband. I look at Michael and giggle, "Hi, love."

He mouths, "I love you," as Devon hooks my ankles on his shoulders and slides his cock back into me.

"Ohhh, god!" I cry out as his throbbing cock fills me. Devon immediately jackhammers into me, and my tits jiggle with every thrust. Michael reaches out and pushes the top of my dress down, causing my breasts to bounce free as Devon plows into me. I'm sure this looks filthy, but the smile on Michael's face says he's enjoying the show.

I'm close enough to the side of the table that when Chris moves next to my head, stroking his cock, I'm able to turn and take him into my mouth. I greedily suck on him, my mouth working in time with Devon's thrusts. Having Devon's cock in my pussy and Chris's cock in my mouth sends me soaring, my mind consumed by pleasure. I thought what we did the other day was the filthiest thing I've ever done, but being fucked on a table in front of my husband tops everything.

Devon's thrusts become more desperate, his grip on my thighs bruising as he chases his own release. "I'm going to fill you with my cum," he grunts, his pace relentless. "I'm going to mark you as mine, right in front of your husband."

His words are so filthy they send me spiraling into another orgasm. My body convulses as the pleasure rips through me. I scream, but my cries are muffled by the shaft in my mouth. Devon's body stiffens, and he groans, his cock pulsing inside me as he unloads. Chris follows suit, his cock swelling in my mouth as his salty cum coats my throat.

I collapse against the table as the pleasure fades, spent and shaking. When Chris pulls out, I look over at my husband. Michael has an almost pained expression on his face as he stops stroking himself through his jeans.

Devon slides out of me, and he helps me lower my legs and sit up. He kisses me deeply before murmuring, "Good girl, but we're not done with you yet. First, you're going to clean me off."

Oooh, I want to taste him. He helps me off the table, and I sink to my knees on the hard deck. I eagerly suck on his half-hard cock, tasting myself as I clean him off. My mind is still fuzzy, and I find myself lulled into a happy place as I lavish his cock with attention, making sure to swirl my tongue along the veins of his shaft. The longer I suck on him, the harder he gets.

"That's it, baby," Devon groans, his hand tangling in my hair. "Suck my cock with that pretty little mouth of yours. Make me hard again so I can fuck you some more."

I gurgle around his cock happily, loving the feeling of being their fuck-toy. I've never felt so desired, so wanted, and it's intoxicating. Devon seems to know exactly how far to take the dirty talk, and it leaves me feeling warm and tingly.

When Devon's had enough of my mouth, he pulls out and picks me up, setting my ass on the surface of the table again. I wrap my legs around him as he slides into my pussy, filling me up once more.

I expect him to fuck me on the table, but he picks me up and holds my ass, turning around so that Chris can come up behind me. I hear a pop top from a bottle of lube, and it takes me a moment to realize what's happening. Holy shit, Michael must have told them what I wanted. I guess my wish really was his command.

But wait, are they going to fuck me standing up? Devon moves me up and down his cock and I cling to his shoulders as Chris positions himself behind me. Huh, I guess so.

"Such a beautiful ass," Chris murmurs, his fingers massaging the lubricant around my tight opening. "I can't wait to fuck it."

The change in Chris once he gets turned on makes my head spin. I love it when he stops being shy and starts talking dirty. When he slowly pushes a finger into my ass, working me open, the pleasure short circuits my brain.

"That's it," he murmurs, his finger moving in and out. "Relax and let me in. I'm going to make you feel so good."

Once Chris deems me sufficiently lubed up, he positions his cock against my ass. "You want this?" he asks, his voice thick with lust.

I pant, "Yes, please fuck me. I want to feel both of your cocks at the same time."

Chris pushes inside me, and my head spins as the pressure hurts at first and then eases. The feeling of both of them inside me at the same time is indescribable, and I moan as I'm consumed by pleasure.

The men have me positioned so that Michael has a side view, and I look over at him, resting my head on Devon's chest as the two guys fuck me.

Michael's eyes are filled with lust, and I can tell he's loving every second of watching this.

The two guys work my holes, their cocks moving in and out of me in a rhythm that has me seeing stars. I can barely breathe, every inch of my body electrified with bliss, every nerve ending overloaded. I'm drowning in sensation, my mind struggling to comprehend the sheer intensity of the pleasure rippling through me.

"Such a good little fucktoy," Devon growls, his breath hot against my ear. "Look at you, taking both of our cocks. So fucking sexy. You love this, don't you? You love being our little slut, our plaything."

Every word he speaks heightens the ecstasy coursing through my veins, and I'm too overwhelmed to answer. My body quivers as I ride the razor's edge of orgasm, and I bury my face in his neck, my eyes screwed shut as I brace for the impending eruption.

The guys start moving faster, and the sensation is amazing. I can hear how wet my pussy is with each thrust of their cocks, and the thought is incredibly arousing.

"That's it, baby," Devon groans, his thrusts becoming erratic. "Come for us. Come all over our cocks."

His words push me over the edge, my body convulsing as I explode. I look over at Michael, our eyes meeting as pleasure crashes through me, every muscle in my body quivering as wave after wave of euphoria washes over me. I can barely hang on as the guys keep thrusting, my body wracked with pleasure.

Suddenly, Devon's body tenses, his cock pulsing as he spurts deep inside me. His rhythmic contractions send me crashing over the edge again, my mind unraveling as I clench around his shaft, milking him for all he's worth.

A few moments later, Chris climaxes, his body shuddering against mine as he shoots his load into my ass. We're all breathing hard, the heady scent of sex thick in the air as we bask in the afterglow of our debauchery.

Chris pulls out first, and Devon sets me back on the table carefully before withdrawing. He keeps his arms around me until he's certain I won't fall. I gaze up at him, my head spinning.

"You're amazing. Thank you," I mumble, still dizzy from my orgasms.

Devon has a mischievous glint in his eye. "Trust me, the pleasure was all ours."

Michael approaches, and Devon steps back so that Michael can put his arms around me. He grins at Devon. "Go enjoy the rest of your evening. I'll take it from here."

"Absolutely," Devon says as he tucks his cock into his jeans and zips up. "Thanks, gorgeous. I had a blast."

"It was nice meeting you," Chris says with a smile, and I echo it back to him. "It was nice meeting you too."

Michael holds me close, I smile at him, grateful for his support. The guys walk around the side of the house, leaving us alone.

"Are you okay, love?" he asks, his brow furrowed with concern.

I lean against him, still a bit lightheaded. "Mmm hmm," I mumble. "Do I look wrecked?"

He chuckles. "Oh, yes. And It's hot as hell."

He kisses me softly, and I melt into him. God, I love my life.

Chapter 5

When Michael's kisses become more insistent, I can tell he needs me. I pull out of his arms to lean back on the table. I prop myself on my elbows and give him a saucy grin. "So are you going to fuck me here or inside?"

His eyes flash with desire as he trails his fingers up the inside of my thighs and rubs my clit. "Maybe both. You're my freeuse slut, after all," he says, his voice thick with lust.

Mmm, that I am. I moan as he plays with the wetness between my legs. He seems fascinated, but I want more than just his fingers.

"Fuck me, please. I need you," I whimper, grinding my pussy against his hand.

Michael pulls his cock out of his jeans and lines it up with my swollen opening, rubbing his tip over it and up to my clit. He gently taps the head of his cock against my clit a few times before slipping it back down to my hole. The teasing is so fucking arousing, I feel like I could come just from this.

His eyes lock on mine as he inches inside, pushing in gradually. It's such a contrast to the frenzy of earlier, and I revel in the connection. He pushes me back as he laces our fingers together, and presses my hands flat on the table by my head as he fully enters me, the friction lighting up my already sensitized nerves. His hips roll against me, his pubic bone hitting my clit in a way that makes me see stars.

I gasp as he buries himself inside me, his cock stretching me just like I like. "I love you," I sigh contentedly.

"Love you too," he murmurs, as his strokes become longer and more urgent.

Closing my eyes, I savor every moment. He lets go of my hands so he can caress my body and knead my breasts. I grasp the edge of the table and moan as I arch into his touch. Everything he's doing feels wonderful.

Michael's tempo increases and his thrusts become more powerful, sending sparks through me. The familiar warmth blooms in my core, and I moan as the pleasure builds.

"That's it," Michael groans. "Come for me, sweetheart."

As if on command, I come, my body quaking beneath him as I reach my peak. My legs wrap around his waist as I clench around his length. The orgasm is stronger than I expect, and the world disappears as I'm consumed by the bliss.

Michael's grip on me tightens, and he shudders as he explodes. I feel his cum bathing me as his cock pulses. We stay locked together as we come down from our high.

I can feel the cum dripping out of me. Yeah, this table is going to need to be cleaned. I giggle as I realize how I must look—splayed out on the patio table, dress hitched up to my waist and my boobs hanging out while multiple guys' cum leaks out of my pussy.

Unhooking my legs from around his waist, he helps me sit up.

"God, I love you," Michael whispers, pressing a tender kiss to my forehead. "We both need a shower."

"Yeah, a shower would be good. That was fun." I giggle again and reach a hand between my legs. I gather some of the wetness and lick it off my fingers, curious about the taste. It doesn't taste like me. I guess I have too much cum in me.

Michael's eyes glint as he watches me suck on my fingers. I smirk, enjoying the knowledge that he's probably thinking I'm a shameless slut.

"C'mon, my filthy slut. Let's get cleaned up," he says, pulling me to my feet.

A zing of pleasure hits my brain. See, I knew he was thinking I was a slut. "Only if you promise we can do this again someday," I tease, pulling my dress down and straightening it.

Michael grins. "Don't worry, this is definitely not the last time. I'll find someone for you to fuck so I can watch again."

My heart soars at his words. Hell yes, I really am a hotwife now.

The Naughty Hotwife in the Wild

Book 8

Lacey Cross

CHAPTER 1

I stretch languidly on the couch, my body still humming with satisfaction whenever I think of last week's escapades with Chris and Devon out on the newly finished deck. My husband Michael is sitting at the kitchen table, sipping his coffee and scrolling through his phone. I study him, admiring the way his T-shirt clings to his broad shoulders. God, I love that man.

"Hey, babe?" he calls out, not looking up from his phone.

"Mmm?" I respond, my mind still replaying the delicious memories of Devon's and Chris's hands on me.

"What do you think about a camping trip this weekend? Just you and me, two nights under the stars."

I blink, caught off guard. "Camping?" The thought of bugs, dirt, and sleeping on the ground doesn't exactly thrill me. But then I remember how amazing Michael's been lately, letting me explore my desires and become a hotwife. He's given me so much freedom and pleasure. The least I can do is humor him with a camping trip.

"You know what? Sure, why not?" I say, sitting up and running a hand through my messy blonde hair. "It could be fun, right?"

Michael's eyes twinkle with excitement. "You won't regret it, I promise."

I'm unable to resist his boyish enthusiasm. "Hmm, maybe. But you owe me a spa day when we get back."

He laughs, getting up to join me on the couch. "Deal," he says, pulling me into his arms. His lips find mine, and I melt into him, my body instantly responding to his touch.

I bet he has something planned for this trip. Knowing Michael, it's bound to be more than just roasting marshmallows and telling ghost stories.

Breaking off the kiss, I trace lazy patterns on his chest and ask, "So, when do we leave?"

"Friday afternoon," he replies as his hands cup my ass. "That gives us a couple of days to get ready."

My mind is already racing with what to pack. "All right, I'll start making a list. But first..." I straddle his lap, grinding against him. "I think we need a little preview of our outdoor adventure, don't you?"

Michael chuckles. "I like the way you think."

As we lose ourselves in each other, I tell myself not to get my hopes up for anything grand. This really could be just camping.

The next couple of days fly by in a blur of preparations. I get off work earlier than Michael does, and I'm packing our bags when he walks into the bedroom Friday afternoon.

There's a lusty glint in his eye when he says, "I've got a surprise for you," and pulls a small box from behind his back.

My heart races as I take it from him. Oooh, I like gifts! Inside, nestled in tissue paper, is a sleek, black butt plug. I raise an eyebrow at him. "And what exactly do you have planned for this?"

He grins, his voice dropping to a husky whisper. "I want you to wear it on the drive up. Get you nice and ready for what I have planned."

A shiver of anticipation runs through me. "Oh really? Are you going to tell me what we're doing?"

Instead of answering, he takes the plug from me. "Pull your panties down and bend over."

I guess the fun is starting now. I comply, bracing myself against the bed with my panties at my knees and my sundress up around my waist. He squirts lube onto the toy and his hand before his fingers, slick and cool, circle my asshole. I moan softly, wishing he was fucking me right now, but we probably don't have time.

"That's it, baby." He works the plug into me. "Nice and easy."

The stretch is delicious, and by the time the plug is fully seated, I'm panting with need. When I stand up, Michael spins me around, brushing his lips over mine as he unzips his pants.

"Fuck, you're so hot," he growls, lifting me onto the bed so I'm on my hands and knees. Hell yeah, guess we have time after all! The butt plug shifts inside me, sending a jolt of pleasure straight to my core.

Michael grasps my hips firmly, and I can feel his cock, hard and ready, against my entrance. With one swift motion, he sinks into my pussy, and I cry out in delight. The added pressure from the plug makes every thrust more intense.

"You feel amazing." He pulls out almost entirely before slamming back home. The force propels me forward, and I have to brace my hands on the mattress to stop myself from collapsing.

The plug in my ass seems to amplify every sensation, making my nerve endings sing with each movement. I can feel the veins of his cock as he thrusts in and out, the friction igniting a fire in my core that threatens to consume me entirely.

"Oh my god," I moan as pleasure ripples up my spine.

He continues to fuck me relentlessly. "You like that, baby? You like feeling me deep inside you?"

I'm incapable of forming words as the pleasure builds, so I only nod. Michael's hand snakes around to my front, his fingers finding my clit and rubbing slow, torturous circles. The added stimulation drives me wild, and I can feel my orgasm building. It's a tidal wave of sensation threatening to crash over me.

I want more. I need more. Pushing back against him, I meet him thrust for thrust, desperate to feel him even deeper. "Harder," I beg, my voice barely recognizable. "Fuck me harder, Michael."

He responds immediately, and he slams against me with renewed fervor. The sound of our bodies slapping together fills the room.

"God, yes," I moan, my muscles coiling tighter with each thrust. "Just like that. Don't stop."

Michael continues doing exactly what I like as the tension builds. His voice is rough with desire. "Come for me, baby. Let me feel you come all over my cock."

His words are my undoing. With a cry that's half-scream, half-sob, I tumble over the edge, my body convulsing with the force of my orgasm. Waves of pleasure wash over me, each one more intense than the last.

Michael continues to fuck me through it, his movements becoming erratic. "Fuck, you feel so good."

With a final, powerful thrust, he buries himself deep inside me, his body shuddering as he climaxes. The warmth of his cum fills me, prolonging my own orgasm as I milk every last drop from him.

For a moment, we stay like that, our bodies joined and our breathing ragged. Then Michael gently pulls out, his fingers tracing the curve of my spine as I flop onto the bed.

"Holy shit, that was intense." My body still tingles with aftershocks.

Michael laughs, pulling me into his arms. "Just wait, babe," he says, a wicked glint in his eye. "The fun's only just beginning."

I giggle, "Well, that's one way to start a camping trip."

He laughs with me before getting up. "No time to relax, lazybones. We have to pack."

Oh god, how can he fuck me like that and then expect me to have the energy for anything? I give myself a moment longer before forcing myself off the bed to clean up and finish loading the car.

An hour later, we're on the road, the butt plug a constant, delicious reminder that he has more plans for me. As we drive deeper into the woods, I daydream about what might happen. He wouldn't edge me all weekend after giving me such a wonderful orgasm, would he? The dang plug is keeping me needy and ready to burst, so I'm not sure he could edge me. I might come as soon as he touches my clit.

We pull into the campsite just as the sun is setting. As Michael parks the car, I spot a familiar truck nearby. My heart skips a beat when I see Devon and Chris setting up a tent.

I turn to Michael with a huge smile. "You invited them?"

"I told you I had plans, didn't I?" He grins and kisses me.

Oooh yeah, I think I might enjoy this camping trip after all.

Chapter 2

As we step out of the car, Devon and Chris glance up from their work. Devon's eyes lock onto mine, and he gives me a slow, predatory smile. My body instantly reacts as a tingling warmth envelops me.

"Well, well," Devon drawls, straightening up to his full height. "Look who decided to join the party."

"Hey, Sasha. Michael." Chris stops hammering a tent stake to give me a shy wave.

Michael wraps an arm around my waist, pulling me close. "Hope you guys don't mind us crashing your camping trip," he says with a wink.

Devon laughs. "Oh, I think we can make room for you two."

I shift slightly, the butt plug reminding me of its presence. The thought of what might happen this weekend sends an electric tingle racing down my spine.

Michael gives my ass a playful squeeze. "Let's get set up."

As we unload our gear, I can feel Devon's and Chris's eyes on me. Every time I bend over to grab something, my dress creeps up and exposes my upper thighs. I know I'm giving them a good view. The sexual tension in the air is palpable, and I'm already aching to get a cock inside me.

Once our tent is up, Michael works on starting the fire while Devon and Chris chat with him. I excuse myself to change into something more comfortable.

In the privacy of our tent, I decide to wear a pair of tiny shorts and a tank top that barely contains my breasts. I debate for a moment whether to keep the butt plug in, ultimately deciding to leave it. The constant stimulation is driving me wild, and I love the secret thrill it gives me.

When I emerge from the tent, I'm met with appreciative glances from all three men. Michael's eyes darken with lust, while Devon and Chris don't even try to hide their enthusiasm.

Devon gives a low whistle. "Damn, girl. Are you trying to start a forest fire?"

"Just trying to stay cool in this heat," I giggle and settle onto a log next to Michael.

Chris hands me a soda, his fingers brushing mine longer than necessary as he murmurs, "Well, you're certainly raising the temperature around here."

As the night progresses, the tension in the air continues to build. We share stories and jokes, but there's an undercurrent of desire that has me squirming in my seat. Every time I move, the plug sends jolts of pleasure through me, and I have to bite my lip to keep from moaning out loud.

Eventually, Michael stands up, stretching languidly. "Well, I don't know about you guys, but I'm beat. Think I'm gonna turn in. You coming, babe?"

He gives me a meaningful look, and I know this is part of whatever he has planned. I nod, standing up a bit unsteadily. The constant arousal has left me feeling delightfully fuzzy.

"Night, boys," I purr, letting my gaze linger on Devon and Chris. "Don't stay up too late."

As soon as we're in our tent, Michael's on me, his lips crashing against mine as he lowers me down onto our sleeping bags. He growls, "Do you have any idea what you've been doing to those guys all night?"

I moan as he grinds against me, feeling his hardness through his jeans. "Why don't you tell me?"

Michael's eyes glint with mischief in the dim light of our lantern. "Oh, I'll do better than that. I'll show you."

He flips me onto my stomach, yanking down my shorts. His fingers find the base of the plug, and he gives it a gentle tug. "You've been such a good girl, wearing this all day." He works it out of me. "I think you deserve a reward."

I whimper as he removes the plug, feeling suddenly empty. But then there's the cool liquid of more lube before I feel the blunt head of his cock rubbing against me. I have to bite down on my pillow to muffle my moan as he sinks into my ass.

He sets a torturously slow pace, each thrust flooding me with pleasure. I'm so worked up and already close to coming.

"Please, I need more," I beg, pushing back against him.

Michael continues his slow, deep thrusts. I need a little more stimulation to come. I'm a writhing, needy mess beneath him.

Just when I think I can't take anymore, Michael speeds up. The pleasure zips through me as I moan louder. I'm making enough noise that I know the pillow isn't going to hide what we're doing, but I don't care anymore.

"Touch yourself and come for me," he groans.

I move a hand down and furiously rub my clit as my toes curl in pleasure. When I finally come, I cry out as ecstasy rushes through me from my fingertips to my toes. Michael shudders a moment later, and pumps me full of cum.

My head is swimming when he pulls out and slumps down next to me. I snuggle against him as he strokes my back.

We're both quiet for a minute until I giggle. "If all the camping trips were like this, I might start begging you to take me more often."

He laughs. "Yeah, 'cause you're a little slut who enjoys being the center of attention."

Mmm, he's got me there. What's not to like about a weekend of pleasure in the forest?

We lay there cuddling for a few minutes until Michael pulls me to my feet. "I'm beat. Let's go get cleaned up so we can sleep."

I murmur my agreement and as we leave the tent, Devon and Chris are still by the campfire. I can feel myself blushing furiously as they both smile at us without saying a word.

When we get back from the campground's showers, Devon and Chris are getting ready to head into their tent. Devon says goodnight to us and adds, "I hope you plan on sharing her tomorrow."

Michael laughs. "If she's a good girl, I will."

Devon chuckles with him and disappears into his tent. I'll be the best girl there is if it means I get multiple cocks tomorrow. The thought sends a bolt of arousal straight to my core, and it takes me a long time to settle down once we're snuggled in our sleeping bags. When I finally drift off to sleep, visions of multiple dream-men using all my holes dance in my head.

The morning light filtering through the tent walls wakes me up and my pussy thrums with need as the memories of last night come flooding back. My dream, along with all the sexual tension from yesterday, has me ready to take on everyone's cock before breakfast.

Michael stirs beside me, a slow smile spreading across his face as he takes in my flushed appearance. "Morning, beautiful." He leans in for a kiss. "Ready for a hike?"

Uh, what the hell? That doesn't get a cock inside me. I raise an eyebrow. "A hike? Really?"

He brings his hand down to cup my breast and gently tweaks my nipple. "Trust me, it'll be worth it."

Hmm, it better be. I expected today to be a marathon of cocks in every hole. A hike wasn't in my plan. I should have known camping might have been too good to be true.

As we emerge from our tent, Devon and Chris are already up and about. Devon's gaze travels up and down my body, taking in the tiny shorts and tank top from yesterday that I put back on for our hike.

"Morning, sunshine," he drawls, handing me a can of cold-brew coffee. "Sleep well?"

I take a sip, enjoying the way my body responds to his voice. "Definitely, especially after the workout Michael gave me."

Devon's eyes cloud with lust, and I smile to myself as I take another sip of the coffee. Good, now he's thinking about fucking me.

Chris joins us, and his shy smile contrasts with the hungry look he gives me. "I'm ready for a hike."

I want to sass them all and tell them it's good THEY are, but then I remember I need to be a good girl today. I don't want to risk them edging me and not letting me come later.

As we set off into the woods, I try to stay cheerful. I'm not a fan of hiking, so to amuse myself I tantalize the guys by continually bending over to examine flowers or rocks and wiggling my ass. I know my plan is working when I catch Devon and Chris's glances lingering on my backside.

About an hour into our hike, we come to a small clearing. The trees provide a natural screen, hiding us from any potential passersby.

Michael stops. "I think this is a pleasant spot for a rest, don't you?"

Before I can respond, Devon moves behind me and wraps his powerful arms around my waist. "I couldn't agree more," he murmurs, his lips brushing against my neck.

When Chris moves in front of me, his usual shyness is replaced by a look of pure lust. "You've been teasing us all morning," he says, his voice a deep rumble.

I glance at Michael, silently seeking his permission. He nods, settling himself against a nearby tree. "Show them what a good girl you can be, baby."

Desire pulses in every nerve ending and I blow him a kiss a moment before Devon spins me around, crushing his lips to mine while his hands squeeze my ass. I can feel his hardness against my stomach, and I moan into his mouth like a needy slut. Maybe I enjoy hiking after all, if it ends like this.

Chris moves in close behind me, sliding his hands under my tank top to cup my breasts. "God, you're so sexy," he groans, grinding his cock against my butt.

Devon breaks off the kiss, and commands, "On your knees, slut."

I comply immediately, sinking to my knees on the mossy forest ground while he unzips his pants. His cock springs free, thick and hard, and my mouth waters at the sight. Without hesitation, I take him into my mouth, moaning around his length.

Chris kneels behind me, tugging my shorts and panties down to my knees. His fingers find my dripping pussy. "Fuck, she's soaked."

"That's because she's been a good girl," Michael says from his spot by the tree. "And good girls get rewarded."

As if they preplanned this, Devon kneels in front of me as Chris pulls on my hips, forcing me to get on all fours. I'm still sucking on Devon's cock, and I'm ready to get another hole filled. Jesus, this is filthy.

I feel Chris line himself up with my entrance, and then he's sinking in, stretching me deliciously. The combination of his cock in my pussy, Devon in my mouth, and knowing how slutty this looks has me seeing stars.

Devon fists his hand in my hair, guiding my movements as I suck him. "That's it. You love being a cumdumpster for us, don't you?"

I moan around his cock happily. Oh god, I love the degradation, and knowing that Michael is watching makes me want to prove just how good of a cumdumpster I am.

Chris sets a punishing pace, his hips ramming against me with each thrust, forcing Devon's cock further down my throat. The forest is filled with the sounds of our passion—skin slapping against skin and muffled moans.

I'm lost in a haze of pleasure as Devon and Chris use me. Michael's voice cuts through the fog. "Make her come. I want to see her fall apart."

Chris reaches around, his fingers finding my clit and rubbing circles around it. My orgasm builds rapidly from the added stimulation, and I moan continuously around Devon's shaft.

"That's it," Devon groans, his cock hitting the back of my throat. "Come for us. Show us what a good little slut you are."

His words give me a jolt, and I come with a muffled scream around his cock. My body convulses, as my orgasm rips through me like wildfire. Feeling me come sends Chris into a frenzy as he continues to plow my pussy.

Devon pulls out of my mouth, stroking himself furiously. "Where do you want it?" he pants.

"Face," I gasp out between Chris's relentless thrusts.

Devon groans, his cock twitching as he paints my face with his cum. The sight seems to trigger Chris, and he slams into me one last time, emptying himself deep inside me. My head spins as he spasms, unloading every last drop into my pussy.

As we catch our breath, I become aware of Michael's presence beside us. He kneels down, gently wiping Devon's cum from my face with the hem of his shirt. "You did so good, baby." He gives me a soft kiss. "Such a good girl."

I love it when he calls me a good girl. It makes me want to be their fucktoy all weekend for the praise... which might be the point.

We clean up as best we can with what we have, adjusting our clothes so we're somewhat presentable. As we start the hike back to camp, I'm still humming with desire. I hope this isn't the end of Michael's plans. This is the best camping trip ever.

CHAPTER 3

The hike back is a delicious torture. Neediness swirls in my core, and every step reminds me of what just happened in the clearing—the ghost of Devon's cock in my mouth, the lingering ache from Chris fucking me. I catch Michael watching me with a knowing smirk, and I blow another kiss at him.

As we approach the campsite, Devon's hand brushes against my ass, giving it a firm squeeze. "Hope you're not too worn out." His voice is low enough that only I can hear. "The night's still young."

An expectant tension coils in my gut, and I have to bite my lip to stifle a moan. God, I wish he'd just bend me over the picnic table and use me right now. Don't make me wait for later.

Back at camp, Michael suggests we all clean up before dinner. "Why don't you go first, babe? Take your time."

I nod, grabbing my toiletries and a change of clothes before heading to the campground showers. I feed quarters into the shower and step into the stall. The hot water cascading over me feels heavenly. I take my time, putting in a few more quarters so I can savor the warmth as it soothes my pleasantly sore muscles.

While I'm rinsing the shampoo from my hair, I hear the bathroom door open and close. Footsteps approach my stall, and suddenly the curtain is pulled back. I gasp, instinctively moving to cover myself, but relax when I see it's Michael.

He has a towel with him, and he quickly removes his clothes and sets his stuff down on a nearby bench. When he steps into the stall with me and closes the curtain, he's grinning. "Thought you might need some help."

Before I can respond, he's on his knees in front of me, his hands gripping my thighs. "Spread your legs for me, baby," he commands softly.

I brace myself against the shower wall and spread my legs as Michael leans in, his tongue finding my clit. I moan softly, aware that we could be caught at any moment. The danger only adds fuel to my lust.

Michael works me with his mouth, his tongue alternating between broad strokes and focused licks to my sensitive bud. "Such a good girl," he murmurs against my pussy. "Letting Devon and Chris use you in the woods. You love being our little slut, don't you?"

"Yes." I rock my hips against his face. "God, yes."

He increases the pressure of his tongue, slipping two fingers into my still-sensitive pussy. The dual stimulation has me spiraling towards an orgasm.

"That's it, baby," Michael encourages. "Come for me. Let me taste how much you love being used."

Holy fuck, he's really getting into the dirty talk. His words catapult me over the edge, and I come with a muffled cry, quivering from the strength of my climax. Michael laps up my release, licking me through the aftershocks until I'm a trembling mess.

As he stands, he wipes his mouth with the back of his hand. I can see his cock jutting straight out. I grip it firmly and rub him. "What about you?"

He catches my hand, bringing it to his lips for a kiss. "Later," he promises. "This was just for you. Now finish getting cleaned up. We've got plans for tonight."

My mouth drops open in delight as he steps out of the shower. He dries off and gets dressed, winking at me before he leaves. There's a restless neediness inside me, and I wish he had fucked me. But if he wants to torture himself and wait for later, that's on him.

I finish my shower quickly, knowing the hot water is going to end any second. When I get back to camp, the guys have started a fire and are in the process of cooking dinner. The smell of grilling meat makes my stomach rumble, reminding me that I haven't eaten since breakfast.

As we sit, eating and chatting, I can feel Devon's eyes on me. They keep wandering to my cleavage that's barely contained by the low-cut sundress I've changed into. Chris's cheeks pinken every time he looks at me, and it makes me almost giggle at how adorable he is. For a guy who does a good job of taking what he wants in the moment, he seems unsure of himself otherwise.

After dinner, as we're cleaning up, Michael pulls me aside and kisses me. "You've been such a good girl today. Are you up for a little game?"

I nod, my body already responding to his touch. "What kind of game?"

He grins, reaching into his pocket and pulling out a small remote. "Remember that new toy we bought last month? The one that can be controlled wirelessly?"

My eyes widen as I realize what he's suggesting. The vibrator he's talking about is designed to be worn internally, stimulating both my G-spot and my clit. And with the remote, anyone can control it.

"You want me to wear it now?"

Michael nods. "I want you to go put it in, and then we're going to play a game of poker. You're going to sit there and watch, and whoever wins each hand gets control of the remote for the next round."

The thought of being at the mercy of all three men sends a naughty zing through my entire body. "Okay," I agree, taking the vibrator from him.

I duck into our tent to insert the toy, moaning softly as it settles into place. When I emerge, the guys already have the game set up on the picnic table.

As they start to play, I'm hyper-aware of the toy inside me, waiting to spring to life at any moment. It's not until the third hand that someone finally uses the remote.

I'm daydreaming about having one of their cocks in me when suddenly, the vibrator buzzes to life on the lowest setting. I gasp, my eyes darting to Devon because he won the last hand. He smirks at me and turns the dial, ramping up the buzz in my pussy.

I'm flushed and dizzy as the game continues. The intensity and pattern of the vibrations change with each hand. Sometimes it's a low, constant buzz that I can almost ignore. Other times, it's a pulsing rhythm that has me squirming in my seat, desperately trying to hold in my moans.

By the time they're on the last hand, I'm a wreck. My panties are soaked, and I'm so close to coming that I'm afraid the slightest touch might set me off. Chris wins the final round, and as he takes control of the remote, I brace myself for what's coming—expecting them to turn it up full blast until I explode.

To my surprise, he turns the vibrator off completely. I blink at him in confusion, but before I can say anything, he stands up.

"I think it's time we took this somewhere more private," he says, his usually shy demeanor replaced by something more commanding. "Sasha, come join me in my tent."

I look to Michael, and he nods, a smile on his face. "Go on, baby. You deserve it."

As I follow Chris to his tent, I can feel the other men's eyes on me. Are they just going to sit out there and listen? The thought is naughty, and if that's the plan, I'm going to give them plenty to hear.

Inside the tent, Chris wastes no time. He pulls me into his arms, kissing me with an urgency that makes my head spin. "God, you're so hot," he groans against my lips.

He stops kissing me long enough to peel my sundress off, and then he lowers me down onto his sleeping bag. He kneels and pulls my panties down my legs, and I reach down to hold the vibrator in place against my pussy. The moment feels oddly intimate, despite knowing that only the thin wall of the tent separates us from Michael and Devon.

He sits back on his heels, reaching for the remote from his jeans pocket. He turns the vibrator back on to its highest setting.

I cry out, my back arching off the sleeping bag as the intense vibrations short circuits my brain. Ohhhh, holy fuck. Chris takes his clothes off as he watches me writhe.

"You're so fucking beautiful," he murmurs, positioning himself between my legs. "I can't wait to feel you come around my cock."

He moves the toy aside, keeping the vibrations focused on my clit but leaving him room to slide in. With one swift motion, he plunges into my pussy. The vibrator and the pleasure of his cock make me squeal and thrash. Chris speeds up and each circle of his hips has my muscles quivering until my vision blurs and rapture consumes me. We surge together and I rock my hips in time with him.

"That's it," he grunts, his fingers digging into my hips. "Show me how much you love being fucked."

The combination of his words, the relentless pounding of his cock, and the vibrator still buzzing away against me quickly pushes me towards the edge.

"Oh god," I whimper, clinging to his shoulders and wrapping my legs around him. "I'm going to come!"

He captures my lips in a bruising kiss before saying, "Do it."

His permission is all I need. I come with a scream, convulsing as wave after wave of pleasure crashes over me. Chris follows soon after, burying himself deep inside me as he empties himself with a low groan. I feel his cum paint my insides as I float in euphoria.

As we lay there, panting, I marvel at how this shy, sweet guy transforms in the bedroom. It's a side of Chris I never would have expected, but one

I'm definitely eager to explore further. Someday he's going to have a very happy partner if he continues to bring this level of heat.

Just as we're coming down from our high, the tent flap opens. Devon pokes his head in, a wolfish grin on his face. "Room for one more?"

Chris nods, and Devon strips off his clothes, I wonder if Michael is still by the fire. I had thought he wanted to go camping for himself, but this trip is turning out to be the best idea he ever had.

Devon lies down and pulls me on top of him. As I bounce on his cock and moan, I decide Michael is the best husband in the world. And we still have one more day to go.

Chapter 4

The next morning, I wake up with my arms wrapped around Michael. It was late when Devon and Chris were done with me. Michael still wanted to wait when I tried to coax him into fucking me. Something tells me I'm going to get a hard pounding by the time we're done on this trip.

I try to extricate myself without waking Michael, but it doesn't work. He blinks at me and smiles. "Sleep well?"

"Mmm, eventually," I reply with a grin. "Did you enjoy listening last night?"

Michael kisses me softly. "Hearing your pleasure is so damn hot."

His words send a ping of delight through me, and I lean in to deepen the kiss. As we break apart, I can feel his hardness through our sleeping bags. Pushing him onto his back, I straddle him and grind against his cock. "Want me to take care of that for you?"

I'm already wet this morning, and this sleeping bag is going to need a thorough washing when we get home, but I don't care. My own sleeping bag is probably covered in cum since I didn't shower after the guys were done using me last night.

He groans, his hands gripping my waist. "As tempting as that is, I want to wait. I have a feeling Devon and Chris will be up soon, and we have more plans."

As if on cue, we hear movement outside our tent. "Morning, lovebirds," Devon calls out, his voice gruff with sleep. "Hope we didn't keep you up too late last night."

I feel a blush creeping up my cheeks, but Michael just laughs. "Nothing we couldn't handle."

Devon yawns and I hear the cooler open as he fishes out something to drink. Michael kisses me again, drawing my attention back to him. "Let's get up, babygirl. The day is starting."

I climb off him reluctantly and gather my shower supplies. I leave the men at the campsite and speed clean myself. Today is not a day to waste time. I want a cock in me ASAP.

The guys are all sitting around the picnic table, nursing cans of cold brew coffee and planning the day ahead. I can't help but marvel at how comfortable this all feels. There's no awkwardness, no jealousy—just a group of friends enjoying each other's company...with some incredible benefits.

"So," Michael says, setting down his empty can, "I was thinking we could go for a swim in the lake today. It's supposed to be pretty hot."

The suggestion is met with enthusiastic agreement, and we quickly clean up and change into our swimwear. I munch on a granola bar for breakfast as I slip into my bikini—my sexy red one that leaves little to the imagination. Michael keeps tossing appreciative glances at me, and something tells me this won't be an innocent swim. Thank god the campground is pretty deserted this weekend.

The lake is a short hike from our campsite, and by the time we arrive, the sun is beating down on us mercilessly. The cool water looks incredibly inviting. Yesterday, I was reconsidering my dislike of hiking, but today I'm back to thinking it sucks.

Devon doesn't hesitate, stripping off his shirt and pants, and diving in with a whoop. Chris follows suit, while Michael hangs back with me on the shore. Both of them are wearing swim trunks and I admire their muscular forms as the water glistens on their chests.

"You okay?" Michael asks, his hand resting on the small of my back.

I nod, leaning into him. "Just thinking about how lucky I am," I reply, watching Devon and Chris splash around in the water. "Thank you for this weekend. For everything."

Michael kisses me softly. "Anything for you, baby. Now, why don't we join them?"

We pull our clothes off, down to my bikini and his swim shorts, and wade into the water. The coolness is a blessed relief from the heat. Devon swims over to us, his blue eyes sparkling. "How about a game of chicken?" he suggests, nodding towards Chris.

Before I can respond, Michael's hoisting me onto his shoulders. I squeal in surprise, gripping his head for balance. Devon does the same with Chris, and soon we're engaged in a playful battle, trying to knock each other off. It's pretty hilarious seeing Chris on Devon's shoulders, and it makes me admire Devon's strength even more.

As we wrestle, I'm acutely aware of Michael's head between my thighs, and the way Chris's hands feel on my shoulders as he tries to unseat me. The innocent game quickly turns sexual.

Eventually, Chris manages to topple me, and I fall into the water with a splash. When I surface, I find myself face to face with Devon. He pulls me close and moves his hand between my legs to rub my pussy under the water. "I think it's time we take this game to the next level."

I glance over at Michael, who's watching us with undisguised lust. His smile tells me he's totally fine with the direction this is going. Devon cups my chin and turns my head towards him before his lips crash against mine. His tongue demands entrance as his hands knead my ass cheeks. I moan into the kiss as I open my mouth for our tongues to swirl together. I'm desperate to get a cock in me, so I wrap my legs around his waist as he moves us into deeper water.

I feel a second set of hands snake around me from behind and squeeze my breasts, and I realize Chris has joined us. He presses up against my back, his lips finding the sensitive spot on my neck that makes me shiver.

"God, you're so fucking sexy," Chris says as he plays with my nipples through my bikini top.

Devon breaks off the kiss. "What do you say we give your husband a show?" he asks, his voice husky with desire.

I nod eagerly, too turned on to form words. Devon reaches between us, pushing my bikini bottom to the side. In one swift motion, he enters me, filling me completely. I grip his shoulders and use the buoyancy of the water to ride him.

The water adds an extra dimension to the sensation, making every movement feel more intense. Chris continues to play with my breasts, pinching my nipples through the thin fabric. I cry out in pleasure, my head falling back onto Chris's shoulder. His cock is hard against my back, grinding against me and I love how dirty this feels.

Devon sets a steady rhythm, his powerful strokes driving me closer and closer to the edge. I'm vaguely aware of Michael watching and stroking himself through his swim trunks.

"That's it," Devon says, his pace increasing. "Let everyone see how much you love being fucked. Show your husband what a good little slut you are."

His words make me explode. I come with a loud cry and the intensity of my orgasm triggers Devon's. He groans as he empties himself inside me.

When my brain is finally working again, I become aware of Chris's still-hard cock pressing against me. When Devon slides out of me, I unhook my legs from around him and turn to face Chris, giving him my sexiest smile.

"Your turn," I purr, reaching down to free his cock from his swim trunks.

Chris doesn't need any further invitation. He lifts me easily, and I wrap my legs and arms around him as he slides into me. Devon takes up Chris's previous role in supporting me, his hands on my hips, guiding my movements. The three of us rock together, and I glance over at Michael. He's watching us with an expression of pure lust. Knowing he's enjoying this spurs me on, and I increase my pace, chasing another orgasm.

Chris buries his face in my neck. "Fuck, Sasha," he moans. "I'm close."

"Me too," I pant, grinding down on him harder. "Oh god, me too. Fill me up."

My words seem to trigger him, and he bucks wildly, crying out as he comes. The feeling of him pulsing inside me makes me come again, my vision whiting out with the intensity of it.

I'm not sure how long I ride his cock as the euphoria fries my brain. All I know is I'm crying out as pleasure ripples through my entire body.

As we come down from our high, I become aware of Michael approaching us. He pulls me into his arms, kissing me deeply.

"You're amazing," he murmurs against my lips. "So fucking hot."

I can feel his hardness through his trunks, and I reach down to stroke him. "NOW is it your turn?"

Michael doesn't hesitate. He pulls me towards the shore, laying me down on a large, smooth, sun-warmed rock. As he pulls open my legs, I can see Devon and Chris watching us, their eyes dark with renewed desire.

"Show them," Michael sinks into me in one smooth stroke. "Show them who you really belong to."

"Ooooh, god!" I cry out as he drills into me, my oversensitive body singing with pleasure. The knowledge that Devon and Chris are watching, that they can see how thoroughly Michael owns me, adds an extra layer of excitement.

Michael's finger finds my clit, rubbing tight circles as he pounds me into oblivion. "Come for me, baby," he commands. "Let them hear how good I make you feel."

I scream as my orgasm hits, my back arching off the rock. Michael follows soon after, groaning my name as he empties himself inside me.

We lie there, spent, and I can't help but laugh. "I think we're crazy."

He gives me a soft kiss on the forehead. "Crazy with lust, maybe. It's not over yet, baby. We've still got one more night."

As we make our way back to camp, I can't imagine how this trip could get any better. I'm never going to look at camping the same way again.

CHAPTER 5

As the sun begins to set on our final evening at the campsite, we're all gathered around the fire, the crackling flames casting a warm glow on our faces. I'm nestled in Michael's lap, his arms wrapped securely around me, while Devon and Chris sit across from us.

"I can't believe it's our last night already," I sigh, leaning back against Michael's chest. This trip has been pretty damn fun, despite my initial hesitation.

Devon smirks. "Well, we better make it count, shouldn't we?"

Chris nods in agreement, his usual shyness replaced by a look of determination. "I think we should play a game."

Michael's arms tighten around me slightly. "What kind of game did you have in mind?" he asks, and I can hear the amusement in his voice.

Chris grins, reaching into his pocket and pulling out a familiar-looking remote. My breath catches as I realize it's the control for the vibrator I'd worn during our poker game. "I was thinking we could put this to use again, but with a twist."

My skin prickles with growing excitement as I ask, "What's the twist?"

Devon leans forward, his blue eyes intense in the firelight. "The game is called 'Edge Sasha.' You'll wear the vibrator, and we'll take turns controlling it. The goal is to keep you on the edge of orgasm for as long as possible, without letting you come."

Oh fuck, this game sounds horrible and awesome. My pussy clenches at the thought, and I can feel myself getting wet already. "What happens if I come?" I ask, trying to keep my voice steady.

Michael chimes in. "If you come without permission, you'll be punished. And if you're a good girl and hold out until we say you can come, you'll be rewarded."

Yeah, they didn't just come up with this game. They had this pre-planned. But I'm not complaining.

I glance at the three men, and I can see the bulges growing in their pants. "Okay," I agree, my voice shaking with excitement. "I'm in."

Not that I'd say no, plus this game seems like a win/win to me. Like, oops I came by accident! What's the worst they can do? Edge me some more? I might just come again.

Michael helps me up, and when I make a move to take the vibrator and go to the tent, Chris just laughs and pulls me to him. "I'll be putting it inside you."

Mmm, I like it when Chris gets demanding. He hands the remote to Devon before sliding his hand with the vibrator down the inside of my shorts and panties. I can tell he's pretending he has to adjust it just perfectly and using it as an excuse to brush against my clit. I close my eyes and moan, enjoying the simmer of pleasure in my core. When Chris finally removes his hand, I'm breathless as I settle back into Michael's lap.

"Let's set some ground rules," Devon says. "We'll each get five minutes with the remote. No touching Sasha directly—this is all about the vibrator. If she comes before we tell her to, the game ends and she gets punished. If she makes it through all our turns, she gets to choose her reward. Agreed?"

We all nod, and Devon says, "I'll go first."

The vibrator comes to life, starting on a low, steady pulse. I gasp, my thigh muscles tensing at the sensation. Devon watches me, slowly increasing the intensity over the course of his five minutes. By the time his turn is over, I'm squirming in Michael's lap.

Chris takes the remote next, and his approach is completely different. He alternates between high-intensity bursts and complete stillness, never letting me settle into a rhythm. It's maddening, and I have to bite my lip to keep from begging for more. By the time his five minutes are up, I'm fighting to not orgasm. Oh shit, this is harder than I thought it would be.

When it's Michael's turn, I brace myself for what's to come. He knows my body better than anyone, knows exactly how to bring me to the edge without letting me fall over. He starts with a low, constant buzz, gradually ramping up the intensity until I'm on the verge of orgasm. Just when I think I can't take anymore, he backs off, leaving me trembling and desperate.

When he passes the remote back to Devon, I almost protest. I thought it was only one round per guy! Devon looks at me before he turns it on. "Want to say something?"

The tiny smirk on his face keeps me quiet. "Nope, all good."

Oh god, I'm fucked. We go through several rounds like this, each man finding new ways to torment me with the vibrator. I'm a writhing mess, my skin flushed and covered in a light sheen of sweat. My clit is throbbing, my pussy clenching around the vibrator, desperately seeking release.

"Please," I whimper during Devon's third turn, my hips bucking involuntarily. "I need to come. Please let me come."

Devon chuckles. "Not yet. We're not done playing with you."

As we enter what feels like the hundredth round (but is probably only the fourth or fifth), I'm not sure how much more I can take. The world is fuzzy, and I feel like I'm drowning in a sea of pleasure. Every nerve ending in my body is on fire, and I might explode at any moment.

It's Chris's turn with the remote, and he's been steadily increasing the intensity throughout his five minutes. It seems like Chris picked up

Michael's tricks, and I'm trembling with the effort of holding back my orgasm.

"Oh god," I moan, my hands fisting in the fabric of my shorts. "I can't ...I'm gonna..."

Just as I feel myself about to tip over the edge, the vibrations stop abruptly. I cry out in frustration. I'm not sure if I love them or hate them at the moment.

"Fuck," Chris breathes heavily as he watches me struggle to regain control. "That was close."

Michael's arms tighten around me, his voice soothing in my ear. "You're doing so well, baby. Just a little longer."

Since Michael is busy holding and soothing me, Devon takes the remote again. I'm a quivering mess and my entire body is coiled tight, ready to snap. Devon starts with a low pulse, slowly building the intensity.

"You want to come, don't you?" His eyes lock on mine. "You're desperate for it. I bet you'd do anything to come right now."

I nod frantically, beyond words at this point. Devon grins, cranking up the vibrator to its highest setting. The sudden intensity has me arching my back, a strangled cry escaping my lips.

Michael caresses my side soothingly. "Soon, baby."

The seconds tick by agonizingly slowly. Just when I think I can't take it anymore, when I'm sure I'm going to come whether I have permission or not, Devon speaks up.

"You've been such a good girl. You can come now."

As soon as he says the words, I explode with a scream that probably echoes through the entire forest, I come harder than I ever have in my life. Bursts of color sparkle along the corners of my vision, and I convulse as energy cascades through my body. The vibrator continues its relentless assault, prolonging my orgasm until I'm sobbing with the intensity of it.

Finally, mercifully, the vibrations stop. I collapse against Michael, my pussy still twitching with aftershocks. As I slowly come back to myself, I become aware of the three men watching me with a mixture of awe and lust.

"Holy shit," Chris adjusts himself in his pants. "That was the hottest thing I've ever seen."

Devon nods in agreement. "I believe you've earned a reward. What would you like?"

I take a moment to catch my breath, my mind racing with possibilities. Finally, I look up at Michael, a slow smile spreading across my face. "I want all three of you," I say, my voice hoarse from screaming. "At the same time."

Michael's eyes widen slightly. "Are you sure, baby? You can handle that?"

I feel a renewed surge of desire. "I'm sure."

Devon and Chris exchange glances, then start stripping off their clothes. Michael helps me to my feet, leading me towards our tent. As we step inside, I can feel the anticipation building. This might be the closest thing I ever get to my gangbang fantasy, and I'm going to enjoy every minute of it.

We quickly remove our clothes and when the other guys come in, Chris lies down on his back on the sleeping bag. Oooh, am I getting Devon in my ass? I straddle Chris and sink onto his cock, moaning as his length massages my sensitive nerves. Chris plays with my nipples as Devon moves behind me. I hear the squeeze of a lube bottle, and I almost joke about them having been prepared this weekend, but Chris distracts me by pinching one of my nipples.

Devon applies pressure to my shoulder, and I lean down and kiss Chris while I feel Devon tease a finger against my asshole. My pussy clenches around Chris, making him moan. Devon continues to rub the sensitive nerves around my ass with his finger until I start to relax. As he breaches the tight ring of muscle with the tip of his finger, I gasp and instinctively rock back, wanting more. He takes his time working me open, adding more lube as needed to ease the process.

Michael joins us, kneeling beside me as he watches Devon work. "Are you ready for him, baby?" he asks softly, his hand gently brushing my cheek.

"Yes," I breathe, my body humming with lust. "I need it."

Devon adds a second finger alongside the first. The stretch is delicious.

"Oh, fuck, you're so tight," Devon groans, withdrawing his fingers and positioning the head of his cock against my ass.

When Devon pushes in, the fullness is incredible. I feel impossibly stretched, yet I crave more. Chris moans as Devon bottoms out and they move in tandem, driving me wild. I'm flooded with pleasure as I'm filled in both holes. Michael stands up, gripping the base of his cock, and I turn my head and open my mouth so he can feed it to me.

I moan around his shaft, loving being stuffed in all my holes. I suck Michael as he gently fucks my throat, relishing in my pussy getting hammered into submission while my ass takes it deep. Chris holds onto my hips for leverage, and the sound of our moans fills the tent.

Devon's hands cup my breasts, squeezing my tits roughly. "Such a perfect little slut," he murmurs, his hips banging against me. "Taking all three of us."

I shudder with pleasure, losing myself in the sensations. Every nerve in my body is alive, singing with desire. I suck on Michael's cock with renewed vigor, swallowing him down until his pubic hair brushes my nose. I bob my head in time with the movements of the other men, allowing them to set the pace.

"Fuck," Michael groans, his hand gripping the back of my head. "I'm close."

Devon increases his pace, and knowing everyone is so close to coming catapults me over the edge. I scream out my pleasure as I come around both men inside me. My ass squeezes down on Devon so hard that he releases instantly with a guttural cry, filling me with his hot load. I greedily swallow down Michael's cum as it spurts down my throat, and Chris moans as he explodes deep in my pussy. It feels like our orgasms last forever as the guys keep pumping me full of cum.

The euphoria lasts until it becomes too much for all of us and we fall apart. Michael catches me as I collapse into his arms. I can feel Devon's and Chris's cum leaking out of me and I shiver from aftershocks of my orgasm. I feel a deep satisfaction knowing I made them all come.

We're silent for a moment and then Devon jokes, "I think this has officially been the best camping trip ever."

Chris chuckles softly. "No argument here."

I smile at the guys as Michael helps me get my clothes on for the short walk to our tent. As Michael and I head to our tent, I nuzzle into his warmth, sighing happily.

"Thank you," I mumble, my eyelids already heavy with sleep. "For everything."

Michael kisses me tenderly. "You're welcome, baby. Rest now. I love you."

The last thing I remember is snuggling against him and whispering, "I love you too." Then darkness takes me. I sleep the deep and peaceful sleep of the thoroughly used.

Chapter 6

The morning after our intense finale, I wake up feeling refreshed. Michael is already up, packing our gear outside the tent. I stretch and sigh, savoring the memories of last night's activities.

As I emerge from the tent, squinting in the bright morning sunlight, I see Devon and Chris breaking down their campsite as well. They both look up as I approach, matching grins spreading across their faces.

"Morning, sunshine," Devon calls out, his eyes roaming appreciatively over me. I'm suddenly aware that my legs are bare and I'm wearing nothing but one of Michael's oversized T-shirts and shorts.

"Sleep well?" Chris asks, a hint of shyness creeping back into his demeanor now that we're in the light of day.

I nod, and give him a satisfied smile. "I did. It was wonderful," I reply as I saunter off to get some coffee in me.

As we work together to clean up our campsites, there's a comfortable camaraderie between us all. The sexual tension is still there, simmering just beneath the surface, and it's an enjoyable feeling after so much sex this weekend.

Once everything is loaded into our respective vehicles, we gather for a final goodbye. Devon pulls me into a tight hug, his lips brushing against my ear. "This was one hell of a camping trip. I hope we can do it again sometime."

Chris is next, his embrace warm and surprisingly confident. "Thank you," he says softly. "For everything."

I thank them, and as we pull apart, I catch Michael watching us with a smile. He steps forward, shaking hands with both men. "Thanks for joining us, guys. It's been...educational."

We all laugh at that, and with final waves and promises to keep in touch, Devon and Chris climb into their truck and drive off, leaving Michael and me alone.

As soon as they're out of sight, Michael pulls me into his arms, his lips finding mine in a deep, passionate kiss. When we finally break apart, both breathless, he rests his forehead against mine.

"So," he says, a hint of mischief in his voice, "was the trip everything you hoped for?"

I circle my arms around his neck, and reply honestly. "It was more than I ever could have imagined. Thank you for making it happen."

Michael cups my ass, and I can feel his growing hardness pressing against my stomach. "You know," he says, "we don't have to leave just yet. The campsite is paid for until noon."

A thrill of excitement ripples straight to my core. "Oh? And what did you have in mind?"

Without warning, Michael lifts me up, my legs automatically wrapping around his waist. He carries me over to the picnic table, setting me down on the surface. "I think," he says, tugging my shorts off, "that I'd like to reclaim what's mine."

I moan as he brushes my panties aside and fingers my already wet pussy. I lean back on my elbows as he strokes me. "Yes," I moan, rocking my hips against his hand. "Please, I need you."

He doesn't need any further encouragement. He pulls his cock out of his pants and slides inside me, immediately setting a punishing pace.

"You're mine," Michael growls. "No matter who else touches you, who else fucks you, you'll always be mine."

"Yours," I cry out and use the table for leverage to meet him thrust for thrust. "Always yours."

We move together frantically, the table creaking beneath us. The knowledge that someone could walk past adds to the dirtiness. I'm still sensitive from the night before and my orgasm builds rapidly.

"Oh god, I love you," Michael pants, his thumb finding my clit.

"I love you too!" I cry out as my orgasm hits, my pussy squeezing around him. Michael follows soon after, groaning my name as he unloads ropes of sticky cum deep inside me.

As we come down from our high, still tangled together on the picnic table, I laugh at how we must look. "I think we've officially christened this campsite."

He chuckles. "I'd say this trip was a resounding success, wouldn't you?"

I nod with a contented sigh. "Absolutely. And on top of this wonderful trip, I get a spa day."

Michael laughs as he helps me off the table. "I suppose you do."

It doesn't take us long to finish packing up, and as we climb into our car and start the drive home, I'm already thinking about our next adventure. Yep, Michael has totally turned me into a slut.

"So," I say casually, glancing over at Michael while he drives. "You know, if you ever wanted to do this again with more of your friends, I'd be down for that."

"More friends?" The tone of his voice tells me he's surprised. "You want more than three guys at once?"

"Mmm hmm, but only if you're okay with that."

The side of his mouth curves up. "Well, I suppose if you continue to be a good girl, I might consider it."

Relaxing against the backrest, I'm bathed in a warm glow of satisfaction. Oh yeah, someday I'm totally getting a gangbang now that I've put the thought in his head. It might not be next week, but one thing's for sure—being a hotwife has definitely invigorated our marriage. I'm excited to see what happens next.

Naughty Hotwife Unleashed

Book 9

Lacey Cross

Chapter 1

It's date night, and Michael's cryptic request to "dress sexy" echoes in my mind as I stand before my closet. What would he think is my sexiest outfit? His secretive planning for tonight's date has me curious, and a delicious shiver runs down my spine. I'm sure it's too much to hope that he's planned a gangbang for my ultimate fantasy. He loves to share me, but I'm not sure he's up for anything beyond three guys at once. Too bad...though, maybe I shouldn't assume he doesn't want to watch me get railed by a bunch of men. It's not like I've ever asked him.

I giggle at myself as I slip into a pink silk dress. It's one that clings to every curve like a second skin. My recent indulgences have filled out my figure in all the right places—my breasts threaten to spill over the neckline and my ass looks particularly tempting. I style my blonde locks in soft waves down my back because I know Michael loves it that way. A few swipes of mascara make my blue eyes pop, and I opt for subtle, natural gloss for my lips. I mean, if Michael's surprise is anything like his last one, I might be sucking off a couple of guys by the end of the night.

Stepping into the living room, I find Michael waiting, his broad shoulders accentuated by a green button-down. His eyes widen as they rake over my body, a low whistle escaping his lips.

"Wow." He crosses the room in two quick strides and wraps his hands around my waist so he can pull me flush against him. "You're a vision."

Desire pools low in my belly, and I flush from the compliment. I love how after all these years together, we still find each other hot. "You clean up pretty well yourself, handsome."

His growing arousal is evident, pressing insistently against my hip, and I reach down to stroke him through his pants. "Ready to spill the beans about our destination?" I ask, batting my eyelashes playfully.

Michael's boyish grin makes my heart skip a beat. "Not a chance. You'll see soon enough."

Dang it, rubbing his cock while asking him the question didn't weaken his resolve. I pout, but there's no real disappointment behind it. "You know how I feel about surprises."

His laugh is rich, and my body tingles as he slides his hands down to cup my ass. "Trust me, baby. You're going to love this one."

His confidence is infectious, and I practically buzz with excitement as we head out. Ever since I became a hotwife, Michael has been planning adventures for me. I know whatever happens tonight is going to be kinky and fun.

As we drive, Michael keeps one hand on the wheel, the other on my thigh. His thumb traces lazy circles on my bare skin, each touch sending sparks of electricity through my body. I can't shake the feeling that tonight is going to be different. There's a glint in Michael's eye that speaks of carefully laid plans. My body hums with anticipation, desire coiling more tightly with each passing moment. A part of me hopes his plans include Devon and Chris—my favorite duo, who built the deck in our backyard and then railed me against it—but even if tonight is just Michael and me, the mystery is making this special. I'm his, completely and utterly. And tonight, I have a feeling he's going to remind me of that fact.

As soon as we're out of our neighborhood, he pulls the car to the side of the road. Uh, what're we stopping for? I peer out the window as Michael turns to me, his eyes dark with desire.

"What—" I start, but his mouth crashes into mine, silencing my question. His hand grips the nape of my neck, holding me in place as his tongue explores. My gasp of surprise turns into a moan as heat blooms between my thighs.

"Couldn't wait," he murmurs and trails his fingers up my leg, pushing my dress higher. I shiver as he traces the edge of my panties.

My eyes dart to the empty street. I spread my legs to give him better access as I give a weak protest. "Hey, someone might see us."

He chuckles, "Good," as he pushes my panties aside and slides a finger inside me. I cry out and relax against the backrest as his thumb finds my most sensitive spot.

"Fuck, baby. You're drenched," he growls. "Ready for tonight?"

I don't even know where we're going, but I'm ready for whatever it is. I gasp as he slides another finger inside me. My hips move of their own accord, rocking against his hand as the pleasure builds.

"That's it," he urges. "Ride my fingers. If you come like a good girl, I'll let you fuck another guy tonight."

His words send me over the edge. Ooooh, yes! I convulse around his fingers as waves of ecstasy crash over me. He doesn't stop, drawing out my orgasm until I'm shivering and panting.

"Good girl," he praises, withdrawing his hand. I'm floating down from my high as I watch him with hooded eyes while he licks his fingers clean. Desire surges through me at the erotic display. My husband has turned so dang kinky since I became a hotwife. I love it.

"That was just a warm-up, baby," he says, his tone suddenly serious. "Tonight, you're my sexy hotwife goddess. Got it?"

I nod, still breathless. He leans over to kiss me once more, softly this time. "I love you. Remember that."

"I love you too," I whisper back.

The engine roars to life, and we're moving again. My body thrums with residual pleasure, and my mind races. Who is he going to have me fuck tonight?

CHAPTER 2

The restaurant he takes me to pulses with energy: the clink of wine glasses and the murmur of intimate conversations. Michael's eyes glint across the table as I savor the last bites of my dessert, anticipation zinging through me. I feel like I'm being fed so I'll have energy for whatever he has planned, and I love it. I'm his hotwife goddess tonight, ready to fulfill his every wicked desire.

As we leave the restaurant, Michael's hand on the small of my back is like a hot brand, searing through the thin silk of my dress. His touch is possessive, sending shivers rippling across my skin. The rumble of his voice makes me weak in the knees. "Wait until you see what I have in store for you."

The drive to a familiar gated community is a blur of heated glances. Michael's friend, Jake, owns a house here, and we've attended several of his parties. My heart pounds as Michael pulls up to the clubhouse, a beautiful building lit up with twinkling lights along the walkway. Sultry music pulses from the open windows, and I can hear people laughing. The party is already in full swing.

"It's Jake's birthday tonight," Michael explains.

I smile, recalling that Jake's birthday parties are always a touch wild and full of fun. Wait, Jake is single. Is Michael intending to gift me to him? My body buzzes at the thought of fucking one of Michael's close friends.

Just as we're about to enter, Michael stops me with a firm grip on my arm. I turn to face him, and he pulls me into a deep kiss. Breaking away, he says, "Whatever happens tonight, you have my permission to enjoy it. I've arranged some surprises for you."

Oooh, now this sounds kinky. A thrill runs through me at the implications. "Okay, my love," I reply softly, and we step inside. We're immediately greeted by familiar faces and warm welcomes. Michael guides me through the crowd, his hand steady on my hip. Among the guests are Michael's closest friends, and Jake, the birthday boy, stands out with his infectious smile.

"A dance for the birthday boy, Sasha?" Jake asks, extending his hand.

I glance at Michael, feeling a surge of lust at the idea of him watching me dance with someone else. He nods, giving his approval. "Have fun, baby."

With a sense of excitement, I let Jake lead me onto the dance floor. For a moment, I wonder if I'm about to find out I'm his birthday present. I wouldn't mind a chance to ride him, especially with his charming curly brown hair and muscular build, honed from years of playing football.

As the music quickens to a fast beat, our bodies move in sync, each motion more seductive than the last. I lose myself in the heat of the moment, feeling Michael's gaze following every move I make. How did I never realize how erotic it would be to have him watch me with other guys?

Jake's hands explore my curves, lingering briefly on my hips and grazing my ass. His body presses against mine as he murmurs, "You're on fire tonight." But it's the weight of Michael's stare that has me aching, my skin flushed and tingling.

The night turns into a haze of grasping hands, wicked smiles, and dirty whispered praise from Michael's single friends as I'm passed between them. Each guy I dance with turns me on even more because I can tell

Michael told them to tease me however they wanted. My husband knows me so dang well, and I wholeheartedly consent to the naughty thrill of being so wanton in the middle of a room full of people.

When I dance with Harry, his hands brush the underside of my breasts. When it's Tom's turn, his thigh slides between mine and we're dirty dancing with me grinding against him. The dance with Damien is slow as he plasters my body against his, giving me a delicious zing of pleasure when I feel his hard cock brush against me.

Through it all, Michael watches indulgently. To anyone else, he looks relaxed, but I can see the undercurrent of desire in his movements. It makes me bolder as I run my hands over his friend's shoulders and backs, trying to make Michael react.

I catch glimpses of the other wives watching me—some scandalized, others intrigued. Their stares only fuel the fire within me. They probably think I'm acting like a slut, but someone only needs to look at Michael to know it's with his permission. My wondering if everyone thinks I'm a slut makes the flirting from all the guys turn me on even more. A fleeting thought of Devon and Chris sends a shiver down my spine, and I wish they were here. I can almost feel their calloused hands on my skin, their powerful arms enveloping me.

When Michael comes to claim me, I'm dizzy and breathless. He bites at my neck, sucking hard. "That's my good girl," he rasps, grinding his hardness into me. "You've got them all salivating after what's mine."

Arousal surges through me so fiercely I fear my knees will buckle. The rest of the world fades away. Nothing exists but his touch and the press of his body against mine.

Michael's hand slides between my legs, and I gasp and glance around to make sure no one is watching. No one is, and I notice the birthday boy is having a blast with a sexy brunette.

"Please," I whimper, my voice needy. "I want you so badly."

His fingers find my slick, scorching heat, and his groan reverberates through me as he feels how wet I am. "Oh, I know exactly what you need, baby," he says darkly. "And you're about to get it. Every. Last. Inch."

My body is electrified, throbbing, aching for a cock. Tonight, I'm his in every way imaginable. His to control, to share, to claim. And I've never been more ready to surrender.

CHAPTER 3

Michael's hand grips mine as he leads me through the crowd. His purposeful stride tells me wherever we're going is pre-planned. The music thrums in my chest, matching the rapid beat of my heart. Every nerve in my body tingles with anticipation. If I hadn't just seen Jake out on the dance floor, I'd assume I was about to become that birthday gift. But since Jake is busy, I mentally chant, "Please be Devon and Chris," but I can't ask who I'll be fucking tonight—the music's too loud.

We reach a door, and Michael pauses. His eyes, dark with desire, lock onto mine. "You want this, baby? You want to fuck someone else while I watch?"

I grin, heat flooding my core. "Hell yes. Open that door."

He does, and I step inside. The bright light takes a moment to adjust to, but then I see them. Devon and Chris.

I squeal, delighted. My husband knows me so well. Devon is leaning against a table in a kitchenette area, while Chris sprawls on a couch across the room.

Devon's eyes rake over me, and my body responds instantly. I sashay towards him, pressing close enough to feel the heat radiating off his skin. I tilt my head up, giving him my best flirty smile. "Hi."

He doesn't hesitate. His lips crash into mine, and bliss ripples through my core. Between kisses, he growls, "I've been thinking about fucking you all day. Chris can use your mouth, but that pussy of yours is all mine."

My mind blanks while my nipples harden. When I can think again, I feel wetness pooling between my thighs. Fuck, that's hot.

"Mmm, yes please," I murmur, desperate to be their slut for the night.

Devon leads me to the couch and Michael follows, taking a seat at the opposite end from Chris. The party's muffled sounds filter through the walls, but my focus narrows to the men around me. Chris's eyes light up, darting to my breasts before looking up. "Hey, Sasha. How're you doing?"

I'm so turned on I can barely think, but I manage a flirty, "I'm good, but I bet I'll be even better soon."

I glance at Devon, and his eyes flash with lust. "Chris," he says with a sly smile. "Consider yourself lucky. Tonight, Sasha's going to give you a treat while I fuck her from behind."

My lips press together, suppressing a giggle. As if Chris didn't know he was here for something sexual.

Chris blushes, looking down. "I'd like that," he murmurs, and suddenly, I want nothing more than to give him the best blowjob of his life. You'd think by now he'd be used to fucking me and not so shy.

He raises his eyes again, focusing on my tits, and my heart rate speeds up as his gaze caresses my curves. I can't wait until he gets comfortable and really opens up his wild side. I just have to get him turned on enough.

Devon presses down on my shoulder, and I know what he wants. I kneel a little awkwardly in my heels and settle between Devon's widespread thighs before staring at the bulge in Chris's jeans. I know from past experiences that Chris's cock isn't as thick as Devon's, but it's still going to be a tight fit in my mouth.

The room is hot, or maybe it's just the heat radiating from my core. I lick my lips as Chris caresses his growing bulge—taunting me. Oh yeah, I need to get my lips around his cock. My pussy throbs, and I'm desperate to have both my holes stuffed.

Chris's voice is commanding as he points to his cock. "Take it out, slut."

There it is—that dominant edge that sends a shiver down my spine. I hold his gaze as I slowly reach for his zipper. My fingers graze his hardness through the denim, a lingering touch that makes him suck in a sharp breath. I ease his zipper down, revealing his cock, already hard and standing at attention. I wrap my hand around his shaft, feeling him pulse against my palm. A bead of pre-cum glistens at the tip, and I watch, entranced, as it slides down his shaft. Mmm, I want to taste him.

I fit my lips around the head of his cock, enjoying the thought that I'm their toy to use. Before I get too involved, I give a quick glance at Michael. He's leaning back with one arm along the headrest of the couch, looking prepared to enjoy the show. He winks at me and if the tip of Chris's cock wasn't already in my mouth, I would blow him a kiss.

When I suck on the head of Chris's cock, he groans, a deep, resonant sound that vibrates through his chest, and places a firm hand on the back of my head. He pushes me gently but insistently, guiding me further onto his cock. His dominance sends a thrill down my spine. I savor the velvety smoothness of his skin, contrasting with the hardness beneath. The musky scent of his arousal is intoxicating.

I suck him deeper into my mouth, feeling the pulse of his shaft. I moan softly at the taste of his pre-cum. It's salty and slightly bitter tonight but far from unpleasant. The taste mingles with the heat of his body, creating a heady mix that leaves me craving more. I want to make him come.

Devon kneels behind me and removes my high heels before sliding his hands up my thighs. He pushes my dress to my waist, and I wiggle my ass at him playfully. When he spanks me, I yelp and jump, causing Chris to moan loudly. The sudden sting on my skin sends a shockwave of mixed pleasure and pain through me, making my head spin. Devon's hand lands firmly again, and I feel a warmth radiating across my skin, each smack resonating through me. The sensation makes my mind fog with desire, and I arch my back, craving more.

As Devon continues to spank me, the rhythmic sound and the burning heat on my skin consume my every thought. My mind blurs, fixated solely on the pleasure and the need to satisfy both men. Chris moans as I suck on him enthusiastically, fueled by a need to make him blow his load deep in my throat. The room whirls around me, but all that exists is the connection between the three of us. I'll do anything to please them, to make them both lose control.

When Devon stops spanking me, a desperate hunger for more stirs within me, but then the cool air hits my exposed ass as he tugs my panties down to my knees. Oh god, yes, I need his cock now. He kneels behind me, teasing me as he rubs the head against my ass cheeks, coating me with his pre-cum.

A wave of shame and desire crashes over me—I'm such a slut. I danced and flirted with a bunch of men, and now here I am, on my knees, with a cock in my mouth and another man at my ass, ready to be used. I moan as I bob my head, taking Chris deeper, reveling in the pleasure of being treated like a fucktoy.

I steal another glance at Michael, and he's riveted. His eyes smolder with desire, and the bulge in his jeans is unmistakable. He's aroused by seeing me like this, and that knowledge fuels my excitement. I hope he gives me a rough fucking when Chris and Devon are finished using me.

As Devon continues to rub his cock against my ass, pleasure coils tightly in my core. I'm teetering on the edge, and I might come the moment he thrusts inside me. Hell, if he doesn't fuck me soon, I might just orgasm without his cock in me.

Chris distracts me from what Devon is doing by grabbing a fistful of my hair and pulling sharply. I whimper as he thrusts deeper into my mouth. Hell yes, the aggressive side of Chris has finally emerged. Devon slides his hands over my breasts, groping them through my dress, while Chris's momentum makes his balls slap against my chin. I moan in pleasure from the rough treatment, and the vibrations run up Chris's length, making him curse and quicken his pace.

I'm in slut heaven as Chris uses my mouth roughly. I always wished Michael could be a little more rough with me, but I never knew how much I'd enjoy it. But one of the main reasons it's fun is because I feel safe with Michael here. I can let go and just experience the pleasure as the men use my holes.

When Devon slides inside me, I hum in delight, and Chris groans. The thickness of Devon's cock always takes me by surprise, which is funny considering how many times I've fucked him now. When Devon bottoms out, I gurgle happily around Chris's shaft as pleasure zips through my body.

Devon fucks me slowly at first, giving me time to adjust to his size as Chris keeps pumping into my mouth.

I gasp as Chris pulls my hair again.

Devon hisses, "Be a good fucktoy and take our cocks."

I let out a soft moan of pleasure as Devon rocks in and out of me slowly while Chris takes complete control of my mouth. I briefly think about the party outside the room. With only a wall between us and the partygoers, everything we're doing seems extra filthy. Would Michael's other friends be shocked to find out what's going on in here? Thinking that they would be shocked gives me another naughty zing. Yeah, I want to feel like a complete slut in front of his friends.

Chris releases my hair and leans back, savoring the moment. Each powerful thrust from Devon drives Chris's cock deeper into my throat. Devon withdraws and slaps my ass cheek with his cock. I let out a desperate moan, and Chris squeezes his eyes shut in raw pleasure as he pistons his hips upward, riding my mouth with increasing intensity.

Devon chuckles and slams his cock back inside of me. "Does the fucktoy want me to cover her in cum?"

I can't answer easily around Chris's cock and my whimpering "yes, please" is muffled. Out of the corner of my eye, I can see Michael watching and rubbing his cock through his jeans. I'm being a good slut for him, for all of them.

Devon growls, "What's that? You've got to beg for my cum if you want it—unless you want me to come all over your ass."

I whimper loudly at Devon's words. I want to beg, but the cock in my throat is making it difficult. When I groan, Devon responds with another sharp slap on my ass. I jump and yelp around Chris's cock, causing Chris to moan again.

"Fine, I'll just do whatever I want," Devon growls and grasps my ass cheeks so hard it's almost painful as he slams into me repeatedly. The exquisite combination of pleasure and pain sends shockwaves of pleasure rolling through my body.

The intensity and suction from my mouth is too much for Chris, and he hisses loudly before blowing his load. His cum coats my tongue, distracting me from the pain. As Chris floods my throat, Devon's cock pulses like he's going to explode. Nooo, wait, he can't come yet. I need to come! I'm too busy licking and cleaning up Chris to voice my thoughts.

Before Devon comes, he pulls out. Why did he stop? Devon takes a fistful of my hair and yanks me off Chris's softening cock, and I moan in pleasure. The room tilts from not having my holes stuffed, and I glance at my husband. Michael is leaning forward, his eyes wide with anticipation.

Devon lets go of my hair and drags my panties off, before picking me up and carrying me over to the table by the kitchenette. Mmm, I love how strong he is. He positions my body so that I'm lying on my back, my ass at the edge of the table. When he hooks his arms under my thighs, spreading my legs apart, his eyes are glazed with desire, a wild and desperate expression crossing his face as he thrusts into me. I moan deeply, pleasure surging through me as he pumps his hips with an ever-increasing pace.

Holy fuck, this is wonderful. I can feel the wetness coating my inner thighs as he pounds into me, harder and more intense than ever before.

While he drills into me, I tease my nipples through the thin fabric of my dress. Each thrust into my pussy shakes the table, and I can feel my breasts swaying with every motion. I can't see Michael from here, but I hope he's in a spot where he can watch the action.

Devon puts my ankles on his shoulders, changing the angle of his entry. Each thrust sends waves of intense pleasure through me. Every time he bottoms out, it hurts in a pleasurable way that causes my pussy to clench around his cock. Devon closes his eyes and I can tell he's lost in the pleasure of fucking me.

I'm on the brink of orgasm when he opens his eyes again and starts with the dirty talk. "You're a filthy cum slut who loves taking all our cocks."

I whimper, "Yes," knowing I really am. Hell, I want a gangbang's worth of cocks inside me.

"You love being used as a fucktoy," he continues as he slams into me.

I whimper again, unable to form words, and think about a line of men using me.

Devon pulls out and spanks my clit with the tip of his cock, causing me to mewl out from the unexpected zing of delight. My mind is so far gone, I can't do anything but moan as he continues to slap his cock against the sensitive bundle of nerves. I writhe from the pleasure, knowing I'm going to explode soon if he keeps this up.

I grip the edges of the table and hold on when he slams his cock back into my pussy. "You're a desperate slut for my cum. Admit it."

Fuuuuuck, I love his dirty talk. I whimper and chant, "Yes, Yes, Yes," as I arch my back, aching for him to fill me with his cum.

"I'm going to coat every inch of you," Devon pants. "You're going to be dripping with it by the time I'm done with you."

"Oh god, yes!" I cry out, my face contorting in ecstasy. The pleasure builds to an unbearable peak, radiating out from my core. My entire body shakes and quivers, tingling with an electric charge. I feel like I'm drifting away on a cloud of pure bliss.

Squeezing my eyes shut, my toes curl tightly and my back arches sharply. Sparks dance along the corners of my vision when Devon pulls out almost all the way and slams back into me. I scream as I explode. Waves of intense pleasure crash over me, and for a moment, I lose myself, drowning in an ocean of rapture.

"F-fuck!" I gasp out, trembling through the aftershocks. My inner walls pulse with fierce spasms as Devon presses his pelvis against my sensitive clit. I moan softly, eager to take everything he's willing to give me.

Devon speeds up, jackhammering into me until he jerks against me and groans. I can feel his cock pulsating as he coats me with ropes of warm cum. I shudder in pleasure as he fills me.

When he's done, he pulls out and collapses over me. I'm blissed out, unable to speak. His cum and my wetness leak out of me, but I'm too dazed to care where it's landing. I'm a filthy slut, and I love it.

He kisses me softly, and murmurs, "That was amazing."

I'm still recovering from the mind-blowing orgasm, and I can't even nod. All I want to do is relax until my brain functions again.

Devon effortlessly lifts me up and carries me to the couch. Michael holds his arms out, and Devon transfers me to Michael's lap before sitting down between the two guys. I rest my head on Michael's shoulder and offer Devon and Chris a dreamy smile. "Did you guys enjoy that?"

Chris laughs, "Oh yeah. Couldn't you tell?"

Michael chuckles, and I snuggle closer to him. I give Chris a wide smile. "Maybe a little."

Chris shifts his position, and I can see the bulge in his jeans. Ooooh, he's hard again. A flutter of delight in my core makes the brain fog dissipate, and I act without thinking. I get up and climb over Devon, positioning myself across Devon's lap on my stomach. This gives me access to Chris's crotch, and I tug on his zipper, opening his pants to get to his cock again.

When I close my lips around the head of his cock, Chris moans and places a hand on the back of my head, forcing me down until my mouth is full. Ohhh, guess I'm going to deep-throat him again. He's gentle this time, so I relax my throat and let him guide my head up and down his shaft.

I didn't expect to be blowing a guy twice in one day, but this is my kind of filthy. Devon caresses my ass before slipping his hand between my legs to brush against my clit. His light touch against the swollen bundle of nerves creates a swirl of pleasure in my core. Holy shit, I think I could come again.

My body tightens, and I throw all my energy into sucking Chris's cock as Devon finger fucks me and rubs my clit, making my body quiver in ecstasy. I can tell when Chris is close to coming again because he holds my head steady and pumps into my throat in quick strokes.

"Oh fuck," Chris gasps as he thrusts one last time and floods my mouth with his cum. I swallow as much as I can before he slips out of my mouth with a groan.

I swallow the rest of his cum, savoring every last drop, and wipe my mouth with the back of my hand. A hunger for more stirs within me—I think I'm addicted to making them cum. Devon's fingers continue their relentless assault, and I squirm against his hand, desperate for another release. When he hits that perfect spot, I explode in pleasure. A surge of raw electricity courses through my veins. I scream from the sheer bliss of it all, my body trembling with delight.

The waves of ecstasy overtake me, and my mind is mush once I come down from the high. Devon is a master at making me come with his fingers. That was amazing.

When Chris gets off the couch and moves to the kitchen area to clean up, Devon rolls me onto my back across the cushions. The tip of his cock probes my entrance, and I moan in ecstasy as he sinks inside me again. This time, he fucks me nice and slow.

Devon trails soft kisses down my neck as he whispers, "You're such a good girl taking all our cum. You look so gorgeous right now."

His praise short-circuits my brain. All I can do is moan as he continues.

"Our perfect little cumdumpster, ready for all the cum she can get."

Oh god, he's right. I'm desperate for every drop. My eyes widen and pleasure ripples through me as I imagine a circle of guys covering me with cum—like a cum fountain...all for me. My gangbang fantasy where I'm a used, sloppy mess at the end. The mental thoughts overwhelm me, and I can tell I'm going to come again at any moment.

Devon continues to thrust into me, and I grip his arms as he fucks me slowly, each thrust causing a delicious friction against my sensitive clit. He kisses me again, and I wrap my arms around him and let go. My mind clears of everything except the feeling of his cock and the growing inferno of pleasure.

I'm floating in bliss as Devon growls, "If you want to come again, you better do it now."

"Yes. God, yes," I moan and arch into him.

Devon's movements become more forceful, and I can tell he's almost there. I let out a long moan of pleasure as I rock my hips, silently pleading for him to release his load.

Devon groans, "Time to fill our slut with cum."

Each thrust feels better than the last, and I become a ball of pure ecstasy. He hammers into me, and I come again as I cry out, "Yesss!"

Devon roars with pleasure as his cock twitches and jets of cum coat my inner walls. We both quiver as we ride out our pleasure. I'm still trembling with aftershocks when he pulls out. Devon collapses beside me on the couch with a groan. I feel used in the best of ways.

Michael starts clapping. "Nice show, everyone."

I giggle at Michael and Devon laughs with me. I blow a kiss to Michael. "Thanks, love."

Michael helps me stand up as Devon and Chris gather their clothes, putting themselves back together. I'm a bit wobbly, my body still humming with the remnants of pleasure, and Michael wraps his arm around me, steadying me. I lean into him, breathing in his comforting scent.

Once Devon is dressed, he walks over and takes my hand. He kisses it gently and says, "You were incredible, Sasha. Thank you."

I smile softly at him, still feeling a bit out of it, and murmur, "Thank you, too. It was amazing."

Chris approaches us. He looks shy again, which is endearing after the face fucking he gave me tonight. "Thanks. That was...wow," he says, scratching the back of his neck.

I grin at him. "My pleasure, Chris. Literally."

The guys chuckle, and Devon claps Michael on the back. "Thanks for having us, man. It's always a good time."

Michael nods. "Thank you both for agreeing to give Sasha a fun night."

Chris waves goodbye to us and Devon leans in to give me a soft kiss on the cheek before they both leave. Once they're gone, Michael pulls me closer, and I snuggle up against him. He strokes my hair gently, and I can feel his heartbeat against my cheek. "You were so sexy tonight. Watching you enjoy yourself like that...it always drives me crazy," he tells me.

I look up at him and grin. "Oh yeah? Well, I hope you're ready for me because the night isn't over yet," I tease.

His eyes darken. "Let's get home first. I want to make you scream again."

His words kick up a pleasant buzz in my core, and I giggle as we retrieve my panties and straighten my clothes. Yeah, I'm ready to have my husband's cock in me now.

CHAPTER 4

As we drive home, I replay the night in my head—the way Devon and Chris touched me, the way Michael watched, the pleasure I felt. It was exhilarating. I turn to look at Michael, his eyes focused on the road.

"What are you thinking about?" I ask him in a soft voice.

He glances at me and smiles. "How sexy you looked tonight. How much I enjoyed watching you. How lucky I am to have you."

I smile back at him, my heart fluttering in my chest. "Mmm, I'm the lucky one." I reach out to squeeze his knee. "I have a husband who understands me and loves sharing."

We drive in silence for a while, the city lights passing by in a blur. As we pull into our driveway, Michael turns to me, his eyes filled with desire. "I need you."

A thrill runs through me at his words. "Then let's hurry and get inside."

The door to our house barely closes behind us before Michael's hands are on me. He pushes me against the wall, his lips crashing against my mouth in a fierce, possessive kiss. I moan and wrap my arms around his neck, pulling him closer.

His hands roam over my body, getting reacquainted with every curve. He squeezes my breasts, thumbs brushing over my nipples, sending a jolt of pleasure straight to my core. I'm still dripping from multiple loads of cum, and I can feel myself getting wetter.

He breaks the kiss, his breath ragged. "You're mine," he growls, his eyes locked onto mine.

"Yes," I gasp, my hips grinding against him. "Always yours."

He fumbles with his pants while he kisses my neck, and when his cock is free, he grabs my thigh, pulling my leg up. My wet panties don't slow him down as he pushes them aside. He thrusts into me, hard and deep, making me cry out in pleasure.

"Oh god," I moan as I wrap my legs around him and hang on to his shoulders. Every thrust is a claim, a reminder that I belong to him. His hands tighten on my hips, his cock filling me completely. The pleasure is intense, my body still sensitive from the multiple orgasms from earlier.

"Mine," he grunts with each thrust, his body slapping against me. "Mine. Mine. Mine."

I've never seen him like this, and knowing that he got this turned on while watching me with other men spirals me into another orgasm. I scream in pleasure as ecstasy ripples from my fingertips to my toes as he fucks me through my orgasm.

Once I come down, Michael lets go, his cock pulsing inside me as he finds his release. I shudder as his warm cum mixes inside me with Devon's. Fuuuck, this is filthy.

Michael's entire body quivers as he slumps into me, pressing me into the wall. "I love you," he whispers, his voice raw and filled with emotion.

"I love you too. So much."

We stay like that for a moment, panting as our heart rates slow. When Michael pulls out, he helps me stand and then brushes away the strands of hair stuck to my sweaty cheeks. "Did you have a good night, baby?"

I giggle, practically drunk from pleasure. "I think so..."

Michael chuckles, his eyes crinkling at the corners. "Come on, let's get cleaned up and into bed."

In the bathroom, we take a shower together while he gently cleans between my legs. I feel a surge of love and gratitude for his care. I really married the most wonderful man.

Once we're cleaned up, we crawl into bed. I lay my head on his chest, listening to his heartbeat, feeling content. But as the haze of pleasure begins to fade, a familiar desire starts to burn within me.

I prop myself up on my elbow, looking down at him with a mischievous grin. "So, when do I get my gangbang fantasy?"

Michael's expression is amused as he draws lazy circles on my back. "You're insatiable, aren't you?"

I press my lips to his chest, murmuring, "You love it."

He shifts suddenly, flipping me onto my back. His weight presses me into the mattress, and I relish the feeling of being pinned beneath him. He gazes down at me with lust.

"What if we make your fantasy a reality?"

The words hang in the air between us as my heart skips a beat. "For real?"

He nods, giving me a slow grin. "My friends you danced with tonight? They're ready to fuck you. All of them."

My mind races, recalling the men who flirted with me on the dance floor. One, two, three...four. Four men. The thought sends a jolt of electricity straight to my core. Oooh, hey, and I'll be able to give Jake a belated birthday gift.

"Plus Devon and Chris," Michael adds, his voice husky with desire.

A moan escapes my lips before I can stop it. Six men. Six cocks. All for me. My pussy clenches at the thought, already aching to be filled.

"Yes," I breathe, my hips grinding against Michael instinctively. "God, yes. I want that. I want them all."

He chuckles, the sound low and dirty. "That's my girl. My naughty, cock-hungry wife."

I pull him down for a kiss, pouring all my desire into it. When we break apart, I'm panting. "When?"

"Soon," he promises. "I'll set it up."

He rolls off me and pulls me against him. I melt into his side, my body humming with anticipation. "Thank you," I murmur, nuzzling into his neck.

As sleep begins to claim us, I daydream about six pairs of hands on my body, six mouths tasting my skin, and six cocks stretching me open. And Michael, watching it all, orchestrating my pleasure.

I drift off with a smile on my face, dreaming of the delicious debauchery that awaits me.

The Naughty Hotwife's Desires

Book 10

Lacey Cross

CHAPTER 1

The hiss of the coffee maker greets me as I enter the kitchen, its carafe freshly filled. Michael's back is to the counter, and his fingers slide across his phone screen before he sets it face down. The movement is too quick to be casual. There's a smirk playing on his lips; thirteen years of marriage have taught me to read his face like a map, and right now, every line points to mischief.

"What are you up to?" I ask, suspicious.

He shrugs. "Maybe something for our anniversary next weekend, or maybe nothing."

Uh-huh, right. I raise an eyebrow. "Come on, spill it."

"Wouldn't you like to know?" he teases as he tugs me to him. The counter edge presses against my back as his hands settle at my waist. "Patience was never your strength."

I play with the collar of his shirt. "Then stop testing it."

"But where's the fun in that?"

I push at him, playfully. "Tell me."

His thumb brushes the skin where my shirt meets my yoga pants, and when his lips ghost across my neck, I almost forget what information I was attempting to get out of him. He knows this weakness.

"Soon," he whispers.

I moan, "No, now," as he nibbles at my neck. The words are more of a plea than a demand.

He captures my mouth, stealing any argument. He squeezes my ass and I moan again as he kneads the globes. Wetness grows between my legs as I get more desperate.

When he stops kissing me, satisfaction gleams in his eyes. "No, later."

"You're impossible."

His laugh rumbles through his chest. "Always." And then he moves his mouth to my ear. "But only because you love it."

God, I do love it. Before I can respond, his lips crash onto mine, urgent and demanding. I gasp into his mouth and he swallows it with a growl. He cups my breasts, playfully kneading them while he explores my mouth. His tongue twirls with mine, sending jolts of pleasure coursing through me. I melt into him as the kiss deepens. His stubble scratches my chin, and each flick of his tongue stokes a fire within me, making me crave more.

Right when I'm about to go for his cock, he stops kissing me. "You'll find out soon enough. I promise."

"That's not fair." I give him my best pout.

He chuckles, "My little hotwife slut is going to like it."

Oooh, I am? He pushes me backwards to the nearest wall, and I can feel his hard cock through his sweatpants.

"Michael—" I start, but he silences me with another kiss.

I moan into his mouth, arching my body against his. He knows exactly what he's doing, exactly how to drive me wild.

He pulls back. "Yep, you're going to love it," he repeats as he grips the hem of my yoga pants and yanks them down to the floor. My panties follow quickly, and as I step out of them he frees his cock.

When he slides his length between my pussy lips without sinking inside me, he groans, "Oh, fuck. So ready for me."

I can't speak, he's sizzled my brain already. I wrap my legs around him and he lines his cock up with my entrance. His first thrust is smooth, and slow, pinging all my pleasure points. We moan together as he sinks deeper.

He fucks me steadily until I'm crying out with every thrust as the pleasure builds to an unbearable peak.

"You're such a dirty little slut," he growls as he drills into me.

"Yes," I gasp. "Your dirty little slut."

My words spur him on. He picks up speed, fucking me hard, and I can feel my orgasm building, coiling deep in my belly.

"So close," I whimper. "Don't stop."

Michael grunts, his pace becoming erratic as he chases his own climax. The wet sounds of him fucking me fill the air. With a few more hard thrusts, he drives us both over the edge. I cry out, my pussy clenching around him as waves of pleasure crash through me. He comes with a groan, his hips jerking forward as he fills me with his cum.

As we come down from our high, we're both breathless and panting. Michael presses his forehead against mine. "I can't wait to see how you like your surprise."

I blink while my brain takes a moment to process everything. "You're really not going to tell me?"

"Trust me. It will be worth the wait."

I want to grumble some more, but I'm too happy to put up a fight. Plus, he always has great surprises. I can be patient...I hope.

Chapter 2

I have the day off from work, and I'm sprawled on our leather couch. My phone sits on my stomach, rising and falling with each frustrated breath. Michael's been impossible all week—and annoyingly irresistible. Every time I try to get information about our anniversary plans, he just gives me that knowing smirk. The one that infuriates me and makes me want to kiss him at the same time. He's been more aggressive lately and I've been here for it. Quick fucks wherever he can catch me.

But honestly, I'm dying here. But he just doles out those hints with a cheeky grin and then fucks me roughly over the nearest surface, leaving me needy and more confused than before.

This morning, he fondled my ass while I was making coffee. "Just two more days," he whispered. "Think you can handle something big?"

Then he just walked away, leaving me trembling and wet before my first cup of coffee. Bastard.

I can't take it anymore. I grab my phone and call Erin, needing someone to talk to, to distract me from my sexual frustration.

"Well, if it isn't my favorite friend," Erin answers, amusement in her voice.

"I'm going to murder my husband," I huff out without any greeting. "He's been dropping hints about the gangbang fantasy all week. You know, the one he promised me someday? But he won't confirm anything."

"Mmm, sounds delicious," Erin purrs. "What kind of hints?"

I shift on the couch, remembering. "Last night, he had me bent over the kitchen counter, telling me how sexy I look when I'm being fucked from behind. Then he started talking about how good I am at taking cock, and how much he loves watching me..."

"And?"

"And nothing! He got me right to the edge and then stopped, kissed my cheek, and said 'Patience, baby.'" I groan at the memory. "I nearly screamed."

"He's got you wound up tight, doesn't he?"

"You have no idea. This morning I found a new bottle of lube on my vanity with a note that said 'Just in case.'" I press my thighs together, feeling the familiar ache. "I don't want to get my hopes up, but at this point if it's not a gangbang, I'm going to be sad."

"You love it though," Erin says, and I can hear her grin. "The not knowing...it's making you crazy in the best way."

"Maybe," I admit, trailing my fingers along my collarbone. "But what if I'm reading too much into it? What if it's not what I think?"

"Sasha, when has Michael ever disappointed you? That man worships you. Whatever he's planning, it's going to be amazing."

I think about how attentive Michael's been lately. "He did surprise me with a new remote-controlled toy yesterday. Said he's got plans for it this weekend."

Erin laughs. "He's going to drive you absolutely wild beforehand. Smart man."

"Too smart for his own good," I mutter, but there's no real malice in it. "I just hope I can make it two more days without spontaneously combusting."

"You could always take matters into your own hands. Give yourself a little relief."

I remember Michael's words last night. "He made me promise not to touch myself today. Said he wants me desperate for it."

"Damn." Erin whistles. "He really is good at this game."

"Tell me about it." I stretch, feeling a twinge in my pussy that I can't satisfy yet. "Thanks for letting me vent. I needed this."

"Any time. And hey? Make sure you call me after. I want all the dirty details."

That makes me laugh. "Will do."

Everyone needs a friend who wants the details of an upcoming hypothetical gangbang. After hanging up, I stretched out on the couch, daydreaming about what could happen this weekend. Whatever Michael has planned, one thing's for sure—he's doing a good job of turning me into a needy slut beforehand.

My phone dings with a text. It's from my husband.

Michael:

> Still thinking about you bent over the kitchen counter. Hope you're being good.

I groan—just two more days.

CHAPTER 3

The night has finally arrived. I stand in front of the full-length mirror, my hands smoothing over the black fabric clinging to my curves. The pants hug my legs like a second skin, and my off-shoulder top reveals just enough to make promises my body aches to keep. I've chosen a strapless bra and the tiniest black thong—because sometimes the sexiest things are the ones that stay hidden. For now.

"How much longer are you going to make me wait?" Michael's playful voice comes from the doorway. I catch his reflection in the mirror. He's wearing dark jeans and a fitted black button-down that makes my mouth water.

"Patience," I tease, turning to face him. "You can't rush perfection."

"Perfection?" He kisses the spot below my ear that he knows I love. "You're always perfect, though I prefer you naked."

He nibbles on my neck, causing me to squeak, "Hey, don't mess with me if you want to leave soon."

"Worth it." He cups my breasts, his thumbs brushing my nipples. "You have no idea how sexy you look right now."

I press against him, feeling his growing hardness. "Mmm, I think I have some idea."

His kiss is hungry, demanding, making my knees weak. One hand tangles in my hair while the other grabs my ass. I moan into his mouth as he grinds his cock into my thigh.

"Maybe," he murmurs, "we should skip tonight's plans."

I pull back, laughing, "Not a chance. Not after all your teasing this week. You promised me something special."

"That I did." He steps back, adjusting himself with a grimace that makes me giggle. "And you're going to love it. But first..." He reaches into the nightstand and brings out the sleek black box of the new vibrator he gave me. "I want you to wear this."

A thrill runs through me as I take the box and open it. The vibrator is small, sleek, and discreet—designed to be worn internally. I look at Michael, my eyebrow raised in question. "You want me to put it in now?"

His gaze burns through me. "Yes, now. You need to be ready for whatever happens tonight."

I bite my lip, feeling a rush of excitement. I take the vibrator out of the box and hand it to him. "Then you have to help me," I say, turning around and putting my arms on the top of our dresser, bending over slightly.

Michael reaches around and unbuttons my pants. I wiggle my hips, helping him slide the pants down to my knees. His fingers hook into the waistband of my thong, peeling it down just enough to expose my pussy.

I close my eyes in anticipation, and hear him open a bottle of lube. When the slippery silicone brushes my clit, I jerk slightly from pleasure. I whimper as he rubs my clit with the toy—almost like he's pretending he can't find the right spot.

When he finally pushes the vibrator inside me, I moan as it settles in place.

I can tell he's enjoying my reaction when he chuckles. "Good girl. Now, let's go. We don't want to be late for your surprise."

I tug up my thong and pants, feeling the vibrator inside me. As I put on my favorite pair of sandals, he picks up the toy remote and turns it on a low setting. Every movement I make sends a tiny jolt of pleasure through me. Oh god, I'm going to be mentally fucked before long.

Michael takes my hand, leading me towards the door. After all the teasing and sexual frustration this week, I'm hyped up from excitement. Whatever he has planned, I know it's going to be amazing. The wait is finally going to pay off.

"Michael." I lean forward in the passenger seat, peering through the windshield at the sprawling building before us. The neon sign—"Glow Golf"—casts multicolored light across the empty parking lot. The building itself is massive, decorated with oversized golf balls and clubs painted in vibrant colors that pop even in the darkness. The vibrator inside me makes it difficult to think, but I manage to ask, "Why are we at an indoor mini golf course?"

Michael kills the engine, turning to me with that sexy half-smile that always means trouble. "Did you think I was going to tease you about multiple guys all week and then not deliver?"

The pleasure from the vibrator swirls in my core. I squirm slightly, trying to stop myself from coming right here. "I hoped not."

"Well." He runs a finger down my arm. "Tonight's your chance to earn it."

Um, what's this? "Earn it?"

"Damien owns this place," Michael explains. "He's one of the guys you danced with at Jake's birthday party. The one with the Mediterranean look and the slight silver at his temples."

I nod, picturing Damien's sexy, sophisticated demeanor.

"He's closed it down for us tonight." His hand finds my thigh, squeezing gently. "Everyone's inside waiting."

"Everyone?" My pulse quickens at the thought.

"All the guys you danced with that night," he confirms. "Plus Devon and Chris."

Mmm, nice. "And what exactly do I need to do to 'earn' it?"

"If you win you get your gangbang. All of them, however you want them."

Heat floods between my legs. "And if I lose?"

"Then you only get to pick one." He kisses me softly before continuing. "Don't lose."

A grin spreads across my face. Mini golf? I've got this in the bag. Years of family vacations and college date nights have made me a pro.

"Ready?" Michael asks, sliding his hand higher up my thigh.

I grab his wrist, stopping his teasing touch. "You have no idea how ready I am."

CHAPTER 4

I push open the heavy doors of Glow Golf, and my senses are immediately assaulted in a good way. The place is like a psychedelic playground of black light and neon, with phosphorescent paintings covering the walls and geometric patterns glowing along the baseboards. The air hits me first—cool, and slightly sweet, like someone's been burning vanilla candles. Music pulses through hidden speakers, just loud enough to be heard but it won't impede conversation. My skin prickles with goosebumps, though I'm not sure if it's from the temperature—or, you know, maybe it's the damn vibrator buzzing in my pussy. Michael kept it on low the entire drive, but I can tell I'm a wet mess between my legs. I need a cock in me ASAP.

The course sprawls out before me, each hole a different fantasy scene. There's a rainforest-themed area where Devon's leaning against a massive UV-reactive tree, the neon paint making his silver hair gleam almost ethereally. Another area winds through what looks like an underwater paradise, complete with glowing coral and fish that seem to swim across the walls.

"Welcome to my humble establishment." Damien appears beside me. His cologne—something spicy and masculine—mingles with the vanilla air. He's wearing a blue button-down and I have to force myself not to stare at how it clings to his chest.

Chris and Tom are by the drink station, which has been set up to look like a tiki bar complete with LED-lit plastic ice cubes in the punch bowl. Chris is fidgeting with his golf club, that boyish energy barely contained, while Tom sits at the bar like he's posing for a magazine shoot, his sleeve tattoo creating fascinating shadows in the unique lighting.

"The lady of the hour," Harry calls out, his eyes crinkling at the corners as he approaches. He's wearing a deep green shirt that somehow looks both casual and expensive. "We were starting to think you'd gotten cold feet."

"More like fashionably late. A girl's got to make an entrance."

Jake whistles low, pushing off from where he'd been examining a putting green that looks like the surface of the moon. "That she does." His curly hair is particularly wild tonight, like he's been running his hands through it.

Devon appears at my side. "A drink for the guest of honor," he says, pressing a cool glass into my hand.

"Liquid courage?" I ask, raising an eyebrow. The ice clinks as I take a grateful sip—it's just cold water. I almost laugh but hold it in. Yeah, I don't actually need any liquid courage. I'm ready for them all to get a hole-in-one with me as the golf course.

Devon's gaze fixes on me, a knowing smile tugging at his lips. "Ready to start?" he asks, gesturing towards the first hole.

Oooh, he's not wasting any time and the buzzing from the vibrator in my pussy means I'm not interested in small talk either. I set the glass down on a nearby table. "Yep, let's get the party started."

The first hole looks deceptively simple—a winding path through the underwater scene. But I can see subtle slopes in the artificial coral that will make putting tricky. I'm lining up my shot when I feel Devon's presence behind me. The heat of him makes me hyper-aware of every inch of my body.

"The trick," he says, as he glides his hands down my arms to adjust my grip on the club, "is all in the hips."

Normally I might get annoyed at a guy trying to tell me how to play mini golf, but I'm enjoying the attention too much. His touch leaves trails of fire on my skin, and I have to bite my lip to hold back a whimper. Plus, if I pretend helplessness, they'll be in for a surprise when I win.

"I thought the trick was actually hitting the ball," Tom quips from nearby, his dimples showing as he grins. He's perched on a decorative rock, the position highlighting his muscular thighs in his fitted jeans.

I swing, watching as my hot pink ball weaves through the neon obstacles, finally coming to rest near—but not in—the hole. "Not bad," I say, straightening up and accidentally-on-purpose pressing back against Devon's chest.

"Not bad at all," Damien comments as he steps up and takes his shot, the fluid movement making his designer clothes stretch in all the right places. His ball rolls straight into the hole with a gratifying clunk.

Oh shit, he's good. What if I can't win after all?

We gather around the second hole—a jungle-themed challenge with UV-painted vines hanging from the ceiling and tiny LED fireflies twinkling in the foliage. The putting green winds through what looks like ancient ruins, complete with tiny waterfalls that create a gentle burble in the background.

"Watch out for the trap," Harry warns, pointing to a hidden dip in the course. I catch a whiff of his woodsy cologne that makes me want to bury my face in his neck.

Chris appears on my other side, practically bouncing on his feet from excitement. "I found that out the hard way earlier," he admits, rubbing the back of his neck sheepishly. "Three putts straight into the water."

I'm about to take my turn when Tom's hands land on my shoulders, kneading gently. "You're too tense," he says, his fingers finding knots I didn't even know I had. "Golf is all about relaxation."

"Is that what we're calling this?" I manage to ask, melting under his skilled hands. "Because I'm pretty sure this stopped being about golf about thirty seconds after I walked in."

Seven different chuckles sound around me. Yeah, no one thinks we're playing golf. Michael catches my eye and takes the small remote from his pocket. My breath catches as he slowly turns the dial, and the vibrations become stronger. Heat floods my cheeks as I try to maintain my composure. The night is young, the course is private, and I'm surrounded by seven men who are all looking at me like I'm dessert.

I attempt my next shot, but my hand trembles as a wave of pleasure courses through me. The ball rolls to a stop near a glowing plastic fern. "Oops," I giggle as Michael increases the intensity again. "Looks like I need more...practice."

The third hole is a space-themed nightmare of black holes and asteroid fields, all glowing with phosphorescent paint. I'm trying to focus on the seemingly simple course, but Harry's standing so close to me that it's disrupting my concentration.

"The angle's crucial here." His hand brushes my lower back, feather-light. "You want to..." He trails off as I shift my weight, pressing back against him slightly.

"Want to what?" I ask innocently, looking up at him through my lashes. I watch his throat work as he swallows.

Tom laughs from somewhere close by, and then appears. "You're going to kill the poor man before he gets to finish his lesson."

I swing, but Tom chooses that exact moment to stretch—his shirt riding up to reveal a strip of toned abdomen—completely throwing off my concentration. The ball goes wide, bouncing off a neon Jupiter and ricocheting off a planet before rolling under a table.

"Distracted?" Tom asks with amusement. He hasn't bothered to fix his shirt.

"Nope, that was all planned" I lie as I retrieve my ball, making sure to give them all a good view as I bend over.

While the men take their turn, Michael catches my eye and winks. He knows exactly what I'm doing, the little show I'm putting on. His approval makes me bold, and I decide to up the ante.

"I think I need some hands-on instruction for the next hole," I announce, looking around the group. "Any volunteers?"

Six hands go up immediately, and I can't help but giggle. This is fun.

The next one is a twisted maze of mirrors and neon lights, creating infinite reflections of all of us. I can see myself from every angle—and so can they. Tom steps up, his hands settling on my hips. "This one is all about control."

His thumbs make small circles along the exposed skin above my pants line, and I have to stifle a gasp. In the mirrors, I can see Devon watching us intently. I try to focus on the ball, but Chris chooses that moment to bend down and adjust something on his shoe, his t-shirt pulling tight across his shoulders. In the mirrors, the movement is multiplied infinitely, and I'm treated to a kaleidoscope of rippling muscles.

"Eyes on the ball, Sasha," Devon jokes. His voice seems to come from everywhere in this mirror maze.

I take the shot, but Harry clearing his throat—a sound that shouldn't be sexy but somehow is—makes me jump. The ball careens off three different mirrors before rolling to a stop nowhere near the hole.

Yeah, fuck. Maybe I don't have this one in the bag after all. Between the men and the vibrator in my pussy, this is delicious torture.

The men all take their turns as I get more and more worked up just being near them.

"Next hole?" I manage to say, my voice only slightly breathless.

Devon's hand is on my lower back. "Ready for more...instruction?"

The emphasis he puts on that last word makes it clear we're not really talking about golf anymore. Not that we ever were.

The fifth hole is a twisted fairy tale scene, complete with glowing mushrooms and what looks like a castle in the distance. I'm barely paying attention to the actual game anymore—not with Devon's hand on me and Chris moving to stand in front of me.

"I don't think she's learning anything about mini golf," Harry observes dryly.

"Oh, we're playing mini golf?" Jake asks, grinning as he watches from his perch next to a glowing tree trunk.

Michael gives me a subtle nod. He's enjoying this as much as I am—watching these men circle closer, the flirting becoming bolder.

The game continues, but we're all just going through the motions now. The real game is in the lingering touches and heated looks.

And I'm winning that game hands down.

CHAPTER 5

By the time we're on the last hole, I'm ready to be done with mini golf. I don't even know who won, but if I get multiple cocks in me, I'm going to announce myself the winner. I'm standing ready to take my shot when Devon and Chris move in beside me.

Devon cups my ass, sending a jolt of electricity through me. "Sasha, we need something from you. Tell us what you want."

Oh god, it's so filthy when they make me admit my desires. Tonight is even worse because of how many guys there are and what I want them to do to me. My entire body flushes as I open my mouth. "I want..." I start, and then look around the group, meeting each of their gazes. I focus on Michael last—my amazing husband.

"I want you to use me and make me scream in pleasure."

A collective groan resonates through the group. Devon's hand tightens on my ass before he slips his fingers between my legs, rubbing my pussy through my pants and forcing the vibrator to shift. I whimper from the pleasure of the vibrations as Chris's teeth graze my neck.

"You heard her," Michael says, his voice firm from the seat he took close to us. "Give her what she wants."

Looks like we're skipping the last hole. Not that I mind. I can't resist the urge to tease. "Let's call me the final stretch," I say with a playful grin. "I need someone to drive it home."

Devon laughs, "Well, I'm always here to help," and then he crashes his mouth down on mine. Mmm, finally! I rock against him, desperately wishing we were both naked. Behind me, Chris rubs my pussy through my pants. Waves of pleasure ripple through me—from the vibrator, and from knowing what's about to happen.

I feel another set of hands on my hips. I didn't even notice that Chris had moved aside, and now it's Tom at my back. "You're so fucking sexy," he murmurs as he fondles my breasts.

Damien moves next to me and brushes his thumb along my cheek. "You want to be our little fucktoy?" he asks. His voice is a low growl.

"Yes, please," I gasp. "I want to be a fucktoy tonight. Use me."

Hands are everywhere—touching, teasing, driving me wild. I'm passed from one set of arms to another. Each man takes his turn kissing me, touching me, and making me moan. Devon's hands find the hem of my shirt, his fingers brushing the sensitive skin on my sides as he slowly lifts it up. My breath hitches as the cool air hits my stomach, my breasts still covered by my bra. He tosses the shirt aside, his gaze fixed on my newly-exposed skin.

"So beautiful," he moans as he slips his finger underneath the fabric of my bra to tease my nipples. I sway into his touch, wishing he was sucking on a nipple. Chris groans and grasps my hips firmly as he grinds his cock against my ass.

Tom steps in, replacing Devon, and he reaches for the clasp of my strapless bra. With a deft movement, he unhooks it, and the bra falls to the floor. My breasts spill free, and Tom cups them, his thumbs grazing over my nipples. I moan as I tilt my head back, resting it on Chris's solid shoulder.

I smile at Jake as he kneels next to me, peeling my pants down my legs. "You know, tonight is kind of like a belated birthday gift for you."

He raises an eyebrow, playing along. "Oh, really? And what kind of gift am I getting?"

"Guess you'll have to finish unwrapping it to find out," I tease, stepping out of my sandals so I don't get tangled up.

Jake looks at me with a wicked grin as he traces the lace of my thong before pressing a kiss to my hip bone. "It's a wonderful gift."

He hooks his fingers in the waistband of my thong and yanks it down. I'm naked now, surrounded by these men, their hands and mouths exploring me. I'm consumed by the delight coursing through my body. And I love all of it.

Tom slips his hand between my legs, removing the vibrator from inside me. He takes it over to Michael. My husband turns it off and puts it into his pants pocket.

Tom licks his fingers and grins. "She tastes delicious." His words send a jolt of desire through me, the dirtiness of it all making me even hotter.

Michael knows what I want, what I need. He guides me with his words. "Baby, get on your hands and knees."

My heart rate speeds up as I lower myself to the floor, thankful the industrial carpeting gives a little padding. I hear the rustle of clothing as the men start to strip. I'm trembling with anticipation, and getting wetter by the second. Being on the ground in front of seven men is degrading, yet it turns me on. They could all line up and I'd suck on their cocks one by one and just ask for more. Imagining them actually doing that makes me feel slutty, submissive—and I revel in it.

Harry steps up, naked, and his cock is hard. I open my mouth eagerly. My lips stretch around his girth and explore the velvety texture as I brush my tongue along his thick veins. The taste of him—salty and musky—fills my mouth as I take him deeper. He groans in pleasure and it makes me feel powerful.

I feel hands on my waist. A cock presses against my pussy. I push back, eager to be filled. I'm not sure who it is, but when the person groans, I recognize Devon's voice. He thrusts in and his hips smack against my ass.

"Fuck, you feel so good," Devon growls. His grasp tightens, anchoring me in place.

Chris sinks to the floor next to me and stretches out on his back. I almost laugh when he moves his head underneath me to suck on my breasts. I wasn't expecting this, and when his tongue flicks over my nipple, I gasp. Fuck, I bet this looks raunchy from Michael's viewpoint.

Tom stands beside me with his cock in his hand. Jake is next to him, his fingers tangling in my hair, guiding my movements as I suck Harry's cock.

"That's it," Jake murmurs. "Be a good fucktoy and take him deep."

Oh god, this is amazing. Pings of bliss radiate up and down my spine as they use me for their pleasure. The rapture builds and builds until I can't hold back anymore. I come hard, my body shuddering with my orgasm. But they don't stop; they keep fucking me, drawing out my pleasure.

The men swap places, and it's Tom in my pussy while Jake is in my mouth. There's no time to think, I'm just a ball of pleasure as they work me over. The room echoes with the wet sounds of flesh on flesh, the raw scent of sex thick in the air.

When the guys switch positions again, I get a glimpse of Michael. His face is a mask of desire, and I can tell he's enjoying the show.

"Look at you, Sasha," Michael's voice is thick with pride and lust. "You're taking every cock in this room like you were made for it."

A hand grasps my hip, another takes control of my head. I'm man-handled, positioned. Devon slides beneath me, his cock hard and ready. Michael's voice becomes deeper. "Ride Devon. Show me how you fuck him."

I straddle Devon and sink down onto his length. He groans and grips my thighs. I feel every ridge, every vein as he fills me. My body is slick with sweat and need as I start to rotate my hips.

Michael stands and moves closer. He grips my chin, turning my face towards him. "Good girl," he praises. "Now suck Jake's cock too."

Wow, I didn't expect Michael to be directing the action, but it feels right.

Michael goes back to his seat as Jake brings his cock to my mouth. I open wide so he can slide it past my lips. He tastes salty, feels smooth against my tongue. I find a rhythm, fucking and sucking in tandem. My vision fogs from pleasure and I can feel my orgasm building.

Michael's occasional directions are a filthy soundtrack. "That's it, Sasha. Fuck Devon's cock with that tight pussy. Suck Jake harder. You're a goddess like this."

Time loses meaning. I'm a vessel for pleasure. Now it's Chris fucking my pussy enthusiastically. The ecstasy is overwhelming, and I come hard, my body convulsing with waves of pleasure. Damien replaces Jake, his cock long and well formed as he plows into my mouth. The intense stimulation builds again, and I feel another orgasm approaching, ready to consume me entirely.

I'm lost in the pleasure, and Michael's voice sounds far away. 'You look so gorgeous when you're being used like this. I want you to come as many times as you can, baby."

I'm a whirlwind of motion, a toy passed from man to man. I'm fucked, used, my body a plaything for their pleasure. It's glorious.

"Switch," Michael groans. Someone lifts me and turns me. Now I'm on my back with my legs spread wide. Devon's between my thighs with his cock poised at my entrance. Harry kneels next to me, his cock ready for my mouth.

Michael's voice is a growl. "You're going to come, Sasha. You're going to come with Devon's cock in your pussy and Harry's cock in your mouth. And you're going to scream my name when you do."

Oh god, that's my filthy husband for you. Devon thrusts into me, hard and deep. Harry fucks my mouth, his cock hitting the back of my throat. The pleasure builds into a tidal wave. I'm going to drown.

"Michael—" I moan around Harry's cock, the name a plea, a prayer.

"Come, Sasha," he commands. "Come now."

And I do. I scream his name as my body quivers. Pleasure detonates, annihilates me. My nerve endings sing in delight as Devon hammers into me, fucking me through my orgasm. The other men gather around, their eyes fixed on us as they stroke their cocks.

"Fuck, that's hot," Tom groans as he speeds up his hand, jerking his cock furiously.

"You're so fucking sexy," Jake adds, and my body tingles from their appreciation.

The room is a symphony of moans and groans. I'm lost in a haze as the pleasure builds to an unbearable peak. When the guys swap around again, it's Damien between my legs. He pushes my knees to my chest and enters me, hammering home like he's trying to win a competition.

The night wears on, and I'm taken higher and higher. Each orgasm is more intense than the last and my body is a trembling mess of exertion and pleasure. But I crave more. I want to be filled in every hole.

As if sensing what I want, Damien lies on the floor and pulls me on top of him. I don't waste any time fitting my pussy against the length of his cock, trapping it between our bodies as I glide along his shaft, not letting him inside me. He groans and grabs my hips, forcing me to hold still.

"Stop being a little tease," he grumbles, and I giggle as I reach between us to guide him inside me. As I sink down onto his cock, we both moan.

Michael watches, his gaze fixed on me like a predator. I love being the center of attention with Michael overseeing this all.

Jake approaches with a lube bottle in hand. "You want me in your ass?" he asks, his voice rough with desire.

I nod, my breath coming in short puffs. "Yes. Fuck yes."

Jake kneels behind me and I lean down to kiss Damien as Jake applies the lube, his fingers circling my tight hole, preparing me. I feel the cool liquid, the pressure of his fingers. He starts with one finger, gently pushing in, and

I groan at the intrusion. He finger fucks me slowly, allowing me to get used to the sensation. My body tenses slightly, but it feels good.

When I say, "More," I can hear the desperation in my voice.

Jake obliges, adding another finger, stretching me open. I can feel the burn, the slight pain, but it only heightens my arousal. I push back, trying to take his fingers deeper.

"Please," I moan, my forehead resting against Damien's chest. Damien strokes my hair, his touch soothing as Jake continues to prep me. Jake adds a third finger, and I whimper from pleasure. He fucks me with his fingers, his movements slow and deliberate, driving me mad with need.

"I need your cock in my ass," I beg. "Please, Jake."

Jake makes a low, throaty sound. "Such a needy slut," he teases, but he doesn't stop the motion of his fingers. My body is on fire, my need consuming me.

"Please," I whimper while my body shakes from pleasure. "I need all my holes filled."

Hearing the filthy words come out of my mouth thrills me. Being able to say exactly what I want and knowing I'll get it is the best anniversary gift Michael could give me.

Finally, Jake removes his fingers, and I feel empty, desperate to be filled again. He replaces them with the tip of his cock, applying pressure. I grip Damien's shoulders, my nails digging into him.

"You're okay, it's okay, you're safe with us, Sasha," Michael says from his chair, his voice steady and calm.

I will my body to relax. Jake pushes in, groaning, "Fuck, you're so tight," as he moves slowly, carefully.

Tom kneels next to me. I turn my head so I can take him in my mouth. This is it, all holes stuffed! As all three men thrust into me, my brain short circuits from pleasure. Tom holds onto my head, guiding my movements on his cock while Chris steps up next to him. Damien helps hold me up as I stroke Chris's cock. When I see Devon on the other side of us, I reach my free hand out trusting that Damien will support me. Devon takes my hand and wraps my palm around his cock. I stroke both men while my head whirls from the pleasure overload.

"That's it," Michael's voice barely penetrates my haze of lust. "Take them all."

I'm a mess, just one massive ball of rapture. My world has shrunk down to include just me and the guys. The sounds of our pleasure filling the air, and I'm lost in the sheer bliss. I feel another orgasm building, every thrust amplifying the pleasure. I'm surrounded, consumed, overwhelmed.

And then it hits.

The orgasm doesn't just crash over me, it explodes through every cell in my body. It's a tidal wave of ecstasy, more profound than anything I've ever experienced. My body convulses with the force of it, every muscle tensing and releasing in sheer bliss. Waves of pleasure radiate from my core, spreading like wildfire and consuming me. It's a full-body experience, a symphony of rapture that leaves me trembling.

I feel the men's releases coming in quick succession, each one heightening my pleasure. Damien's orgasm is first, and as he fills my pussy with his warmth, it sends shivers up my spine. Jake follows closely, his groans deep and guttural as he climaxes and pumps my ass full of his seed. Tom explodes in my mouth, shuddering as he comes. I try to swallow him all down, but I'm cum drunk already and some dribbles out.

Devon and Chris groan together and Devon's cum hits my face while Chris paints my back with his load. Harry must have stepped up at some point because he furiously jerks over me until his cum rains down on me. I close my eyes in bliss and enjoy the sensation of all their cum dripping on and out of me as we all shudder through our orgasms.

As the waves of pleasure slowly subside, I become aware of the men around me, their breathing ragged. Their hands are on me, gentle and reverent—so different from the frenzied passion of moments before.

When I open my eyes, Michael is standing over me. His gaze is filled with love and he's smiling. "Happy anniversary, baby."

I smile back as I'm filled with a surge of love and gratitude towards him. He knew what I needed, what I wanted, and he made it happen.

The other men begin to pull away, their touches turning to gentle caresses as they help me up. I'm shaking, my body still humming with residual pleasure. Devon and Jake support me as I stand, their hands steady on my waist. Harry and Chris are nearby, their grins filled with appreciation.

Harry approaches me, his voice soft. "That was incredible, Sasha. Thank you." He kisses my cheek as the other men murmur their agreement.

Michael takes my hand, tugging me towards him. My body fits his perfectly—like we were made for each other. He wraps his arms around me, and I feel his heartbeat against my cheek, steady and reassuring.

When I feel Michael's hard cock through his jeans, I rub my hand along the length of him. I giggle when it jerks. "Maybe we should go home. I think my wonderful husband needs some relief."

Michael laughs. "I think you're right. But let's get you cleaned up first."

I look down at my arm and realize there's a cum streak showing up under the black light. I imagine my face and back are similarly marked, a filthy badge of honor that shimmers. I giggle again. "Yeah, I'm a mess."

As the other men finish dressing and collecting their things, they say their goodbyes to us. I get another slutty thrill when I thank them for the experience. Yeah, I just thanked a bunch of men for a gangbang. This is a glorious life.

CHAPTER 6

Michael leads me to a nearby bathroom. He wets a cloth that Damien provided and cleans me, his touch tender and caring. As I watch him in the mirror, I feel a surge of love for this man who knows me so well—who loves me so completely.

Once I'm clean, Michael helps me dress, his hands lingering on me as if he can't bear to stop touching me. I lean into him, my body still sensitive and aching in the best way. When we emerge from the bathroom, Damien is the last person left.

"We're heading out," Michael tells him.

Damien looks up from straightening a few items and smiles. "Good night, you two. I'll be here for a bit making sure everything is ready for tomorrow."

"Thanks for everything, Damien. And...good night." I'm too happy to worry about him having to clean up after a gangbang.

Michael takes my hand, lacing his fingers through mine as we make our way out of the building and to our car. The night air is cool and refreshing. I feel a sense of peace wash over me, my body sated, my heart full.

As Michael drives us home, I take his hand, giving it a squeeze. "Thank you for giving me this."

He lifts my hand to his lips, pressing a gentle kiss to my knuckles. "I will always try to give you what you need."

As we pull into our driveway, my pussy flutters in anticipation. The gangbang might be over, but now I want to make sure Michael gets an orgasm as well.

Michael guides me into the house, his hand on the small of my back, his touch possessive.

Once inside, he turns to me with a mischievous smile. "Now, about that relief..."

I'm already aching for him. "Yes, please."

Michael cups my breasts, his thumbs brushing over my nipples, making me gasp. He swallows my moans as he kisses me hungrily. Our tongues entwine, and my hands tangle in his hair.

We stumble our way towards the bedroom, shedding our clothes along the way. By the time we fall onto the bed, he only has to tug off my pants and then we're both naked. I straddle Michael and grind against his cock without him being inside me, enjoying the way he groans at the contact.

"God, you're incredible," he murmurs as he grips my waist tightly. He flips us over, and I'm suddenly underneath him. I look at him in surprise, and he grins. "I'm going to fuck you until you forget your name."

Yeah, that's not going to take much. My head spins as his cock teases my entrance, and I moan as he pushes in slowly, filling me inch by inch. I arch my back and writhe from the pleasure.

"Michael," I moan, wishing he'd fuck me hard, but he's determined to drive me wild. I wrap my legs and arms around him and we rock together in a steady rhythm. It's a deliciously slow fucking that has me clawing at him, trying to pull him deeper.

"More, please," I beg, my voice desperate and needy.

After what feels like an eternity, he picks up speed, his thrusts becoming more forceful. The sound of our bodies slapping together fills the room, mixing with our moans and sighs.

He reaches between us, his fingers finding my clit and rubbing in firm, quick circles. The combination of his thrusts and his touch is too much, and I come apart, screaming his name as the pleasure crashes over me in waves. My pussy clenches around his cock, and I feel him throb inside me as he reaches his own climax. He shudders, and his orgasm seems to go on forever as he pumps me full of cum. Yeah, he needed a release after watching me fuck so many guys.

As we lay there, tangled in each other's arms, I feel a deep sense of love and connection. "That was the best anniversary gift ever."

Michael laughs. "I'm glad you think so because I plan on giving it to you again next year."

Mmm, wow. I grin back, already looking forward to next year. "I *suppose* I might be able to take a bunch of cocks again in a year...if I *have* to."

"That's because you're my little cock-hungry slut," he says with a yawn.

Yeah, he knows I am. I just giggle and snuggle closer to him. For now, I'm content to bask in the afterglow of this incredible night.

"I love you," I whisper, my eyes fluttering closed.

"I love you too," he replies, his voice tender. "More than anything."

The next day, I'm pleasantly sore but incredibly satisfied. Michael is puttering around in the kitchen, and I sit on the couch in the living room to text Erin.

Sasha:

Best anniversary ever!

She responds almost immediately.

I type quickly, knowing that she'll be impressed, especially considering I always used to complain that Michael would never share me when she was telling me of her exploits with her cat's veterinarian and his technician. But Michael sure did surprise me.

After I tell her everything, I set my phone aside and look over at our wedding pictures on the fireplace mantel. We look so young and happy in the photos, but our marriage has only gotten better. And now this incredible anniversary.

Michael better start planning next year's anniversary early—this one is going to be hard to top. Instead of mini golf, maybe laser tag? And maybe he should invite the local football team—you know, for variety.

I giggle to myself. Yeah, I'm a slut. And now I have a whole year to fantasize about another gangbang.

Best. Husband. Ever.

The End

About Lacey Cross

Lacey Cross is a wife sharing erotica writer with over 100 short stories published since she started in 2021. Her stories emphasize the pleasure found from the wife living her best slut life and embracing the hotwife lifestyle. She explores themes of free use, submissive wives with dominant bulls, BDSM...and oh-so-many men.

www.ingramcontent.com/pod-product-compliance
Lightning Source LLC
Chambersburg PA
CBHW020738310726
48969CB00002B/308